Harper Large Print Edition

More Praise for
LITTLE ALTARS EVERYWHERE

"A gem of a book. . . . Wells offers a virtuoso performance."

—*Denver Post*

"Energetic and delicious . . . each voice is unique, independent and right-on."

—*Seattle Times*

"At the Walker family altar, sainthood is a one-way ticket to purgatory, and getting there is half the fun."

—*Columbus Dispatch*

"Wells's people pop with life."

—*Kirkus Reviews*

"Rebecca Wells has written a funny, eloquent and sad novel that easily leaps regional bounds."

—*Washington Post*

"A hilarious and heartbreaking first novel."

—*Booklist*

"Rebecca Wells brilliantly and adeptly moves among the voices, lending depth, honesty, and *reality* to the characters. With an intimate, intuitive sense of comedy, she exposes her characters' crazy, hilarious attempts at keeping reality at arm's length."

—*Bloomsbury Review*

"Rarely do you find a first novel of such power. The author's strange, arresting combination of colloquialism and poetry flows from her eight characters with a force so strong you savor each sentence."

—*Southern Living*

"Wells effectively juxtaposes the innocence and joy of childhood reveries with the pain and guilt of adult memories."
—*Richmond Times Dispatch*

"Displaying acute characterizations and a cast of voices unfailingly sharp, Rebecca Wells's *Little Altars Everywhere* is an exceptional debut. This is a book from the heart, full of voices and memory that sifts through yet another crazy family history to find purity and grace."
—*St. Petersburg Times*

"*Little Altars Everywhere* is a wonder of a book that will make you love the human condition and break your heart. Rebecca Wells is a writer we must celebrate to the fullest extent of the law."
—James Welch, author of
The Indian Lawyer

"Voice and energy are two prerequisites to successful storytelling. *Little Altars Everywhere* displays very strong voices, and the energy fairly crackles off the page. Rebecca Wells is a writer to watch."
W.P. Kinsella, author of
Shoeless Joe

LITTLE ALTARS
EVERYWHERE

Also by Rebecca Wells

Divine Secrets of the Ya-Ya Sisterhood

LITTLE ALTARS EVERYWHERE

REBECCA WELLS

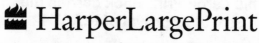 HarperLargePrint

A Division of HarperCollins*Publishers*

First Large Print Edition

ISBN 0-06-093318-6

99 00 01 02 03 RRD 40 39 38

**This Large Print Book carries the
Seal of Approval of N.A.V.H.**

To Thomas Schworer, my beloved
Thomas Wells, my brother
T.G., my guide
and
Lodi, my home soil

ACKNOWLEDGMENTS

The author wishes to thank the Western States Arts Federation, Artist Trust, King County Arts Commission, the Seattle Arts Commission, and the Louisa Kern Foundation for their support during the writing of this book. The author is also grateful to her editor, Mary Helen Clarke, whose patient work helped develop and deepen the book; and to her agent, Jonathan Dolger, who helps keep the faith. Open-hearted gratitude is also given to Brenda Peterson, Joyce Thompson, Jennifer Miller, the Scott sisters—Deb and Torie, Linda Clifton, Mary Koller, Jan Constantine, Maurine Holbert, Donna Lambdin, Bob Corbett, Marilyn Milloy, Darrell Jamieson, Barbara Bailey, and Steve Beaumont. In addition, bouquets of thanks go out to the Bainbridge Island Library and Steve Calhoun at the Louisiana State University Agricultural Extension Service.

CONTENTS

❧ PART TWO

Everything in life that we really accept
undergoes a change.
So suffering must become love.
That is the mystery.
—KATHERINE MANSFIELD

NOTE TO THE READER

I've been thinking lately about the intimacy that exists between us, writer and reader. And the more I reflect, the more grateful I am for this gift, because the process of a book's coming to life is not fully complete until your imagination meets mine on the page. The words evoke pictures and something altogether new is created, something different from the limits of my own skills and imagination. Something that is a marriage between your heart, mind, and body—and mine.

Although inspiration is assumed to be essential to art, in fact, all life requires inspiration. *Inspiration:* literally "to breathe in." To breathe in the life-giving oxygen we need, and also to breathe in whatever divine breath our bodies can receive. When you enter the world of a book I have written, our breaths intermingle, along with whatever celestial breeze might bless our exchange. Breathing in, breathing out; in so doing, if we are lucky or blessed, it all comes to life!

The whole idea of possessing creative work is perhaps as absurd as the ownership of rivers and trees. Helpers and co-conspirators meet me at every turn. I'm graced with all sorts of comfort and aid from my motley crew of angels. Spirits, born and unborn; people near and far; trees; dahlias; the smell of gumbo on the back burner; my cocker spaniel, Lulu; my husband who is sent straight from the Holy Lady as a gift to me, making up for all that is wobbly, wrecked, or lost. Once you, the reader, encounter the words on the page, the alphabet has meaning. So "my" work also becomes "yours."

My closest friends have been known to call me "Rebecca It-Takes-a-Village Wells." They know first-hand what it takes to write a book—at least for me. I never claimed to be a low-maintenance gal, but when I'm writing, it's particularly challenging. I lose things constantly: my watch, my glasses, my papers, my mind. The image of a writer as a solitary person who does it all alone is an illusion, or perhaps a delusion. Too little has been written about the contributions of a writer's loved ones, especially partners, in the creation of a book. Their sight, their touch, their ears, their belief, their patience, the food they hand out to put into mouths when we have forgotten food was necessary—those we love, those who love us, contribute to our work in ways too countless, too precious to explain.

Little Altars Everywhere began as a single short story. I based "Looking for my Mules" on a tale told to me by a person I love dearly. I was working as a playwright and actor while I was writing the story. "You're no writer," sneered the inner critic who tries to sabotage my every move. "You're just a theater person. Who do you think you're kidding?" I wrote "Looking for My Mules" anyway, and a blessed, small literary magazine picked it up, giving me a boost in confidence that I desperately needed.

Slowly, over many years, other chapters began to grow. Then, while performing a burlesque dance in my play *Gloria Duplex* wearing four-inch spike heels, I came out of a flying dismount, landed off-balance, and broke a tiny bone in my left foot called the sesamoid. Small as this bone is, it serves a crucial purpose: it acts for the foot as the knee does for the leg. It hurt to walk. It hurt to stand. It hurt to sleep with a heavy blanket covering my feet. It hurt too much to be onstage. I was side-lined until my foot healed, which took more time than I can bear to think about, even now. I had worked for years to get where I was, and this was devastating to me as a professional actor. You can't afford to be out of the loop. You must be seen, you can't turn down role after role and still expect them to call.

It was scary, depressing, and lonely to lose the career I had trained for and nurtured my entire life in one way or the other. That broken bone forced me to quiet down, sit still, and write, some-thing I've always had trouble doing, because the actor body I inhabit longs to stay in constant mo-tion.

Hidden blessings inside suffering. This is ulti-mately what *Little Altars Everywhere* is about. We are given our lives, our fear, our broken bones, and broken hearts. Breaks create openings that were not there before, and in that space grow the seeds for new creation.

So that at the dark center of suffering that suffuses *Little Altars Everywhere* lies both the luminance of blessing, as well as the seeds for my second book, *Divine Secrets of the Ya-Ya Sisterhood.*

Little Altars Everywhere was originally published by a tiny Northwest press. They gave me the biggest gift anyone could have: the perfect editor for the manuscript, Mary Helen Clarke. We met every Saturday morning at my home on the island, consuming gallons of coffee and tea and baskets of yummies from the local bakery. We stretched out on my bed with drafts of chapters covering every square inch, and howled with laughter over bits we thought were funny. Then we'd try to come up with something even funnier. The sadness we did not have to work on. It came, as sadness usually does, as soon as I sat down and began to listen.

The small press had a correspondingly small budget for publicity, so my husband, our best friend, and I became a public relations firm, and did our damnedest to promote the book. We made up a letterhead on our Mac, maxed out our credit cards at the copy shop, and hit the local and regional media for all we were worth. I'd make follow-up calls to radio and TV and newspapers, pretending to be a secretary just "following up on the Rebecca Wells material we sent you." I have given thanks for my background as an actor more than once!

Receiving the Western States Book Award for *Little Altars Everywhere* brought some money into the coffers of the small press, and helped the book along, not to mention giving me a surge of optimism. Then booksellers began their big-hearted word-of-mouth campaign to sell my book, and I learned to love booksellers as much as I had always loved librarians—book friends, too many to count.

With the publication of *Divine Secrets of the Ya-Ya Sisterhood*, *Little Altars Everywhere* was reissued in paperback, and now, to my great joy, in hardcover. People ask me how I feel, and I say "Happy!" Or, more accurately, I say, "A big fat beautiful *gift* has dropped into my lap, and I hope I know how to treat it right."

I continue to be awestruck and honored by the generosity readers have shown me in sharing their feelings about my books. Especially the gift of extraordinary and heartfelt letters! The wisdom and goodwill of the eighty-three-year-old woman in a tiny town in Minnesota who wrote me to say, "At first I was not going to get your book because the title was so strange. But one of my favorite books also has a strange title. So I read yours. Then I gave it to all four of my daughters. You keep going. I'm going to write Opry [*sic*] and tell her about your books." I received this letter when my book had sold approximately twenty-seven copies.

Or the man in Olympia, Washington who wrote to me with the exact words I craved as the books began selling. "In case you ever wonder if your success is deserved, as humans often do, my vote says it is." I do not know if this reader will ever know how his response tapped into a deep fear in me, acknowledged it, and then comforted me. For whether he is right or wrong, whether we "deserve" anything, he reminded me that I am part of a beloved community that stretches out farther than I can see. This has been the greatest blessing of having my books read widely: the knowledge that I am not so alone, that I am not as orphaned as I once feared. How can a person ask for more than that?

Then there's the joy of meeting readers face to face. I've met people who have changed my life forever—sometimes simply by the inscription that they ask me to pen into their copy of my book. I've met people who know so much more than I do, and they continue to tell me what it is that I have written. Because when you're writing, you are not fully aware of what you are writing. You have no answers. In fact, you're lucky if you can remember the *questions*. Readers find clues, and if you're fortunate, they share them with you.

We are worked on by the work we are helped to create. Compassion works on us, acceptance works on us. If we can see past the myopic confines of the ego that aggressively believes that it alone is responsible for each act of creativity—nay, for life itself—then it is possible to recognize the bounteous goodness and generosity that pours into the making of your fiction as well as your life.

All creativity is a gift. All life is a gift. And what a fetching ecosystem it is. I am given a gift. I am helped to hand it on to you, reader, in the form of a book. As you read, you keep the gift moving, and then hand a new gift back to me— the gift of having been met, of having been seen, of having been listened to.

And so I thank you for holding this book in your hands. My heart's wish is that we both will see what Sidda does when she swings high on the backyard swing—that holy sparks do fly everywhere, especially between writers and readers.

Rebecca Wells
September, 1998

OOH! MY SOUL!
Siddalee, 1991

*I*n my dream, I'm five years old again and it's a summer night at our camp at Spring Creek. Mama and all us kids—me, Little Shep, Baylor, and Lulu—around a bonfire. Mama's gang of girlfriends, the Ya-Yas, and all their kids are there too. Mama goes inside and puts Little Richard on the record player. She cranks the music up so loud it bounces off the pine trees. Then she comes back, takes my hand and says, Alright now, Siddalee: Dance!

Ooooh, My Soul! Little Richard begins, shouting out a warning for the weak of heart. And Mama's already shaking, she's boogying, she's jukin, she's slapping her thighs and rolling her hips like I've never seen her do before.

> Baby baby baby baby, don't you know my
> love is true?!
> Ooooo!
> Honey honey honey honey, get up offa that
> money!

That man sings nasty. Those horns blow nasty. My
body takes over and I'm moving. Sunburned legs shuf-
fle across the ground, head rolls around. I turn in circles, I face Mama and shake my shoulders and hips
faster than the human eye can see. I shake so hard that
freckles jump off my face.

> Baby baby baby baby, don't you know my
> love is true?!
> Ooooo!
> Honey honey honey honey, get up offa that
> money!

My hair flies in my face, it flies in my mouth. Mama
stomps the earth with her feet, I can see her Rich Girl
Red painted toenails against the dirt. I laugh, I spin, I
almost stumble over the other kids—but when I do,
they help me back up and I keep on dancing. Richard,
Little Richard, he's shining like a shooting star, he's the
hottest thing in the Louisiana night sky. He hollers
right up into my four-foot frame, he wails and horns
blow, oh those horns blow!

> Love love love love love
> Ooooh my soul!

Arms and legs have new lives all their own. Every
single part of me dances. And that 45-rpm record plays
over and over and over, and we're singing with Little
Richard now, we're blowing saxophones! And if Daddy
drives up in his pickup, you know he'd yell at us, white
women dancing like that, you know he would! But

Daddy doesn't drive up, and me and Mama go on dancing and all the Ya-Yas and the rest of the kids are yelling and clapping for us! Oh, they yell and clap and hoot and holler! And I know—you can't tell me different: something secret, something sweet, something strong is shooting up from the earth straight into my body, making my limbs quiver, making me crazy-dance all over the place right there in my orange and white sunsuit.

When I wake up from my dream, I'm laughing and my face is streaked with tears. My body feels relaxed, loose, good. And for a minute, I swear I feel Mama in the room. Feel her Jergen's-lotioned hands touching mine. The way they used to when I was little and she'd say, Come here dahling, I've rubbed on way too much, let me give you some moisturizer.

I roll over in bed and I'm 33 years older than in my dream, and I still want to hold Mama's hands. I'm crying and I'm laughing and I still want my mother to come to me and take me in her arms.

Part ONE

WILDERNESS TRAINING
Siddalee, 1963

*O*ne thing I really hate about Girl Scouts is those uniforms. They bring out my worst features—fat arms and short legs. Mama tries her best to give that drab green get-up some style, but I just get sent home with a note because the glitzy pieces of costume jewelry she pins on me are against regulations.

The only reason I joined Scouts in the first place was all because of merit badges. I wanted to earn more of those things than any other girl in Central Louisiana. I wanted my sash to be so heavy with badges that it would sag off my shoulder when I walked. There wouldn't be any doubt about how outstanding I was. When I walked past the mothers waiting in their station wagons outside the parish hall, I wanted them to shake their heads in amazement. I wanted them to mutter, I just don't know how in the world the child does it! That Siddalee Walker is such a *superior* Girl Scout.

I love going over and over the checklists for earning those badges in the *Girl Scout Handbook.* I have eight badges. More than M'lain Chauvin, who constantly tries to beat me in every single thing. I have got to keep my eye on that girl. She is one of my best friends, and we compete in everything from music lessons to telephone manners.

I was making real progress with my badges, and then our Girl Scout troop leader up and quit right after the Christmas holidays. She said she could no longer handle the stress of scouting. She didn't even tell us herself—just sent a note to the Girl Scout bigwigs, and they cancelled our meetings until they could find someone to take us on.

And wouldn't you know it, out of the wild blue, Mama and Necie Ogden decide to take things over and lead our troop. I could not believe my ears. Mama and Necie have been best friends since age five. Along with Caro and Teensy, they make up the "Ya-Yas." The Ya-Yas drink bourbon and branch water and go shopping together. All day long every Thursday, they play *bourrée,* which is a kind of cutthroat Louisiana poker. When you get the right cards, you yell out *"Bourrée!"* real loud, slam your cards down on the table, then go fix another drink. The Ya-Yas had all their kids at just about the same time, but then Necie kept going and had some more. Their idol is Tallulah Bankhead, and they call everyone "Dahling" just like she did. Their favorite singer is Judy Garland or Barbra Streisand, depending on their moods. The Ya-Yas all love to sing. Also, the Ya-Yas were briefly arrested for something they did when they were in high school, but Mama won't tell me what it was because she says I'm too young to comprehend.

At least Necie goes out and gets herself a Girl Scout leader's outfit. Mama will not let anything remotely resembling a Scout-leader uniform touch her skin. She says, Those things are manufactured by Old Hag International. She says, If they insist on keeping those hideous uniforms, then they should change the name from "Girl Scouts" to "Neuter Scouts."

Mama drew up some sketches of new designs for Girl Scout uniforms that she said were *far* more flattering than the old ones. But none of the Scout bigwigs would listen to her. So instead, she shows up at every meeting wearing her famous orange stretch pants and those huge monster sweaters.

The first official act of Mama and Necie's reign is to completely scrap merit badges, because Mama says they make us look like military midgets.

Whenever I gripe about being cut off just as I was about to earn my Advanced Cooking badge, Mama says, Zip it, kiddo. Don't ever admit you know a thing about cooking or it'll be used against you in later life.

Now at our meetings, instead of working on our Hospitality, Music, and Sewing badges, they have us work on dramatic readings. They make us memorize James Whitcomb Riley and Carl Sandburg poems and then Mama coaches us on how to recite them. She calls out, Enunciate, dahling! Feel it! Feel it! Love those words out into the air!

All my popular girlfriends look at me like: Oh, we never knew you came from a nuthouse. I just lie and tell them Mama used to be a Broadway actress, when all she ever really did in New York was model hats for a year until she got lonely enough to come home and marry Daddy.

*   *   *

*O*ur annual Scout camp-out always comes up just after Easter. I just dread it. I'm in the middle of reading a truly inspiring book called *Judy's Journey*. It's all about this girl who's exactly my age, and she and her whole family are migrant workers. They have to travel from place to place, living hand-to-mouth. Judy works in the fields and never complains, and she is brave, and a hard worker, and very popular with all the other migrant kids. Her father plays the harmonica, and her mother is so kind and quiet. I fantasize around fifty times a day about being her instead of me. I would just kill to stay in my room and finish that book instead of going on a stupid camp-out, but you've got to do these things whether you want to or not. Otherwise any chance you have at popularity can go straight down the drain and you will never get it back.

You have to start early if you plan to be popular. Mama was extremely popular when she was growing up. She was elected Most Well-Liked, she was head cheerleader, captain of the girls' tennis team, and assistant editor of the yearbook. Everyone at Thornton High knew who she was. Even though it sometimes wore her out, she said *Hi!* to every single soul she passed in the hall. It was a lot of work, but that is how her reputation was built. Mama understands the gospel of popularity and she is passing it on to me so I won't be left out on the fringes.

*W*e head out to Camp Mary Alice real early on a Saturday morning. It is twenty or so miles from Thornton, in the deep piney woods. They named the camp for this very famous Louisiana Girl Scout who gave up her entire life for scouting. There is a main lodge built of logs with a huge fireplace at one end, long tables set up in the middle, and a big kitchen at the other end. Not far away, at the edge of the woods, there is a screened-in cabin filled with bunk beds where you sleep.

Right off the bat, Necie backs her Country Squire station wagon into the flagpole and bends it in half. I'm inside the cabin unfurling my bedroll when I hear this big uproar. I bolt out the door and—wouldn't you know it—there is the Girl Scout flag flapping in the breeze a couple of inches above the ground! The Louisiana state flag with the mama pelican feeding her babies is right next to it, and the American flag is right next to that.

Mama is laying on the ground kicking her feet up and down, just howling with laughter. Tooty, she yells, quit it! I'm tee-teeing all over myself!

"Tooty" is Necie's Ya-Ya nickname, and all the Scouts flutter around me squealing, Sidda, why is your mother calling Mrs. Ogden "Tooty"? Why is your mother wetting her pants?

Well, I could have predicted that something like this was going to happen. You can't go anywhere with Mama without things getting nuts. If it's going along too smooth she will *invent* something just to stir things up. Sometimes we'll be downtown shopping and everything's going normal, and Mama will put her fingers in her mouth and let out the loudest, most piercing whistle you ever heard in your life. Then everyone gets startled and drops what they're doing and looks around to see where the noise came from. And Mama, she'll just bend over and pretend to be looking at a pair of shoes.

Then she'll lift her head and look around, acting like she's just as puzzled as everyone else. But later, once she gets us in the car, she'll laugh her head off, saying, Did yall see how I shook up those old fuddy-duddies?

And that is only one of her tricks.

Necie sits in the car hooting her head off, too, and finally Mama pulls herself up off the ground and goes over to Necie, walking like Red Skelton.

She says, Good going, dahling. Done like a true Ya-Ya!

Necie says, Vivi, when in the hell did they put a flagpole there? And they both crack up again and Mama lights them each a cigarette.

I stand off to the side behind one of the big loblolly pines, hoping Mama can't spot me, but she yells out: Sidda, dahling, go get me my file out of my purse. I think I've broken a fingernail.

Great, I think, just great. This is going to be a perfect camp-out with my perfect mother, who I wish would shrivel up and blow away. Then I say a quick prayer so I won't burn in hell for having such thoughts about my own mother. It can wear you to a nub, trying to be a popular person and a good Catholic all at the same time. There is no way in the world she can pull this off. It's one thing for her to act half-normal in an hour meeting at the parish hall on Wednesday afternoons, but trying to act sane and sober for a whole weekend is a whole different ball of wax.

So what do our great leaders do? They just walk away from that station wagon and that bent flagpole like nothing ever happened and lead us off on the big hike.

Now, I just hate hikes because they always get me out of breath. Plus, I would rather simply look at the great outdoors than actually be in it. But I step along as quick as I can to keep up with M'lain and Sissy with their Ladybug shirts tucked into their pants. They've both got these neat walking sticks that they found, and their hair is done up in dog-ears, and everything about them is clip-clip.

You've got to understand the social structure of Troop 55. There are

1. The Popular Girls. M'lain and Sissy, and maybe Mimi Plauché. And me, if I do things right on a lucky day.
2. The Almost-Popular Girls. They try real hard but never quite make it. For instance, their leader is Rena Litz, whose father is the manager of the very first K-Mart in Cental Louisiana. She dresses in brand-new clothes all the time but they're cheap-cheap-cheap, and she has an accent from Ohio that sounds like she always has a stuffed-up nose.
3. The Unpopular Girls. At least they love each other.

and

4. Edythe Spevey.

Edythe Spevey is in a class all by herself. She has kind of a crow face with pimples around her big old honker nose, and hair so oily that M'lain says you could wax the floor with her head. (Oily hair is the worst thing you can have at Our Lady of Divine Compassion parochial school. If you have oily hair, you might as well just lie down and die and get it over with.) And— just to top things off—old Edythe wears cheap pointy eyeglasses and crinkled-up shoes. She looks like an orphan, even though we know she has this fat mother who takes in sewing. In fact, just last Christmas, Edythe's mother made her this special holiday dress of green felt that was designed to look exactly like a Christmas tree. Edythe wore it to a Catholic Youth Organization party and the thing actually had little balls dangling off of it, and every time she bent over to pick up the ones that fell off, you could see her underwear. Now, a true Catholic would try to be kind to Edythe, but I just can't. It's too dangerous. You could get lumped in with her, and then maybe even become her, and end up living in a trailer the rest of your life watching *Dialing for Dollars.*

*A*nyway, we're hiking along like little marching rats, and Mama has on her white sunhat and sunglasses, and she's holding the Super-8 like she's shooting a movie in Hollywood. She adores that Super-8 and won't let anyone touch it but her. She films all of us walking through the piney woods, and yells out, Yall *do* something! This is a movie camera!

You can smell the sun hitting the needles and see little mushrooms under your feet. If you quit thinking about everybody and everything, it gets real quiet and private, like swimming underwater with your eyes open. I stop for a minute to feel some bark peeling off a pine like it's the tree's skin. And then I look up and

suddenly realize that Edythe has almost caught up with
me.

She says, Siddalee, did you see that monarch butterfly?

I wouldn't mind seeing a monarch, but I panic at
the thought of being left behind with Edythe. I act like
I don't hear her and take off running to the front of
the group where my popular friends are. The sprint gets
me winded, and I have to pretend I'm coughing, and
palm my asthma inhaler to stop the wheezing.

I pray: God, please don't let me get stuck with
Edythe, and please don't let M'lain see me sucking on
this inhaler like Daddy.

Then Mama says, Okay yall, we're gonna sing now!
And she starts up with her old camp songs that only
the Ya-Yas and their kids know the words to. I wish I
could crawl off and hide from her voice and her legs
marching like she is the general of the world. She sings:

> *I go with the garbage man's daughter,*
> *Slop! Slop!*
> *She lives down by the swill*
> *She is as sweet as the garbage itself*
> *And her breath is sweeter still*
> *Slop! Slop!*

Oh, she just makes me so sick! Who does she think
she is, Mitch Miller? I signal to M'lain and Sissy that
my mother drives me crazy. I've got to let them know
that I am not like her. But then—don't you know it—
they start trying to sing along with her! Stumbling over
the words, acting like they've sung it a hundred times,

when they've never heard it before in their lives. Mama keeps leading the big sing-along, and we march through the woods like in *The Bridge on the River Kwai*. Finally, I start singing too, all loud and full-throated. Mama always says, If you can't sing it good, Siddalee, at least sing it loud.

By the time we stop to cook our food, I'm dizzy from all that hiking and singing. We have to dig out these little pits in the ground and drop hot coals in there, and then plunk our tinfoil packets full of potatoes and vegetables and hamburger meat down in there and let it all cook together. It takes forever and you get dirt under your fingernails and I just hate it. Mama acts like she's an Indian princess in the great outdoors. But I notice that she's got her these little packets of peanut butter crackers that she unwraps and eats, and a Coke that she slips out of her knapsack and gulps down. My throat is all dry and it's too dusty out here. I don't see how my Daddy can stand it, working in the fields all day long.

When we finally finish up eating and head back to camp, M'lain whispers to Sissy and Mimi and me, Yall watch Edythe. Look at how she walks.

And we stare at Edythe the whole way back. She walks all bunched up, like invisible hands are squeezing her shoulders together. It gets me embarrassed just to look at her. I want to go over and hit her on the back and say: Edythe, walk right! Quit being such an I-don't-know-what!

*B*ack at Camp Mary Alice, Mama and Necie get out the Hershey bars and jumbo marshmallows and graham crackers and we make s'mores. I've got to have my marshmallows done perfectly light brown all the way around or I will not eat them. I don't see how anybody can stand to swallow the burnt-up ones. After I get mine just perfect, I slip it off my coat hanger right on top of the Hershey bar. I bite into that crunchy cracker and taste that marshmallow and chocolate down to the tip of my toes.

Mama says, Yall keep rotating those marshmallows constantly and they will roast evenly. When anybody's—even Edythe's—marshmallow falls off into the dirt, Mama laughs and hands them another one. One thing about Mama: She is never stingy with food.

This is the fun part. Around the campfire those flames lick up into the black sky and you can see the stars so good. Mama does what she does best—tell stories. She acts out scary stories, like the one about the old-maid sisters in the big house on Evangeline Street right in Thornton who got eaten to death by giant ants. All their skin got chewed off and the only thing left was their bones and shoes.

Mama says, I saw it with my own eyes when I was about yall's age. Isn't that true, Necie?

Necie nods her head and says, It's the gospel truth.

M'lain whispers to me, You can tell your Mama was a New York actress.

That makes me feel the best I've felt all day. I walk by Mama's side on the way back to the cabin and hold her hand for a minute.

Mama and Necie rig up sheets all around their bunks so they can get some privacy. We take sponge baths and put on our nightgowns, and then we're supposed to go to sleep. M'lain and Sissy and Mimi and I all have our hair rolled up on spoolies, because who knows what kind of things might pop up the next day that will make demands on our hairdos? My legs are twitching they're so tired, but in that cabin with all the other girls, far away from home, and the smell of the pines and the shadows on the screens—well, you couldn't go straight to sleep for a million dollars! All the lights are out except a nightlight that Mama has plugged in at our end of the cabin and a little lamp that lights up Mama and Necie behind the sheets like they're shadow puppets. Moonlight shines down through the trees and you can hear the frogs croaking and the ten-thousand crickets hopping around our cabin like Mexican jumping beans.

I put my head down on the pillow and close my eyes—but then I get that second wind that makes you punchy and giggly and bad. M'lain hits me with her pillow and I'm up in a flash, wonking her over the head, and then Sissy joins in, and Mimi, and we're whacking each other and laughing and screaming and jumping on the beds.

I start tickling Sissy, which always gets her going, and she's yelling, Stop, please! Really, please stop! just like I do when my brother Little Shep or Daddy tickles me.

Cigarette smoke drifts up out of Mama and Necie's cubbyhole, and you can barely hear a Texas late-night station playing Fats Domino on Mama's transistor radio.

Mimi says, I know a nasty joke. Yall wanna hear?

Her joke is all about this man who gets his Thing

stuck in a hole in the floor, and I laugh and laugh even though I don't think it's all that funny. I have seen both of my brothers' Things and they look like turkey necks to me. Like if you're not careful they could get slammed in a door and fall right off on the floor. It's one of the reasons I'm glad I'm a girl with everything tucked up inside where things can't get at it so easy.

The Almost-Popular Girls are playing Go Fish with Girl Scout playing cards. The Unpopular Girls are reading their own individual books, which for a minute makes me wish I was one of them so I could lay up and finish *Judy's Journey.*

Edythe just sits on her bed with her hands in her lap and stares at me. I cannot believe it: She is wearing a housecoat and slippers like a little old lady, and an actual hairnet like a cafeteria server. Why is she looking at me? I am not the ringleader over here in the Popular group. I am barely here myself. I wish she would turn her beady eyes away and stare at someone else!

M'lain and Mimi are playing cat's cradle, and me and Sissy start pretending we're Gidget in the dorm at college. Then do you know what happens? Edythe gets up and walks right over to us on M'lain's bed and just stands there. I can see the way her veins are all purple on her hands. Her face is all red in spots, like she has been picking at it. Why doesn't she say anything? She just stands there looking at me, like she's waiting for something.

Finally I say, Edythe, what do you want?

I think: Oh God, what if she asks to sit on the bed and play with us?

But she says, It is time to go to sleep now. It's way

past our curfew. Yall are breaking the Girl Scouts of America rules.

Well, that just cracks us all up and M'lain says, Hey Edythe, why don't you go on back to your bed and pick your zits?

Then Mimi says, Yeah, but don't aim in our direction!

Edythe looks at me like I'm responsible for the whole world. Then she turns and pads back to her bed and keeps on staring at me. If she doesn't quit doing that, I am either going to lose my mind or have to get up and clobber her!

We start singing "Ninety-nine Bottles of Beer on the Wall," which is an extremely stupid song, but that's how it is when you're in a group. We get all the way down to sixty-eight bottles and then here comes Edythe again. And she puts it all to me again, like I am the ambassador to the Popular Girls (which I definitely am not).

She says, Siddalee, I'm giving yall one more chance. If yall don't go to sleep right now, I'm going to tell your mother.

God, why can't she leave me alone? Edythe Spevey has been tailing me around since first grade. Just because one single time I smiled at her at the water fountain, she has tried to leech onto me for life. What does she think she is, my shadow or something? Does she think we are blood sisters for life?

I would like to reach out and touch the cuff of that awful bathrobe and tell her: Just relax, Edie, everything's okay. To show her she's not really as cootified as we treat her.

But M'lain and Sissy and Mimi are watching me, waiting to see what I'll do. I know they'll banish me forever if I am nice to Edythe. I know how close I am to being kicked off the Popular bunk for life. I've spent a lot of time trying to have a good personality and I will not let Edythe ruin everything now.

Hey Edythe, I finally say, Why don't you go on back to your bunk and eat your boogers for a midnight snack like you always do at home?

Well, that comment really sends my friends, and I'm a big hit. But then I see Edythe's face. It's like something has fallen on it and crumpled it in. Somehow she looks so familiar that I can feel her bones inside my own body. And I start to feel sort of sick.

She turns and walks away and M'lain says, Ten points, Sidda, ten points.

Why don't you shut up M'lain? I say. Then I laugh like I didn't really mean it.

Edythe walks the full length of the cabin to Mama and Necie's cubbyhole. She isn't kidding. She's going to tell on us. If she tells Mama what I said to her, Mama will jerk my arm out of its socket right on the spot. One thing Mama will not stand for is deliberate cruelty. Deliberate cruelty is the reason I got belt-whipped last Thanksgiving and couldn't go to dance class for two weeks because of the marks on my legs.

I tiptoe to the edge of the cubbyhole. My bare feet are cold against the plank floors. I can feel goosebumps on my arms. I pull back one of the sheets just a hair so I can see inside. They're up on the top bunk smoking; Mama is polishing her toenails. I can see the name on the bottle—"Rich Girl Red."

Edythe is looking up at my mother. She says, Mrs. Walker, the nine o'clock curfew is a national Girl Scout rule. It is almost twelve o'clock midnight now. Yall should make them go to sleep, and turn out your light, too.

The blue thermos with Mama's vodka and grape-fruit juice sits on the bedspread between her and Necie. I can smell that nail polish in the clean cool air of the woods. The minute Mama opens her mouth I realize she's had at least four drinks. Her voice is loose and deep and content and amused, and she says: Edythe, don't you ever tell me what to do again as long as you live. Now get your little goody-two-shoes butt back into your bunk before I spank the hell out of you!

Then Mama starts laughing. She sticks a piece of cotton between her toes so the polish won't smear. Edythe does not move.

Honestly, Edythe, Mama says, like she's going to give her the most important advice in the world, If you continue acting this way, you will be *unpopular* for the rest of your life.

I wish I could go someplace far away from the heart of Louisiana. But I just walk back to M'lain's bunk and tell them what just happened. And they all laugh like hyenas.

Mimi says, Boy, your mother sure is cool, Siddalee.

Edythe comes back and climbs into her bed without saying a word. I can see the oyster-colored skin of her arms where they stick out of her old-lady bathrobe. I think about getting up and going to her, saying some-thing, doing something, climbing in the bed with her and just breathing with her. I almost do it, too. I almost comfort Edythe. But the sight of her hairnet just stops me cold.

Edythe doesn't make a peep the rest of the weekend. It rains all day Sunday and even when the Unpopular Girls ask her to sit with them in the lodge, she says no. She just sits by the window and stares out into the woods like something real interesting might happen out there.

That next meeting, all of Troop 55 presents Mama and Necie with a thank-you collage. Mama lets Necie take it home. She says, Necie, I'm sure you have a better place of honor in your home to display this piece of fine art.

At the end of the school year, the two of them volunteer to lead us for another year. But the Central Louisiana Girl Scout bigwigs tell Mama and Necie they already have a more experienced person lined up. They say Mama and Necie deviated from the Girl Scout program, and that it set a bad example for girls our age to see a flagpole get bent up like that. They say that it bordered on being unpatriotic.

One day after school is out, Mama is sitting on the window seat in the den looking at the bayou—"meditating," she calls it. I bring her a Coke with crushed ice without her even asking, and she puts her hand on my cheek and kind of cups it there, like she used to when I was little.

I tell her, I'm quitting Scouts next year, Mama. They're jealous of you. That's why they didn't beg you to stay on. The Girl Scouts of America aren't ready for someone like you.

Mama twists my hair and holds it up off my neck. She studies me, then drops my hair and turns away.

I don't know, dahling, she sighs. Sometimes it's hard to tell what vocation I'm cut out for. Sometimes it's just real hard to tell.

*S*ometime during the summer, I have this dream about Edythe Spevey and me. We're on the swing that hangs from the pecan tree in our back yard. And while we're swinging, it's like Edythe's body is in my body. Her legs kick out from my legs, and her head leans forward out of mine. When I move my arms forward, hers come out of them. We are swinging in this just-right rhythm. We are swinging high, flying way up, higher than in real life. And when I look down, I see all the ordinary stuff—our brick house, the porch, the tool shed, the back windows, the oil-drum barbecue pit, the clothesline, the chinaberry tree. But they are all lit up from inside so their everyday selves have holy sparks in them, and if people could only see those sparks, they'd go and kneel in front of them and pray and just feel good. Somehow the whole world looks like little altars everywhere. And every time Edythe and me fly up into the air and then dive down to earth, it's like we're bowing our heads at those altars and we are praying and playing all at the same time. We just keep swinging and swinging, and in my dream we are swinging at the center of the most popular spot in the world.

CHOREOGRAPHY
Siddalee, 1961

I have fallen in love with my dance teacher. I mean, I really love her. Her name is Charlene Parks, and she came back to Thornton to live with her mama after being a June Taylor Dancer on *The Jackie Gleason Show.* She is tall and slender and pretty, and she used to be Miss Louisiana 1954 before she went off to New York City to be famous. Her long chestnut hair is always up in a dancer's ponytail and she has thick eyelashes and her body is perfect. No bumps on it or hair in weird places or anything. The way she moves, it's like her legs are hooked on different at the hip than other ladies' legs are.

Charlene's Central Louisiana School of the Dance is in a big old cave-like dance studio at the Garnet Parish Community Center. I take tap lessons from her twice a week and I adore it. Only *I* get to take tap. Not Lulu, not Little Shep, not Baylor. Just me.

That dance studio is hot as hell in the summer, even though two huge industrial-sized fans blow like crazy all the time. Mirrors line the walls and ballet barres run the length of the room. The floor is smooth and there's a table at one end with Charlene's record player and piles and piles of popular records and show tunes. At the start of each class, Charlene performs a dazzling show-stopper while we sit on the floor with our mouths hanging open, pulling at our leotards, which are always crawling up our crotches. (What I wish I knew is how real dancers on stage keep from having to pull at their crotches all the time.) As hot and sweaty as it gets in there, Charlene always looks fresh.

She dances in *high-heeled tap shoes,* and I think they are the jazziest things in the world. I would give anything for a pair of my own, but we only get to wear low heels. Charlene uses a lot of George M. Cohan music because it's easy for us to count out. But we also learn numbers to "High Hopes," and "Itsy Bitsy Teeny-Weeny Yellow Polka-Dot Bikini"—a song that my Grandmother Buggy turns off whenever it comes on the radio, because she says it's a sin for such impurity to be on the airwaves.

Charlene's record player has a little knob on the side of it so she can slow the music down to a crawl for us to get the rhythm, while she calls out, Hop-shuffle-slap, hop-shuffle-slap! or whatever the step is. Once we start to catch on, she brings the music real slow-like back up to speed, and we try to actually put the steps to time. That always throws me. Just when I think I have the steps down, the music speeds up, and I forget everything I've learned. I try and try, but I never can dance fast enough and still get it right. But Charlene never fusses, she never pushes. She gives a lot of praise, and I work hard so I can be exactly like her. My riffs and toe-tips and touches are always a little off, though. I just cannot seem to make my left foot cooperate with my right one. It's like there are two separate people on the different sides of my body.

I've worshipped Charlene for months and I have prayed to God for her to notice me. And finally I get to be her pet, which is the best thing I could hope for in this whole town!

This is how lucky I am: Charlene lets me visit her at her mother's house on St. Gerard Street. They live in a big pink stucco Spanish house, the only one like it in the city of Thornton. Charlene's room is the closest you can get to Hollywood without leaving Louisiana. It has a round bed that her mother ordered from Dallas. It's covered with a pink satin comforter, and dozens of little pink and green satin pillows are thrown all over the place. These heavy pink and green flowered curtains hang over all the windows so they can block out the morning sun. Even so, Charlene sleeps with a sleep mask on to block out whatever sunlight peeks through.

On the days when I get to visit Charlene's, I wake up at six A.M.! But Mama won't take me over there until after nine. And then Charlene is still asleep! I can't believe she sleeps *so long*. I have to sit in the kitchen with their maid, Jewel, and wait and wait and wait. Then, when Jewel says it's time, she lets me trail along while she brings Charlene her café au lait in bed. When we get to the edge of the bed, Jewel lets me hold the coffee tray. Charlene turns over and I'm standing there looking at her, making sure I don't spill a drop.

I say, Rise and shine, Miss Sleepyhead! like Mama does.

Jewel walks over to the curtains, and then Charlene

always says, Oh Jewel, will you please just sneak those drapes open real slow-like?

And Jewel pulls those curtains open little by little, keeping an eye on Charlene to make sure she isn't doing it too fast. (Jewel told me one time that there was too much light for Miss Charlene in New York, and that was why she had to come back home. Jewel said she was not fixing to add any more to Miss Charlene's heartache if she could help it.)

Finally, Charlene sits up and lifts that sleep mask up off her eyes and uses it like a headband to push back her hair. (I have been begging Mama for weeks to buy me a sleep mask, but she says, Absolutely not! You're too damn dramatic as it is.) Then Charlene looks over at me and smiles her big lazy just-waking-up smile and asks me, Want to climb in, Sidda?

I hand her the coffee-milk and let myself up on the bed very gently so I won't disturb her. The air conditioner is always pumped up to high all night long, so it is freezing in that room.

Charlene pulls the comforter up over me and says— like it's something tragic: Oh, Sidda! You've got goose-bumps!

Then Jewel goes over to Charlene's big console stereo and says, Miss Charlene, what tunes you want to start your day with?

And Charlene says, Oh I don't know, Jewel, why don't you ask our guest?

And I blurt out, *South Pacific!* No, no, no, play *Carousel,* yeah, *Carousel!* Let's listen to Julie Jordan!

Charlene yawns and starts humming, and when

Jewel has the volume just right, Charlene says, Jewel, how come you're so good to me?

Every single time Jewel says back: Cause your Mama gonna take care of Jewel in her old age.

Everything in that world is pure heaven. I just get lightheaded with all the attention I get from Charlene. But then I start to worry that she'll notice how dumb I am and not like me anymore. I just have to hold myself back from dancing and singing and turning backflips to show Charlene what a fantastic child I am so she will love me forever.

Then my Aunt Jezie comes home from college for the summer. She moves into her old room at my Grandma Buggy's house and immediately she starts making fun of everything Buggy does. When Buggy tells me it's time to wash my hair, Aunt Jezie will say: Mother, the word is "wash" not "warsh." And while we're at it, the word is "rinse" not "rinch." Say it, Mother: *wash* and *rinse.*

And Buggy repeats it after Aunt Jezie, but then she goes right back to her old ways of talking.

Aunt Jezie also thinks Buggy's shoulders are too rounded. She will go over and slap her hand between my grandmother's shoulder blades, and Buggy will stand perfectly straight for a minute. And Aunt Jezie will turn around and say to us, There, doesn't Buggy look less countrified?

It is thrilling to have Aunt Jezie home because she lets me show her all my dance routines. Mama never wants to hear anything about my lessons. When I try to show her Charlene's numbers from *The Pajama Game,*

Mama just says, God, I'll be relieved when you get off this Charlene Parks jag.

One time me and Mama got in this gigantic fight because she wouldn't let me wear the rhinestone tiara that Charlene sent me home with because I was Queen for the Week. All of Charlene's students get to take turns being Queen and it is a very big deal. But Mama said, That tiara is the tackiest little thing I've ever laid my eyes on. You will *not* wear that piece of trash on your head!

Well, I am not about to let anything connected with Charlene get criticized, so I said, Mama, you're just jealous because you can't dance like Charlene.

Mama said, Shut your filthy mouth.

Then I said, Shut *your* filthy mouth.

Which was not like me to say, but I just was not about to let Mama put down Charlene right in front of me. Even though it meant I couldn't go to dance class for a week because of the marks on my legs where Mama hit me with Daddy's cowboy belt. I simply had to defend Charlene.

*A*unt Jezie just wants to hear everything. When I get back from class, I show all my routines to her. If she has the record, she'll stand me in front of her full-length mirror and teach me to sing the words to the dance tunes. Of course Aunt Jezie already knows about Charlene being ex–Miss Louisiana, but *I* am the one to tell her about *The Jackie Gleason Show.* I am also the one who tells her about Charlene's sleep mask and her pink comforter and her little dotted-swiss baby-doll pajamas.

When she's home for the summer, Aunt Jezie and I always do lots of fun things. Sometimes she'll decide at ten o'clock at night that she absolutely has to have a root beer float. And we jump into Buggy's Ford Fairlane and putt on over to the A&W, wearing nothing but our cotton piqué nightgowns. We order from the carhop and Aunt Jezie just dares anyone to say a word about how we're dressed. And we ride horses early in the mornings before the sun gets scorching hot. Aunt Jezie is a great horsewoman. She teaches me dressage and grooming and how to feel what a horse is saying to you. She says, You've always got to be the boss. Once you let the horse take over, then you just might as well forget the whole thing.

One time after dance class, Aunt Jezie comes to pick me up as a surprise. Instead of waiting in the car like Mama does, she walks right up to the door of the dance studio. We are just finishing up our *Yankee Doodle Dandy* routine with all the slaps and toe-tips, and from the corner of my eye I can see Aunt Jezie leaning against the door in her khaki pants and loafers with no socks. I pretend I don't notice her, but I start kicking and hopping furiously to impress her with my talent.

As soon as we finish, I run over to Aunt Jezie and grab her hand. I am panting like a dog, I'm so out of breath. I say, Come on! Come and meet Charlene!

I pull her over to the record player where Charlene is putting stuff away. Charlene looks especially gorgeous. She has on her black leotard with a pink sash around the waist and a matching scarf in her hair. Just the way she stands with her feet kind of splayed out is a wonder to me. (I try to stand like that, so people will think I'm a professional dancer, but Mama always comes along and says, Stop standing duck-footed. You look ridiculous.)

I say, Charlene, this is my Aunt Jezie. She goes to Ole Miss.

Aunt Jezie says, Thrilled to finally meet. The child adores you.

Then she holds out her hand to shake hands with Charlene, although ladies in Thornton never do that. It doesn't faze Charlene though. She has probably seen *every*thing in New York. She shakes Aunt Jezie's hand and they look each other right in the eyes.

Good to meet you, Charlene says, and she reaches her other hand up to touch her hair. Then she does a *tendu* and smiles.

Aunt Jezie says, I want to thank you for the special attention you've been giving Siddalee. She's my protégée, you know.

I chime in, Aunt Jezie teaches me how to sing!

Oh, do *you* sing? Charlene asks Aunt Jezie.

Aunt Jezie laughs and says, I sing passionately to horses, dogs, and children. The general public I avoid.

Charlene laughs back, and Aunt Jezie says, I've enjoyed seeing you on television. How lucky we are to have you back in Thornton.

Charlene does a *plié* and says, It's nice to be back. I *think*.

Aunt Jezie is the one smiling now, and she says, Maybe we should get together sometime and have a laugh or two about this armpit of a town.

Charlene says, I'd like that. God knows there's enough to laugh about.

I want to ask, There *is?* Then I think, Are yall going to laugh about *me?*

But before I can even open my mouth, Aunt Jezie says, *Ciao!* and she leads me down to the car.

She drives straight out to Pearl's Plunge, a concrete pool with spring water, where they have a dance pavilion and all. We swim and lie in the sun all day and eat corn dogs from the concession stand. Every once in a while she reads out loud to me from this book, *The Fountainhead,* all about this architect who everyone misunderstands. I completely forget to ask what she and Charlene are going to laugh about.

*O*ne evening Mama takes Baylor and Little Shep and Lulu and me to Fred's Hamburger Drive-In where we eat at least twice a week. She pulls the Thunderbird into our regular spot facing the wooden fence painted with a hobo eating a huge po'boy. And before Mama even turns off the motor, I spot Aunt Jezie and Charlene across the parking lot. They are sitting in Charlene's mother's Buick Skylark convertible with the top down. I'm so surprised to see them there together. But mainly, I can't believe how lucky it is that we're all here at the same time! I jump out of the car and bolt across the parking lot in their direction, my flip-flops nearly flying off my feet with each step.

When I reach the convertible I stand by the driver's door and say, Hey yall! We're here having hamburgers too!

I think, They'll ask me to eat with them, then take me riding around afterward!

But they just sit there looking all tan, with a basket

of curly-Q fries on the seat between them. Charlene smiles and says, Hello there, Miss Sidda.

But the way she says it, I can tell she is just being polite. You can tell she isn't really glad to see me. Even so, I can't stop staring at how pretty she looks in her pink short-shorts and white ruffly blouse. Mama never wears ruffles. Aunt Jezie sits in the passenger seat acting like I'm nowhere in sight. She just stares in the opposite direction from me and lets out this big sigh.

I don't know what to do next. So I say, Mama says brown cold drinks cause pimples.

I don't know what possessed me to say this and I feel like a complete ignoramus as soon as it comes out. Aunt Jezie reaches down and changes the radio station and Charlene slowly bites into a french fry.

Then Charlene starts to say something, but Aunt Jezie cuts her off and says, Sidda, I believe I hear your mother calling you.

I don't hear anything, I tell her.

Then I realize she is just trying to get rid of me.

My palms are dented in where my fingernails cut into them. I walk back over to Mama's car and I can feel my pride leaking out all over that blacktop parking lot. *They don't want to be seen with me. I embarrass them.*

I climb into the back seat of Mama's car where Lulu and Shep and Bay are all sucking on milkshakes. Mama hands me a strawberry one in a tall frosted glass.

What's wrong, Sidd? she says.

They don't want to talk to me, I tell her, ashamed.

Well, I could have told you that, dahling, she says. But you took off without asking me.

I want to die. I just want to die.

Mama props her foot up on the dashboard and explains, Your aunt, the Queen of Sheba, acts like she's over there on a *date* or something.

She goes on talking, but I blank her out. I am looking at my stomach poking out between the green plaid shorts I'm wearing and my too-tight crop top. No wonder they don't want anything to do with me, I think. I am sickening. I sit in the car, hating myself, and I deliberately suck the milkshake down so fast it makes my head hurt.

It happens overnight, the way Aunt Jezie and Charlene become best friends. One day they barely know each other, and me and Aunt Jezie are having a good summer together and Charlene is teaching me to dance and letting me visit. And then the next thing I know, *they* are doing stuff together every day of the world!

They drive all over Thornton together in that white convertible Skylark looking like a homecoming parade, and Aunt Jezie starts taking Charlene horseback riding instead of me. Every time I call over to Buggy's, Aunt Jezie is out doing something with Charlene! I am the one who introduced them to begin with. Charlene was my friend first! They never would have even met if it hadn't been for me. And now they act like I have evaporated right off the face of the earth. It makes me so sick, I want to get scarlet fever and die and then see how they'd all feel.

Charlene keeps on being as sweet as ever at dance class. When I have trouble with my time steps, she takes me aside and works with me. And she makes me Queen for the Week a second time when I tell her about Mama and the tiara. But I am so mad I can't enjoy any of it. Aunt Jezie just takes all the pleasure out of everything, stealing Charlene away from me like that. I wish over and over that the ugly horse Buggy rented her for the summer would throw her off and stomp her to death.

One night I'm at Buggy's, and my aunt the poot-faced thief goes out with guess-who. Just takes right off and leaves me with Buggy and her dog Miss Peppy. So I tell Buggy I'm looking for my rosary so she will let me go into Aunt Jezie's room. Normally that room is off-limits unless Aunt Jezie gives you permission. Once I get in there, I dump all her perfumes right down the bathroom drain and fill up the bottles with plain old tap water. Then I open her makeup drawer and take out her lipsticks and smash them into the dresser. Then I put their covers back on and put them back in the drawer for her to find them. I hate her guts and I hate all her stuff, too!

A couple of days go by and I spend my time mainly thinking up more ways I can get back at Aunt Jezie. But then she and Charlene come and get me one evening at Buggy's and whisk me right off to the Roxy Drive-In. We have so much fun that I forgive them for every-thing. It's a real starry night with no clouds and there we are in the convertible, which Aunt Jezie says is the only way to go to the drive-in. We rub Six-Twelve all over ourselves and light the mosquito coil and watch *Pal Joey* and sing along to "The Lady Is a Tramp." I get to sit up front between them and eat all the Nutty-Buddies I want. The three of us share a chocolate shake, all sucking right from the same straw, and when I get sleepy, Aunt Jezie takes out one of Buggy's cotton throws and drapes it over me.

We drive home through the sweet night air over the Garnet River bridge. You can smell the water and the cotton poisoning from the nearby fields and the radio is playing "Around the World in Eighty Days." When Charlene bends down and hugs me goodnight in front of Buggy's house, I can smell her hair and it smells so pure.

Then Aunt Jezie and I go inside and fall sound asleep in her big bed. The window air conditioner is turned off, and the attic fan pulls cool air in, making the curtains billow the whole night long like they're waltzing.

I just know for sure that our night at the drive-in means the three of us are going to be best friends from here on out.

But after a few days, I realize I am wrong. They don't call me, don't stop by, don't ask me to go anywhere, anytime, anyhow. The only time I see Charlene is at dance class. Aunt Jezie picks her up afterward and they just zoom off and leave me standing on the curb sweating in my leotard.

So I decide that the reason they're ignoring me is because they're planning a big surprise for me. Something really special—like a trip to New Orleans or a swimming party or my own high-heeled tap shoes. I spend whole days fantasizing about how they're going to surprise me.

One afternoon a couple of weeks after *Pal Joey,* I'm staying over at Sherry Jenkins' house. I tell her all about me and Aunt Jezie and Charlene.

We are best friends, I tell her. We go to the drive-in every night, and ride horses every day, and sit around and talk, and just do everything in the world together. The only reason I have any time to play with you at all right now is because they're so busy preparing this huge surprise for me.

Sherry says, I don't believe you. You're making that up.

Sherry, I tell her, you are so ignorant, you don't know anything.

Then I get my big idea—I'll take her over to Buggy's house and show her where Aunt Jezie hides her lucky horseshoe. Showing off that I know Aunt Jezie's most secret hiding place will prove to Sherry Stupenagel that I'm telling the truth.

But I'm not supposed to walk off my block, Sherry says, like a real whiny-baby.

I say, If you don't come with me, I'm going to tell everyone about that time we saw your parents when they didn't have their clothes on.

That shuts her up. And when we get to Buggy's, there isn't a car in the driveway. It looks for sure like nobody's home.

I want it to seem like a big adventure. I whisper to Sherry, You wait at the kitchen door and I'll go in through the back and let you in.

I sneak around to the back, and I slide open the glass door to the added-on den, where steps lead up to Aunt Jezie's room. The window air conditioner is humming real loud and you can't hear anything else. It's cold and dry compared to the wet heat outside. I get a thrill being in the house when no one knows I'm there. I've never done this before. It makes me feel like I'm the boss.

I eyeball the den like Nancy Drew, looking for a mystery. Then I hear a little gasp coming from Aunt Jezie's bedroom, a sound like someone has just dived into cold water and come up for air.

I think, That's Aunt Jezie in there getting ready to scare me! Every single one of Mama's family loves to sneak up on you from behind and scare you to death.

I tiptoe silently up the white-carpeted steps to Jezie's room where the window unit is blasting out arctic air. When I get to the top step, I drop down on my knees to the carpet. Right in front of me, in broad daylight, are Aunt Jezie and Charlene Parks in the four-poster bed.

Buck naked!

Their clothes are tossed on the chaise longue by the window. I recognize Charlene's powder blue wrap-around skirt. And they don't even know I'm there!

I crawl over by the dresser so I can get a good view of them. They're kissing each other on the face and shoulders, and Aunt Jezie's hand is on Charlene's leg and Charlene is breathing like she's been dancing hard. I can see Aunt Jezie's nipples. They're brown and hard and standing up in little peaks. From what I can see, Charlene's nipples are much lighter, like salmon-pink crayolas. Her hair is loose, spreading out all over the pillow.

I can't get over that hair. I've never seen it look so wild and messed up! Even when she performs her solo from *West Side Story,* her hair always stays up in a neat ponytail.

My face is all hot and I feel twitchy like I have to go to the bathroom or something. I want to go find Buggy and Mama and Charlene's mother and the man who runs the Community Center, and *tell on them!* They shouldn't be doing this! And I also want to climb up there in the bed with them and have them kiss me too, and I want them to let me suck on Aunt Jezie's nipples and to bury my face in Charlene's hair! I want to be grown-up and drive my own convertible and live in a different town where nobody knows Mama or Daddy.

I want so many different things. And the worst part of all is feeling like I'll never get any of them.

Then I remember Sherry. What if she gets tired of waiting for me at the kitchen door? What if she comes back here, and sees what's going on?! God, no one else can know about this! Just me.

I sneak down the steps and ease the sliding-glass door open. Once I make it outside, I break into a run. Sherry is sitting on the kitchen steps just like I told her to. What a little dumb-ass.

I jerk her up and say, Come on! We've gotta get out of here!

We run all the way down to the bayou by City Park. It's scalding hot and the air is thick and damp, but Sherry runs right alongside of me. She will do anything I tell her.

We finally stop on the bank where Little Shep and his in-town friends sometimes crayfish. Sherry keeps saying, What's the matter, Siddalee? What's wrong?

I tell her, Shut up, you are such a moron. You're sickening.

Why are you mad at me? she asks. I didn't do anything.

And then I slap her. Not hard, just a medium slap.
I don't know why I do it. I just have to. And also I
know that she'll let me. She looks at me so innocent, it
makes me sick.

I say, Let's kiss. She looks confused, but she obeys
me. We kiss one long kiss and then I break away. I say,
If you tell anyone about this, I will ruin your whole
life, Sherry, and you know that I can.

She says, I won't tell, Siddalee, really, I promise you.
I won't tell a soul.

Back at Sherry's house that evening we have ice-
cream sandwiches after supper and play cards and then
go to sleep. In the middle of the night it starts raining
real hard, and I wake up because I can feel raindrops
coming in through the open window. I sit up and
watch the rain falling and the lightning shooting across
the sky. It's thundering loud, but Sherry keeps on
sleeping. When the lightning flashes, it lights up her
whole body. It makes her look like she's in a theater
with a stagelight shining on her. Or like she's caught
in a searchlight trying to escape from a Communist
concentration camp. It looks like she could be electro-
cuted at any minute and she wouldn't even know it.

WANDERING EYE
Big Shep, 1962

*S*ometimes I'll turn my head in the middle of the day and out of nowhere I'll still think I hear the sound of Pap's black Ford hitting the gravel road. Then I get a fist in my stomach and my lungs clench up.

My Daddy wasn't really that big of a man. He just *seemed* big. When he walked into a place, he sort of pushed the air out all around him and took up all the air me or Mama or whoever needed. He was a handsome man when I was a boy. Thick head of brownish hair, big old cow eyes. My kids all got his eyes. I got Mama's eyes—hazel. He called them liar eyes.

Pap was a hard worker. Came from an old family—you can check it in *The Walker Family of Louisiana* book. But he was from the country and didn't have quite the education Vivi's family did, and they have never let me forget it. When me and Vivi announced our engagement, Buggy Abbott started crying like someone had died.

It didn't matter that Pap had managed to hang on to three plantations during the Depression, while all the rest of those blue-blood gentlemen farmer friends of the Abbotts lost the shirts off their backs because they didn't want to get dirt up under their fingernails. None of that crowd could take it that my father trucked potatoes to hold on to his land, while the rest of them holed up in their old run-down Civil War houses whining like spoilt babies about Huey Long.

Pap had opinions on everything. And in between being a good man, he could be the meanest sonova-bitch you ever saw. Used to pop me upside the head so hard I didn't know what hit me. My kids think they get whipped? Hell, they don't even know what a whip-ping is. Mama and Pap both whipped. But he was the strong one, he was the one that got carried away. Mama was more of a swatter, like if I'd run out into traffic or sass her real bad. But not Pap. He was a fighter.

One time he lit into me in the front yard. He came at me because I'd left one of the tractors out in the rain. Had just forgot to pull it up under the shed before I left off to go to a picture show in town. Pap didn't even bother taking off his belt, just come at me with his fist. I wasn't ready for it, I'd just got outta the truck and walked into the yard, carrying a sack of Ruston peaches for Mama in my hand. Took me a while to even realize what was happening—you know how you can get caught off-guard. I thought he was just reaching for the peaches. He came at me so hard, he had me on the ground in a split second. Mama was sitting on the porch shelling butter beans. She watched for a while before she stood up and ran down the steps. Out the corner of my eye I could see that bowl fall out of her lap, butter beans rolling across the porch. I could smell those peaches with their full sweet smell, smashed on the ground.

Mama yelled out, Bay, that's enough! Leave him alone!

He turned on her and said, Get away from me before I knock you upside the head too!

She went on back up to the porch. She was wearing that blue printed-cotton housedress, the one with the flowers that looked like bluebells.

He busted me in the eye, knocked one of my teeth loose, and did something to one of my ribs. I don't know if the rib was broke, no doctor ever looked at it. But I couldn't take a deep breath for weeks without hurting. If I coughed, I near-bout fainted with the pain.

I don't care how much my four kids rile me, I never knocked loose one of their teeth. I never broke a one of their ribs. I hope they remember that when they get older. When they count up the things I did and didn't do.

I never gave the drinking a second thought. It was normal as eating in Pap's house. Everybody in the state of Louisiana drank like that, far as I knew. Never thought one way or the other when Mama used to take her "naps" in the middle of Christmas or Thanksgiving dinner. Never said to myself, Mama's not napping, she's passed-out drunk. Never even questioned it the time Pap peed on the goddamn radiator one night instead of in the commode, he was that juiced up. Piss-steam rising up everywhere, Mama leading him out of the room, and me standing at the edge of the door thinking, Maybe he did it to be funny.

My Daddy drank his bourbon as far back as I can remember. Him and Mister Thibeaux used to sit back on the porch of the playhouse and tell stories and drink their highballs in those café glasses Pap bought wholesale by the case. The man was always proud as hell anytime he could get anything wholesale. Sometimes he'd end up with things he didn't even need, just because he'd run across them wholesale. Bought fifteen cases of those little no-good triangle-shaped café napkins one time, just because he got a good deal on them at a restaurant sale. They were too tiny for napkins and he ended up making us use them for toilet paper.

*I*t was a few months ago when I was driving Vivi and the kids home one Sunday evening from Chick and Teensy's that the drinking started crawling across my mind. Vivi and I were both pretty sauced and the kids were cranky and I was driving fast so we could get home. Must of swerved or something because some G.D. policeman pulled me over. I got out of the car to shake his hand before he even asked for my license.

I said, Shepley Walker. What can I do for you, son?

He paused for a minute, then he said, You Shep Walker? Mister Baylor's son?

Yessir, I told him, you got that right.

He looked at my car, then down at his shoes.

I said, What's the problem, officer?

He said: Oh, well . . . I guess there isn't no problem. You know, your daddy got my brother a job with Wildlife and Fisheries. He's been with them for eight years now.

Is that a fact? I said.

He nodded and said, Sorry I bothered you, Mister Shep. Have a good Sunday evening. And he walked back to his car.

I got back in my car and all the kids said, Daddy, what happened? What'd yall do out there?!

I said, Oh, it was a man wanting to talk to me about a dog, been having trouble catching up with me. Old podnah of mine.

Vivi laughed. She said, Shep Walker, you just slay me.

But Siddalee looked at me like: You liar, Daddy, you big liar.

I don't know why I'm thinking about these things—except I got some half-ass idea that if I think enough, I might be able to breathe better. This asthma is a old length of chain that wraps tighter and tighter around my chest every year. In the middle of the night when I wake up, it's all these thoughts that fly at me like cats off the wall. Sometimes I have this dream where I just tell it all, and then this special-made vacuum cleaner comes and sucks all the crap out of my lungs. Stops me from drowning. Clean oxygen reaches deep in my chest like it hasn't for so goddamn long. In the dream I tell it all, and I breathe like a baby. I forget to worry about the next breath, just trust it's gonna come.

*S*iddalee asks too many questions. I don't know where the child gets those thoughts. She pins me to the wall with all the stuff she asks. Sometimes I wish she'd lose her voice. And sometimes I want to go and sit in front of her and ask her questions. I'd like to say: What do you want me to do? Tell me what to do—step by step—to get out of the mess we're in here in this house.

But I know it's foolishness to think my little girl can pull me out of the swamp. I'm ashamed to even admit it. The child was born old, though, and it tempts you.

Siddalee is the smart one. She's the talker. Hell, she's nothing but a kid and she's already using words I never knew how to pronounce right. The child picks up new words everywhere she goes, comes home with them in her pocket. I still can't believe Vivi and me produced something like her. Neither one of us are what you'd call Brains. Although God knows, my wife can sure run on at the mouth.

Siddalee was barely in first grade when they said she had to have that eye operation. Almost paralyzed me just to hear about it. I got mad as hell at Viviane because the wandering eye came from her side of the family. It didn't come from mine. Siddalee's eye—the left one—was wandering off to the outside, making her see double. Hell, what'd people expect of me? People in this parish don't get their eyes cut on. The damn operation had only been performed six or seven times in the world, and that was in places like Boston and what-have-you.

I didn't know what to do. Viviane had lived with it all her life and it hadn't killed her. Hell, when her eye wandered at parties, men thought she was flirting with them. She used to make bets with people that she could see what was going on off to the side without turning her head. She made jokes about it, said she made her beer money in college taking bets in the dorm on what-all she could see with that eye.

I just did not understand why we had to cut on my daughter's eye. But Dr. Claude Hathaway told Vivi about this operation to correct it. Said he could go in there and take a little tuck in one of the muscles that were lazy and that'd do the trick. Siddalee's eye would quit wandering and look straight ahead. Soon as Vivi heard about it, she just had to get it done right away. Just had to.

I said, Well Vivi, why don't we wait awhile, see if it doesn't straighten itself out?

You cheap sonovabitch! she hollered. It's just like you to be too goddamn stingy with a nickel to fix your own daughter's eye!

I said, It's not the goddamn money. I never been under the knife. None of my family has ever been under the knife.

She wouldn't listen to me. She didn't know what I was thinking: *I don't want my little girl to come out blind or gouged up. I'm not cheap, I'm scared. It's the story of my life: not stingy, just a goddamn coward.*

The whole time, Viviane and me fought like dogs. I didn't think about my child, my hands were so full fighting her mother.

Viviane handled it all. I'd never seen her like that, didn't think she had it in her, taking charge like a man. She set up the hospital room, the doctor, jerked Siddalee out of school and put her up in St. Cecilia Hospital. Siddalee's hair was that long red, almost to her waist, and she'd been wearing glasses since she was three, trying to correct that wandering eye.

I wouldn't have a thing to do with it.

I told Viviane, This is on your head. If anything happens to that child, don't come blaming me. You are the one that can't live with the wandering eye. Siddalee's wandering eye doesn't bother me. I can live with the wandering eye.

Viviane and her Mama took over. Buggy moved the four-poster bed into the living room and got it all ready for Siddalee to come home to recover in.

Dr. Hathaway called me the day before the operation. He said, Shep, I'd appreciate it if you'd drop by my office this afternoon, if you have the time.

I said, What for?

I'd just like for us to have a talk before I perform surgery on your daughter, he told me.

I said, I don't have anything to talk about. This is Vivi Abbott's doing. Don't call me up again, hear?

The day they cut on Siddalee's eye, I went out to the duck camp. I cleared and burned some brush. Then I started drinking and cooked a duck gumbo with some birds I had in the deep freeze. I didn't call, didn't go back to town, didn't do a thing. Viviane couldn't get in touch with me and I didn't want her to.

I stayed gone the whole time Sidda was in the hospital. I didn't go up to St. Cecilia's at all. Drove in from the camp to do a little farming, then drove back out there to sleep. Didn't come back until she was home.

They'd set her up in the four-poster bed like she was a little princess. When I got there, her Aunt Jezie was reading *Black Beauty* out loud to her, and I could smell Buggy cooking some peanut-butter fudge. And there was Siddalee. Sitting up in that bed, wearing this little pink satin bed jacket one of the aunts had bought her. Her eyes bandaged from ear to ear. Nothing but white gauze.

I stood at the doorway looking at her, and Jezie just kept on reading, like I wasn't even there. My daughter didn't flinch, didn't have a clue that I was anywhere around. At one point while Jezie was reading, Siddalee asked her to stop for a minute and I thought, *Maybe Sidda knows I'm here.*

But she just laid there still for a minute, then said: Aunt Jezie, would you read that part over again?

I wish Sidda would of sensed me, would of smelled me. Would of known I was near, even though she couldn't see me. But then I'm always expecting too much from the girl, wanting her to know things she can't see. That's not one of the things I'm proud of, it's something I wish I could rip up out of the ground.

I'd bought her some of these velveteen headbands from Bordelon's Drugstore. I remember standing there in the store, thinking: She can rub her hands on the velvet and feel it, even though her eyes are bandaged. I got the salesgirl to gift-wrap them.

I wanted to walk the four steps over to my daughter propped up in that bed and say: Hey, Red! Here's a strawberry-colored headband. I know you can't see it, but just rub your hand on it. Feel? It's gonna look so pretty against that long hair of yours.

But I never walked over to Siddalee laying there in the bed. I just stood right inside the doorway of the living room for a minute, then turned around and walked out.

Buggy and Jezie Abbott both moved into the house

to help Viviane with the kids. They were camped out in the kids' schoolroom, but their stuff was spread out everywhere. You could smell them all over the place. And Buggy had brought Miss Peppy, that rat of a dog, with her. It wasn't my house anymore.

I left the headbands on the kitchen table and went out and checked on some business at the cotton gin. When I got back home that evening, Vivi was sitting at the kitchen counter talking on the phone, describing Sidda's operation blow-by-blow to one of the Ya-Yas, like she'd been the one that got cut on. I walked in to look at Siddalee in the living room. It looked like she was asleep, but I couldn't be sure with those bandages.

Before I knew it, Vivi slammed down the phone and flew into the room. She grabbed me by the arm and pulled me out into the living room.

What do you think you are doing? she said.

Peeking at Sidda, I told her.

You put all the responsibility on me, she said. And I don't want you anywhere near that child now. You stay out of there. Don't you lay a finger on her! I don't even want you talking to her, do you understand me?

I had deliberately not taken a single drink. Wanted to come home sober, wanted to see Siddalee myself—sober.

I said to Vivi, Get off your high horse. That's my daughter in there too.

She screamed, You cheap sonovabitch, you didn't even want to pay for the surgery! I'm the one who handled everything, don't you show up here now acting like you're Ozzie-goddamn-Nelson. You were gone when I needed you. I don't need you now.

She started to slap me, but I caught her hand. It was shaking. I looked at my wife and she looked tireder than usual, thinner.

Then Siddalee was standing there at the doorway between the den and the living room. She was holding on to the doorsill and I could see her feet on the tile floor. I wanted to slip something up underneath those little bare feet because I knew that floor must of felt cold, with her just out of bed. The bandages and her bathrobe made her look like a real short war veteran. It like to tore my heart out.

I let go of Vivi's hand and she went over to Siddalee, put her arm around her. My little girl looked so pale, and someone had braided her hair so it wouldn't get in her face. She couldn't see me anymore.

I started to move toward her, and then she said: Daddy, don't hurt me.

Those words killed me. They stabbed me in the neck. My little girl was scared of me, and my marriage was rotting in the fields.

I said to Viviane, What have you been doing to this child to make her say that?

I went to grab my wife by the shoulders, not to hurt her, but to shake out whatever words she'd filled my daughter with to turn her away from me.

And then the child started crying, terrified. Tears squeezing their way out from under those bandages.

Vivi said, Now look what you've done. She's not supposed to cry. It's not good for her eye. Are you satisfied, Shep? Well, are you?

Then Siddalee was leaning against Vivi. Her legs were shaking under that little robe, goosebumps on her freckled calves. I should of picked her up in my arms and carried her gentle and placed her back into that four-poster bed with all the pillows. But I didn't, goddamn it. I didn't.

And then it was too late, the moment up and went, like time always does. They took the bandages off and Siddalee's eye didn't wander anymore. She had to wear a patch for a little while, but my daughter didn't end up with any scars you could see.

Sometimes, when I'd wake up in the middle of the night wheezing from the asthma, sitting up in the chair because I couldn't breathe lying down, I would think: I can't breathe because of all the things I'm too scared to do. But after getting up and pouring a drink or two, I quit thinking that way. I just kept putting cotton in the ground and hunting and doing what my Daddy raised me to do.

*T*hen one regular day after Siddalee's been back in school a couple months, Pap tells me to go check on the hoe-hands at the lower place. He says, Son, you gotta learn to keep your eyes open. Farming isn't no goddamn New Orleans house party.

That riles me, like he knew it would, him always acting like I'm the biggest playboy in the state of Louisiana. He knows just how to get under my skin. Here I am, a grown man with four children, and he has to watch over everything I do, like I can't tie my own shoes.

I say, Awright, Pap, I'll take care of it.

And my Daddy takes off out of the field. I guess after that he stopped at the post office to get his mail, then drove on home. It was August and sticky hot, getting on toward noon. I guess he figured he'd read his mail and have himself a glass of ice tea. He was sitting in that white rocker out in the breezeway. Had his shoes and socks off to let his feet relax. They say the radio was playing, so I guess he was probably listening to the noonday farm report.

He must of felt the pain in his chest for only a minute before he slumped over and fell out of the rocker. That bottle of nitroglycerine pills he'd been carrying around in his shirt pocket for years didn't do him one bit of good. That bottle rolled out of his grasp over toward that big old pot of hen and chicken that Mama'd been growing forever. He couldn't get his hands on that bottle to unscrew the lid and put one of those pills on his tongue, which might of stopped all the rest of it from happening.

They say Mama was at the Piggly-Wiggly. She drove up in the blue Oldsmobile in a hurry because she didn't want to be late with his noon meal. He always liked to eat his meals on time. She found him there laying in the breezeway.

She tells me she remembers thinking, I got to put this sack of groceries down careful. I got six bottles of RC Cola in here and I don't want to break them.

Chaney, my right-hand man, and his wife, Willetta, are the ones who come out to the field to tell me. I'm standing under that big pecan tree where we always set up the water cooler. When they pull up in the flatbed truck I start to thinking, What the hell is Letta doing out here? She's supposed to be cleaning up at the house.

Chaney and Letta walk over, Chaney's head hanging

down the way it does when he's ashamed. When he gets to me, he takes off his cap and wipes his face with a rag out of his pocket. Your daddy done passed, Mister Shep, he tells me.

What you talkin' about, man? I ask him, thinking maybe he means Pap had driven by in a car.

He says, Mister Baylor Senior done passed, boss. Your daddy dead.

He is standing there with that blue denim cap in his hands, fingering the bill of it. And he's crying like you wouldn't expect a worker like Chaney to do. Letta hands me a cup of water from the cooler. I can taste the tinniness of that water and hear the hoe-hands mumbling in the distance. For a second the specks of cotton I can see out of the corner of my eyes confuse me. They look for a minute like snow in another climate far away from the land where I was born and raised.

By the time I get over to Mama and Daddy's, his body has already been taken to the funeral home. The only thing left is his shoes next to the rocker. Big black broke-in Red Wings sitting there, pair of white socks tucked inside. I bend down to pick one of them up and I can still smell the Ammons' Heat Powder he'd sprinkled on the innersole that morning. I can see how his wide feet had pushed out at the sides of those shoes, just the way my own do.

The funeral feels like a strange political cook-up. Hundreds of Pap's friends from North and South Louisiana are there. Hell, even Russell Long puts in an appearance. And you can't count the number of colored people there, babies hanging on their mamas' hips. Vivi tells me what to wear, and my kids are dressed like little royalty. I think, How did my children turn out to look so damn blue-blooded?

We get home that evening and I go back to the bedroom. I bathe and get ready for bed and don't say nothing to nobody. I climb in the bed with a copy of *U.S. News and World Report*, propping up my pillows like I do so I can breathe.

And then my children start coming back there. I can hear their feet slapping against the wood floor. First Siddalee. Then Baylor, then Lulu, and finally Little Shep. Every one of them, climbing up on the bed with me like we hadn't ever done before. We're not the kind of family that does cozy things. But they all pile up in there with me like a little bird had come and told them to do it. They don't say anything. And I sure as hell don't have any words that can get unstuck from my throat.

Then Little Shep says, Read us what you're reading, Daddy.

And so I start reading out loud from the damn magazine, don't even know what I'm reading about. I just read out loud whatever words are there on the page.

Vivi comes to the door then, rubbing cold cream on her face like always, and I see her look at the five of us. I can smell Siddalee's hair, all clean from just being shampooed, and her eyes are focused on the page I'm reading. Like she understands all about world affairs. Then Vivi walks over and sits on the edge of the bed. I keep on reading out loud, and somewhere in the middle of that article I start to cry. Slow tears, like my body isn't exactly sure how to do it. I keep reading till I can't read anymore, and then my wife takes the magazine out of my hands and lays it on the nightstand. She takes that magazine from me and lays it down, and she does the whole thing like she loves me. She makes that one little gesture with tenderness I've never seen before. Maybe she's been doing things like that all along, and I just haven't seen. Then she climbs up in the bed with us. I can feel all my children's bodies still warm from their baths, and smell the sachet smell of Vivi's gown. They're like little animals, we're all like animals on that bed in the back bedroom. Nobody says much of anything. I know we're all crying, but you can't tell where one person's crying leaves off and the other person's begins.

My Daddy has just died. He's left me three plantations to run. I thought he'd live forever. I am thirty-three years old and half the time I can't even breathe. But this one night with all my family in the bed with me is like living on a safe island. It's the least lonely I've been in my whole life.

I wish I could have more times like this to tell about. I'd give them to my children, gift-wrap them myself to put in front of their eyes.

SKINNY-DIPPING
Baylor, 1963

*I*t's summer at Spring Creek, and Sidda, Little Shep, Lulu, and me are getting so good at stilt-walking that I bet Ringling Brothers is gonna call us before school starts up again. Maybe we'll get hired to perform for a bunch of money and Mama and Daddy will let us travel all over the world. And we'll only come home to Louisiana for trips to Spring Creek.

You have to understand that Spring Creek is heaven on earth for a Louisiana summer. It is always ten degrees cooler than any other spot in the state, everybody swears to it. We talk about it all year long. When things get bad crazy in the middle of winter and the windows are all shut, and Mama has her nervous stomach, she will sometimes say: Hey yall, come over here and let's talk about Spring Creek! And then everything gets a little better.

Every year on the day after Memorial Day, our maid Willetta helps us pack up the car to head out to our camp at Spring Creek for almost three solid months. The T-Bird is stuffed to the gills with our swimsuits, the first-aid kit, tons of Six-Twelve, stacks of funny-books, and the picnic Willetta has fixed for us. And even though there's that hump in the back seat where it's only supposed to fit two, three of us sit back there without pinching or fighting or anything.

Mama says, Oh, I just wish this car was a convertible! Don't yall?!

Yes ma'am! we all say back.

We're so happy to be leaving Pecan Grove. We might live on a nice plantation, but sometimes it can wear you out.

She says, Well, let's just roll down all the windows and *pretend* we're in a convertible!

And we pull out of the Pecan Grove driveway with the car air-conditioner cranked up full-blast and the windows rolled down—which is a sure sign that Mama is ready for a good summer.

All the rest of the stuff that can't fit into the car— the town water in huge glass bottles with cork stoppers, the linens and clean towels, the tractor inner-tubes, folding chairs, ice chests full of food, and the extra rotary fans—Chaney drives all that stuff out in the pickup. He never stays long in Spring Creek because they don't have colored people out there.

Mama begs Willetta to come out every year and stay for the summer, but Willetta says, Thank you, but no thank you, Miz Vivi. I rather have my teefs all pulled out than spend the night in that parish.

Caro with her kids and Necie with hers follow right behind us all the way out there. Mama honks the horn and we wave out the windows, and we're a wagon train heading to summer—leaving all the daddies in town to work and only come out every couple of weeks. Which is fine with me, because Mama and the Ya-Yas are lots more fun without the men around. They don't wear makeup when we're at Spring Creek, just a dab of lipstick and toenail polish. And they don't use hairspray at all. They wear men's big shirts and short-shorts and ratty old tennis shoes, and at night they sleep in teeshirts and panties. They only cook when they feel like it, they read tons of paperback books, and if one of them farts, they laugh their heads off and yell out: Kill it! Step on it! Don't let it get away! When Mama is at Spring Creek, she does only what she wants to.

But when Daddy and the other men come out for a weekend, the Ya-Yas start getting ready on Friday morning. Fixing little appetizers and tweezing their eyebrows, and Mama gets all nervous. It's the only time that Mama makes me put Vitalis on my hair, and she tells us exactly what we can and can't tell Daddy about what we've been doing.

See, Mama and the Ya-Yas all came out to Spring Creek when they were little. All their families had camps and their mamas brought them out here while their daddies worked in town. When they were teenagers, the Ya-Yas just owned Spring Creek during the summers—that's how they put it. You should see the pictures of Mama and Necie and Caro, and sometimes Teensy, how pretty they were then with their hats and sunglasses. Mama drove a Willys jeep and Caro had a red convertible, and they did anything in the world they wanted. We egg them on to tell us stories about the trouble they used to cook up back then.

Spring Creek has always been in a dry parish, the Ya-Yas say. And it's our job to moisten the place up!

Our camp is named *Sans Souci,* which means "without a care." We have a carved wood sign hanging out in front. All you have to say is "Sans Souci" and everybody knows where it is. It's real big and right in the middle of the piney woods, just a short hike away from three different swimming holes.

When we open up the camp at first, it smells the same as ever: all musty and old and good. It is dirty from being empty for nine months. But the Ya-Yas give us our assignments and we get right to work. Daddy-long-legs are crawling out everywhere, and there's so much dust that Sidda has to take out her wheezer.

Mama always has us clean the kitchen up first. She says, A good camper always does her kitchen right from the get-go! She's right, too. Because once we get the kitchen spotless, then we can go in there and wash our hands and eat Letta's ham and cheese sandwiches and lemonade and cookies and kick our feet up while the rest of the place is still a mess.

Mama and Necie and Caro do everything themselves, with only us to help them. They hook up the well, turn on the electricity, and get rid of the dirt-dobbers that have built nests under the eaves. They just take over, and they don't call Daddy or any servicemen to help, even though we do have a phone out there. (That phone is the oldest phone in the universe. If you got hit in the head with that big black phone, it'd knock you out cold and you'd die dead.)

Sans Souci has screen windows running all the way around it. It's like living in a porch the whole time. There are smooth plank floors and a huge, long sleeping porch with three ceiling fans. All the beds are lined up, one after the other, plenty for everyone.

Two-dozen people can sleep at Sans Souci, if they're not picky, Mama says.

Each bed has a little reading lamp just behind your head. And the way the fans hang from the ceiling, every one of us gets this nice little breeze. We never suffocate from the heat unless there's a storm and the electricity goes out. We do our best sleeping at Sans Souci.

We've got a dressing room and a shower in the middle of the camp, but they are awful hot to spend much time in. The toilet is in a little green closet off the side of the sleeping porch, and we keep a thousand funny-books and *Reader's Digest*s in there. You have to pull down on a chain to flush, and the water is brownish from the well. You can't drink that water without boiling it because of all the germs you can't see. There's a little basin just outside the john, and when you wash your face, the water has a tinny smell to it. It's the kind of water that makes your skin squeak. When we get through brushing our teeth, we always have to wrap our toothbrushes in tinfoil so the bugs won't crawl on them.

Oh, but let me tell you, the front room is the best. It's huge and long with a glider at one end and two couches and a rattan chaise longue, which Mama calls her "Throne." And at the other end, there is a long table covered with a yellow-and-white-checked oilcloth, and it doesn't matter what you spill on it because it just wipes clean. You don't ever have to worry about what you break or spill at Spring Creek. It's not like at home, where you get a whipping if you drop a mayonnaise jar on the tile floor. In front of the camp, we have six Navy hammocks strung between the pines around the fire pit. You can lay up in those hammocks all day long and read funny-books. Or get somebody to push you real fast and then jump out and feel like you're flying for half a second. And at night, oh, at night! You can lay there (after you've put on plenty of Six-Twelve) and watch the lightning bugs and the fire, and sometimes we sing and dance and tell ghost stories.

We keep our stilts with our names painted on them under the camp so they won't get rained on and warp. But we keep the huge wooden electrical spool that Daddy got from the phone company outside, no matter what the weather. I can walk backwards on that spool all the way to the gate and back without falling. Me and Sidda can walk on it together like a real circus act. While we're performing on the spool, Necie's kids get Sidda to sing like Little Brenda Lee and they sit there and clap for us.

At Spring Creek, I get to do what I want, when I want. Go to bed when I want and wake up when I want. When I wake up I just put my swimsuit right on without even fooling with clothes. All of us kids share the same clothes at Spring Creek. We just have a big chest full of shorts and tee-shirts and seersucker pajamas and that's it. Mornings are good at Spring Creek. Sometimes when I wake up, the sunrise streams in through the screen windows so full of all these yellows and oranges and pinks, and I lay there in my bed. And before I'm all the way awake, I think that I'm in the back seat of the T-Bird at the Roxy Drive-In watching color spread across the screen! That is just the way it is at Spring Creek.

Mornings at our camp Mama isn't shaking all over, trying to fix a big breakfast like she does at Pecan Grove. I just walk out to the table and there's a bunch of cereal boxes lined up with sugar and peaches. And I get the milk out of the short old icebox that has a good hum to it, and I fix just what I feel like. My throat never closes up on me at the camp. I eat all day long.

I can take my cereal outside and eat in the sun. And Mama and the Ya-Yas are sitting on the steps drinking coffee and smoking cigarettes. Mama rubs the top of my head and says, How you doing, sleepy-bones?

Then she starts singing "Oh What a Beautiful Mornin'!" from *Oklahoma!,* one of her favorite musicals.

Mama leans back on the steps and says: I adore every single one of yall! I adore Spring Creek! This is how I was *meant* to live! No responsibility! I hate responsibility! And she laughs and leans her face back in the sun and says, Yall don't forget to put on your Coppertone! And Lulu, put that zinc oxide on your nose!

I finish my cereal and head out for the creek for a morning swim with Necie and the rest of the kids, eleven of us in all. See, at Spring Creek, Mama isn't the only Mama I have. I've got my pick of whatever Ya-Ya is around. We walk through the woods for our early swim. We go down the hill and I always stop at this little place where water comes out of a concrete culvert and makes a little pool. The farmer who lives by there has got it dammed up. I count tadpoles in there and rinse my face, and on the way back from swimming I stick my feet in there to cool them off. I think it's a magic pool, because one morning I was there and counted twelve tadpoles and when I came back there was nineteen! All kinds of things like that happen at Spring Creek.

The best swimming hole is Little Spring Creek. You've got Big Spring Creek, Little Spring Creek, and Dido Creek, but Little Spring Creek is the best. It has a sandy beach where we lay our towels and stuff, and the ladies set up their chairs and the ice chest. Right around there is the shallow part where the little babies can play. And then there's this big log that divides the shallow end from the deep end. You can sit on that log and watch everything—the ladies rubbing on their oil, big trees on both sides of the creek, dogs sleeping in the sun on the bank, turtles lined up sunning themselves on the slimy log that none of us fool with. We call it the Turtle Log. It's all theirs. We have our log, and they have theirs. You can look down at the deep end where there's a rope swing hung from a huge tree, where you can swing out like Tarzan and holler before you drop down into the water below. You've got to be sure and let go of that rope, though, because one time a little boy whose brother was a friend of my cousin got scared and wouldn't let go, and he hit into the tree and smashed his skull in! We didn't see it, but we all knew about it. So it doesn't matter how scared you are, you've got to let go of that rope and drop down into the deep end.

Your first dive into the water in the morning is the finest thing in the world. It's never too cold. It's Louisiana summer creek water, not some northern-state water—where I've never been, but I know it's so cold it takes your breath away and would give Daddy a heart attack. Little Spring Creek is the kind of water that lets you wake up slow, lets you roll over on your back and float and stare at the clouds without getting the shivers, without having to swim fast to keep from freezing to death. Mama says, This is the kind of water that spoils Southerners for any other part of the country.

All that happens in Little Spring Creek is that your skin comes all alive and maybe a dragonfly lands on your shoulder with the blue-green colors of their wings shining in the sunlight. You don't swat dragonflies because they're the good bugs. They go around eating up the bad ones that itch you to death.

Man, we have the best tractor inner-tubes in the state of Louisiana. They're from my Daddy's farm machinery and Mama painted "Walker" on them with white paint, but we still let other people use them. They're big enough for four of us to sit on, and you can paddle out into the deep end and then—real careful—you can stand up on the inner-tube! Sidda and me do it the best: stand up real slow and hold hands and balance ourselves. We stand there on that tractor inner-tube perfectly balanced, with the sky a big blue tent over our heads. We stand real still and then we start rocking back and forth as hard as we can and still try to stay on. We see how long we can do it and how hard before we fall off. The only thing is, those inner-tubes have got those little nozzles where you put the air in, and if you aren't careful you fall down on them and scrape your body up something awful. Almost every kid in Spring Creek has got one of those long scratches on their bodies. You're just lucky if it doesn't make you bleed, because then one of the Ya-Yas will make you get out and they put Mercurochrome and a Band-Aid on you from the blue tin first-aid kit. And then you have to sit on the blanket with them, and they all say, I just hope he's had his latest tetanus booster.

Anyway, what we usually do is this. We swim in the morning. Then when it starts to get around noon, we pack up and walk over to Spring Creek Shop-and-Skate, which is your only roller rink and grocery store in Central Louisiana. Inside the store it is all cool, with the concrete floor under your feet and the jukebox playing in the skating rink. And they have wooden boxes with screen lids filled with crickets, and next to that they have worms and shiners for fishing. All the Ya-Yas have known Nadine, the owner, forever. And we get our bread and milk from her, and the big blocks of ice that you have to carry out to the car with these big iron tongs. If you drop that ice on your foot you'll be crippled forever, so you better be careful. Then we go back to the camp during the heat of the day, and play with the old slot machine that Mama rigged up so it doesn't cost a nickel to play. And we have bologna sandwiches and Fritos and Cokes and maybe take a nap or do whatever we plain feel like.

Finally when it cools down a little, the Ya-Yas let us go without them back to the skating rink. We rent skates for a quarter. Sidda is all the time playing Nat King Cole on the jukebox. There's this huge fan at one end of the rink that I swear you could get sucked into if you don't watch out. I won't skate down at that end. We put ice-cream sandwiches on Mama's tab, and we eat them sitting on the bench. Then Lulu always goes and gets her a second one, even though she knows we're only supposed to charge one apiece.

I been working on my skating but I'm not what you call the greatest. Little Shep thinks he's so tough, skating backwards and all. He thinks he's King of the Universe in everything he does. At Pecan Grove he answers the phone just like Daddy does, putting his foot up on the kitchen stool and saying "Little Shep Walker here." He wears cowboy boots just like Daddy and acts like he's the boss of the world.

Then before you know it, we're all back in the creek for a late afternoon swim and everyone has cleared out except for only us. We wait until the sun is just starting to go down and then we take our baths. The Ya-Yas all get bars of Ivory soap and we suds up and rub that lather all over our bodies and you can hear the cicadas cranking up. And you suds up your hair, too, then close your eyes and dive into the water and rinse it out. You smell that Ivory and the creek water and see the little bitty ones with their swimsuits off, getting bathed by their mamas. And the Ya-Yas are washing their hair, too, and everybody is laughing and Little Shep and me are making our hair stand up in points.

These are our real baths because we'd run that well dry in no time flat if we all tried to use the shower back at the camp. We get to take our swimsuits off underwater, but only the little ones can just pop up naked.

But then one evening, Caro says, Oh, bathing with a swimsuit on is just ridiculous! And she takes off her swimsuit and flings it over by the towels, and so the older Ya-Yas go right ahead and do the same thing. And so of course all the rest of us take ours off too, and that makes it four mamas and sixteen kids skinny-dipping. We have that whole place to ourselves and they start singing one of their old camp songs:

Once I went in swimmin
Where there were no wimmin
And no one to seeee
Hung my little britches
On the willow switches of a nearby tree
Came a little villain
Stole my underwear
And left me with a smile!

And we're all laughing and Little Shep is trying to sing real deep like a grown-up man and Sidda's long red hair is floating on her shoulders and Lulu is sunburned and Necie's little ones are splashing and jumping up and down. And you can see the Ya-Yas' breasts but they just look like Mama's and it's not a big deal. And we just keep bathing and playing and, oh, it is such a sweet evening. Me and Sidda take that Ivory in our hands and shoot it up into the air and when it lands, it's so pure it floats like on TV. Then Mama gets her famous idea of swinging off the rope swing! Necie stays with the little ones, but all the rest of us climb up on the bank. We get on the rope, two at a time, and swing out buck naked and drop down into the water, yelling *Aiiieeeee!* As long as I'm careful not to get rope-burned, it's exactly like flying. Landing in that water when it's not quite dark yet, just lingering summer light on our bodies and the water and the trees and the crickets and us. It only lasts for a little while because darkness comes, but it feels like it lasts forever.

Then we're back on the bank and the ladies are drying our hair and we're all whining, I'm hungry! I'm starving, Mama! And the Ya-Yas say, We'll be home in a minute—don't worry, we'll get something in your stomach in five minutes.

And would you believe it?! A car with a red bubble light on top pulls up and shines its headlights on us like we're deer in the middle of the road or something! All the ladies scramble to wrap towels around themselves or throw on their swimsuit cover-ups. Mama is reaching for her striped terrycloth one with the hood. And this short fat sheriff gets out of the car and says: What the hell is going on here?

Oh Lord, Mama says, some Baptists must've called and told on us! And the Ya-Yas all start giggling.

Little Shep can't believe an actual sheriff is standing there, and he just walks straight up to the man and touches his gun. The sheriff says, Get your hands away from that, son! That's no toy! That's a real man's firearm.

I know, Little Shep says, lying through his teeth, My daddy's got ten of them. (Which is not true. Daddy doesn't have pistols like that, only shotguns.)

Mama says, Little Shep, come back over here. The sheriff looks at Mama and says, Well, I should have known: Vivi Abbott and the gang. As if yall weren't trashy enough when yall came out here as teenagers, ruining this place with all your carrying-on! Now yall come out here with your innocent little children and expose them to your pervert behavior. I should run yall in on a morals charge.

All the ladies are covered up by now, and I think for a minute that things are going to get bad. And that sheriff is rocking on his heels like he is the King of the Universe.

Then Caro says, Sheriff Modine, I do believe you have put on weight.

Then the Ya-Yas really lose it. They start laughing and they can't stop. The headlights of the patrol car are shining on the Ya-Yas' painted toenails and their wet hair. When I look up, they look like mermaids. How dare this man come and do this to Mama and her friends?

I go over to the sheriff and kick him in the leg. Leave us alone, you chubby! I tell him.

He grabs for me, but Mama comes and pulls me back, still laughing and says: Bay, it's okay, honey, really. And she picks me up, even though I'm too big to be carried. And the ladies are just howling. They gather us all up and ignore that fat sheriff and they lead us over to the T-Bird and Necie's station wagon and start piling us in.

The sheriff is yelling out at us, I don't care *who* your families are! You're not in Thornton now! You're in Spring Creek! We don't act like heathens here. Women like yall shouldn't be allowed to have children!

Once we're in the car, Mama floors it. Necie and Caro are right on our tail, and Mama lays on the horn and blows it all the way out from the creek and halfway down the road. We're all crooking our necks to see if

Sheriff Modine is following us—and he does part of the way. But by the time we reach our turn-off, he keeps on going straight, and then we all start hooting and hollering. Awright! we yell, yaaaay us!

Back at the camp, the Ya-Yas tell us, Now yall go get your pajamas on.

All of us head in and start pulling pajamas out of the chest and putting them on. My skin is all wrinkled from being in the water so long and my fingernails are white.

Lulu says, Baylor, would you rub some Solarcaine on my back? And I do.

And Gavin and Bernard, Caro's twins, start a fight but their big brother Hale, who's Little Shep's age, says, Hey yall cut that out, or I'm gonna give yall two knuckle sandwiches!

And if you think that sheriff scared my Mama and her friends, you are wrong. No. This is what they do. They get out of their swim coverups and put on their shorts and tops and build a fire in the pit, and we all have a weenie roast. Mama rubs Six-Twelve all over us and we turn our hot dogs in the flames, and the ladies help us put mayonnaise and ketchup on the buns. And we have this huge wooden bowl of potato chips and tall cold bottles of Cokes, and the ladies are drinking cold Jax beer out of the red cooler. And we lay up in our hammocks and then somebody goes inside and brings out a bag of Oreos that we lick the centers out of before we eat the cookie part. And the next thing you know the Ya-Yas are pretending to be Sheriff Modine, strutting around the fire, grabbing at their crotches, spitting, clearing their throats. Necie is laughing so hard she falls on the ground and kicks her feet up and down, but Mama and Caro keep on snorting and stomping, making fun of that sheriff's accent, saying: Ah oughta turn yall in ona mahrals chahrahge.

We stay outside with the fire and the stars and the hammocks and the mosquito coils and the lightning bugs. And we sing "Tell Me Why the Stars Do Shine." They teach us to sing it in rounds and we sing it over and over, up into the trees and the sky, and things are so quiet around us. That song is like a bedtime prayer in the night air, and no one is laughing anymore. It's not that we're sad, it's just that it's nighttime and we've had a full day and we're getting sleepy, although nobody wants to break away from our circle around the fire.

I must've fallen asleep, because the next thing I remember, one of the Ya-Yas—I don't know which one—is dusting the sand off the bottom of my feet and tucking me into bed. And the feather pillow is soft and the chenille bedspread is the perfect weight on my body and the ceiling fan is whirring steady. The blades of that fan just circle round and round all night while I sleep. All night long while I dream, that fan keeps me cool. It keeps the bugs from biting me. It keeps the boogey-man away. It stops all the things under my bed from reaching up and grabbing me, like they're always down there waiting to do.

BOOKWORMS
Viviane, 1964

*S*idda can't help herself. She just loves books. Loves the way they feel, the way they smell, loves those black letters marching across the white pages. When Sidda falls in love with a book, she is positive that she is the very first person in the world to have discovered it, poor child. Thinks that no one else anywhere, anytime, has ever heard of the book.

I'll never forget the time she flipped over *The Secret Garden,* which Buggy gave her. She lived inside that book for days. You couldn't even talk to the child. Then, after a while, she went to the library and looked that book up, and when she found out that other copies existed and all kinds of people had their names on the borrower's card, she just broke down in tears. She had truly believed that she was the only one who had ever read that book! After that, everywhere she went she stared at people, trying to figure out which one of them had trespassed on her book.

Of course I simply adore books myself. I get *Reader's Digest Condensed Books* every month of God's world and devour every single one of them. There is nothing

I like better than holing up in my bedroom with a Coke and a Snickers bar and Pearl S. Buck. Pearl S. Buck is magnificent. Oh, the details she puts in her writing. In *The Good Earth,* where she has the man wake up and wash himself before he comes to his wife in the morning—well that just slays me, it is so tender. And he was Chinese, to boot! I should have been a writer myself.

I taught Sidda to read when she was four years old. Before the nuns even got their hands on her. Jezie claims she is the one who taught the child to read, but then my sister would claim she gave birth to my daughter if I wasn't around to contradict her.

I usually take Sidda to the library once a week while Little Shep has his tennis lessons. Sidda took tennis for a while too, but she just could not take the heat. The child did not inherit my abilities on the court. I was the captain of the tennis team at Thornton High. Everybody knows that.

I get the biggest kick out of watching Sidda in the library. She is so serious, the way she carries her library card in that little purse of hers. You'd think she was a grown woman with a Neiman-Marcus charge card. The librarian will make suggestions about books for her age group, but they're always years below her reading level. The nuns tested the fifth graders and said Sidda has the reading skills of a high-school junior. Well, I could've told them that. The child used the word "impeccable" before she even started first grade.

Regardless of her reading level, I cannot allow her to read everything simply because she can. She is just too young. Some of the books that child is able to rip through are not even Approved Catholic Reading. I have to look over her choices carefully to make sure she isn't sinning due to her gift of intelligence. Being a Catholic can be *très fatigué* sometimes.

Sidda and I simply love the City Park Library. They have several good window air conditioners in there, and those floors are waxed so smooth that the wooden chairs just glide when you pull them out from the reading table. For her light reading, Sidda goes into the juvenile section for Nancy Drew or Cherry Ames. Then she crosses over into adult fiction for her more serious stuff. She is in the Great Books Club, which you have to be *invited* to join, and they have their recommended list as well. (Some of the "Great Books" I've never been so much as heard of, so I sometimes wonder just how "great" they really are. I mean, I'm not exactly what you'd call illiterate.)

The child would have died if they hadn't asked her into that club. She always corrects me, saying: *Moth-er, it's not the Great Books Club, it's just Great Books Club.*

She comes home agitated after every single one of the meetings. She cannot stand Mrs. Chauvin, who heads up the thing. Cannot take that woman tearing those books apart like a head of lettuce. To Sidda and me, books are living things with blood and bones, and it breaks our heart when people dissect them. I can't blame my daughter. I don't like Abby Chauvin either. She thinks she is the Lauren Bacall of Thornton simply because she went to Sarah Lawrence.

But I tell Sidda, You have got to try and get along in groups, honey. Even if the woman is asinine.

Sidda's eye still wanders a little, still drifts off to the right. But only when she is very tired. Thank God I got her the eye operation or she might not be able to make out a stop sign. Or she'd be seeing double, not even able to read a sentence straight through. That's the whole reason why I got her the eye operation, not just because a wandering eye is unflattering to a girl, like Shep claimed. He just could not bear it that I knew what to do and he didn't. He couldn't stand the fact that I was stronger than him, that I was smarter. He ups and leaves for the goddamn duck camp every time anything happens in this house, coward of a Baptist that he is. But don't get me started.

Shep does love to read, I will give him that. We fight over who gets to read a new book first. Then, after we've both finished a book, we sit in the kitchen eating ham sandwiches, talking about it. Sometimes arguing just for the fun of it. He never admits it, but he gets just as excited about reading as I do. He hurries in from the fields early when he thinks the *Reader's Digest Condensed Books* is in the mailbox. If I've already run out there and gotten it and started reading, he'll come in and pretend to pout, and try and snatch it out of my hands to make me laugh.

The library will only let Sidda and me check out two books at a time, which drives us nuts. We live in the country, I tell the librarian, we need more than just two books to last us! My daughter and I are fast readers, we are avid.

But the old bat behind the counter says, Two books a patron, that's our limit, no matter where you live.

Sometimes I watch my daughter smuggle an extra

book out, and even though I know I should, I just cannot bring myself to stop her. Sometimes you just have
to reach out and grab what you want, even when they
tell you not to. This is something that I have struggled
with my whole life long.

Another way Sidda gets around the two-book limit
is to also check out books from the bookmobile when
it comes around every two weeks. The Garnet Parish
bookmobile is just an old panel van lined with shelves
of books, with one tee-ninesy nook where a person can
sit down, and a closet where they keep their supplies.
The one thing I'll say for it—it is air-conditioned. If it
weren't, you'd smother to death in there before getting
through four chapters of a dime-store romance.

Sidda made friends with Lenora, the lady who drives
the thing, and Lenora saves books for Sidda, even
though she isn't supposed to. How can you resist a
child like my daughter when it comes to reading? She
is so bright and intelligent, she should have been a boy.
When I want to punish her, all I have to do is take
away whatever book she's involved with at the time and
she suffers madly. See, she goes places when she reads.
I know all about that. When I'm reading, wherever I
am, I'm always somewhere else.

Sidda is always trying to read at the table, but I
wasn't raised that way and I'm not going to let her get
away with it either. If I have to sit there and listen to
all the shit that goes on around that table, then so does
she.

The bookmobile doesn't come all the way out to
Pecan Grove. It stops up at the top of Pecan Road, just
like the DDT truck does. Thornton won't send the

damn DDT truck all the way to Pecan Grove because we're legally outside the city limits, so we have to suffer mosquitoes the size of blackbirds. I'm surprised we don't all get malaria and die. Sometimes my whole life feels like a nightmare where I'm trying to keep bugs from eating my beautiful children alive.

The kids have figured out a way to get one over on the city, though. They ride their bikes behind the DDT truck when it comes out and they let those clouds of white chemicals just swirl around and settle all over them. Their whole little bodies get coated with that fine dust and they come back and play outside till midnight, and don't get one single bite. Like they aren't even in the heart of Louisiana. They beg and beg not to take a bath, just so that DDT will linger on their skin and they can go another day without being bitten to death by the blood-suckers.

So anyway, one night Shep and I have a little too much to drink. He's sunburned from the fields and I'm shaky to begin with. He does something and I do something back. We have this big screaming fight in the kitchen and he scratches out in the truck and doesn't come home that night. Probably just spends the night at the duck camp. I'm used to that.

But he always comes home early the next morning to shower and change into fresh clothes for the day. The next morning, though, he doesn't show up. And I get possessed by the idea that he's been killed in a car wreck the way my own father died, leaving me forever without saying a word. So I get a little upset.

I wake the kids up screaming. Your Daddy is dead! I

tell them. Wake up! We've got to find him. Get up! I can't do this all by myself.

Sidda is my right-hand man as usual and I get her to call the State Police, then Lyle Rotier of Rotier's Bar. Nobody's seen my husband, that sonovabitch. Sidda is all organized. Gets her spiral notebook and a sharpened pencil and writes everything down. She talks like a little adult when the people answer the phone. I have taught all my children impeccable telephone manners.

I fix me a Mimosa and say, Sidda, call his goddamn buddies. Call Sim, call that damn Bernard, call your Uncle Pete.

She grabs the phone list and starts dialing. I take a snippet of a Miltown and sit there at the breakfast table and stare out the window. I'm tempted to bite my nails, but I'll be damned if I'll let Shep Walker ruin my manicure just because he has disappeared.

Then Sidda comes over to me and stands real close. She says, Mama, nobody knows where he is. Nobody has seen Daddy.

I say, He is dead. I'm one hundred percent positive. I can feel it.

I fix another Mimosa and I relax a little. Then I tell Sidda, Hand me the phone. I'll take over now. Go away and play with matches.

She starts that hyperventilating and splotching-up that she does just to get attention and I say, Dahling, I'm just kidding.

She studies me for a minute.

I say, Don't you look at me in that tone of voice. I don't need that, not today.

So she goes on back to her room and I don't give her a second thought.

*W*ell, finally, Shep Walker pulls in around noon asking: Hey babe! Where's my lunch?

And I am so happy to see him get out of that truck with his sleeves rolled up and that sun-bleached blond hair on his arms that I completely forget to kill him, and we start to have the loveliest little midday meal together.

But Sidda runs in, hysterical, and tries to ruin the whole thing for me and my husband, crying and hanging onto Shep. She sobs, Daddy, you're still alive!

Shep looks at her like she's nuts and says, Well yeah, what'd you expect?

I tell her, Would you please leave him alone and stop being so dramatic, Miss Sarah Bernhardt.

Still doing her sob-act, she lets go of my husband and runs out of the room. Shep asks me, What in the world's wrong with her?

I say, She just reads too many books.

Then I give my husband a kiss. A nasty middle-of-the-day kiss that there are far too few of in this world.

My One-and-Only heads out to the fields around three, and the kids are outside. I call up Wayland's to see if they have gotten in the sunhat I ordered. They can be so damn slow getting you something you want in this town. Lulu and Little Shep and Baylor troop in, sweating up a storm.

They lay down in front of the TV to watch *The Little Rascals,* and I ask them, Where is your big sister?

We don't know, they reply without looking at me. Last time we saw her was at the bookmobile.

Now usually Sidda comes straight back with her books and puts the little paper-sack covers on them that she likes to make. (The child can get a little too particular sometimes. I mean, it is not necessary to put book covers over book covers. I don't know where she gets that kind of thing from.) But I am not going to worry. I have worried enough today, I need a rest.

So I take a delicious nap and when I get up, I rub some Pretty Feet on my toes and give myself a pedicure. You've got to keep your feet in shape during the summer if you don't want to look like an ape in sandals.

*W*ell, Sidda doesn't show up for supper. Which is a first. I mean, it's not like we live in a neighborhood, for God's sake. We live at the end of a gravel road on nine-hundred acres. There isn't anybody she can drop in on.

It's getting dark and I start to worry. Shep gets home and he's cleaning up in the utility room. I go in there and tell him, Babe, Sidda's gone.

He says, What do you mean, gone?

I mean we don't know where in the world she is. She's been gone all afternoon.

Goddamn it, he says.

We start off by calling her little girlfriends who live in town. First off, the ones from the Great Books Club. Not one of them has heard a peep from her.

That bitch Abby Chauvin says, You mean you have no idea where your daughter is?

That's right, I tell her, but don't worry your little frosted head about it.

Jesus, Mary, and Joseph, I think, please don't let my oldest child be molested and strangled to death. Please God, don't let her little body be chopped to pieces lying in a culvert off Highway 17.

I'm so shook I can't even mix a drink. Shep has to make it for me. We dial up Buggy. Maybe Sidda's over there, I pray. But Buggy hasn't heard a word from her. Mother says, Light a candle to the Virgin and I'll be right over.

We call Willetta, and she says, Call the sisters up at the school.

So we do. The nuns answer the phone and they have the TV going in the background.

Shep says, So, that's what they do with all the money we give them: buy brand new color-TV sets.

I say, Shut up, babe, we've got more important things to do here than criticize the Roman Catholic Church.

We call her piano teacher and her dance teacher. Not a thing. It is pitch dark outside with no moon and the smell of rain in the air. Shep and I stand out on the carport and he asks me for a cigarette.

I thought you quit, I tell him.

He says, Babe, we're going to have to call the police.

The police! I scream. The police looking for my child. My life is getting more like TV all the time.

The rest of the kids are agitated as hell. Worry shooting through their bodies like electric current. Lulu starts the hair-chewing again. I swear, I don't know where in the world she picked that up. I have to slap her pudgy little hand and say, Honey, cut that out!

Do you want to be bald-headed before you even start dating?

She starts crying and whines, I miss Sidda. Where is Sidda, Mama?

Buggy pulls into the driveway about the same time as the police. We give the officer a description of Siddalee and one of her school pictures.

Then Baylor has to go and rip my heart to shreds, just when it is the last thing I need. He runs into his room and gets this picture he's drawn of his big sister and hands it to the officer. This is Sidda, he tells the policeman. This is what she really looks like.

Then he holds out a white cotton shirt of hers and says: This is what she smells like, if you need to get dogs to trace her.

Sometimes I don't know which child is the strangest: my oldest or my youngest.

I go inside and call up the Ya-Yas. Necie and Caro come over immediately, even though Caro already has on her pajamas. I set out some cheese and crackers and start to fill the silver ice bucket.

I say, Mother, why don't you set out some olives and open a can of artichoke hearts?

Shep says, My God, Vivi, this is not a party.

I scream, Do you want people to starve just because Sidda ran away?!

He looks at me and my best girlfriends like we're some kind of nuts, then he takes his keys down from the hook by the toaster.

Where do you think you are going? I ask him.

Out to look for my daughter, he says.

Damn you Shep Walker, you can't walk out and

leave me to deal with this by myself. You can't do that to me!

I can't just sit here on my butt eating Ritz crackers, he says and walks out the door.

I yell after him, When will you be back?

I don't even have to hear him reply. Necie and Caro answer for him in unison: I'll *be* back when I *get* back.

I smoke eighty-four-thousand cigarettes. I refuse to believe that anything has really happened to my daughter. God will not let anything bad happen to my children. I will not let Siddalee drive me to the insane asylum like she has tried to do hundreds of times.

Mother keeps muttering and praying her damn rosary under her breath, until I finally have to jerk it out of her goddamn hands. I tell her, That's all you've ever done in every single emergency of my life! God, you are worse than having no mother at all.

I'm immediately sick and ashamed of myself and go to Mother and give her a hug and kiss. I say, I'm sorry, Mama, but this is really throwing me for a loop.

That's alright, Viviane, she tells me. I just pray to God that your daughter running away from you is not punishment for the way you treat me.

The bitch.

I stub out my cigarette (although not in Mother's face, as I would like) and I walk down the hall into Sidda's room and shut the door behind me. I stand next to her dresser and close my eyes. I don't reach for the lamp, just close my eyes until they adjust to the dark. I stand there and make myself take ten deep breaths until I can see my daughter's face and her body clearly in my mind. I see her red hair, the brown eyes, the way she lays in bed reading with one eye partially closed. I see her freckles, her lips, the tiny scar on them from when she ran into the wheelbarrow when she was three. I see her arms and hands, her fingernails that I always tell her to push the cuticles back from when she gets out of the tub. I see her stomach, how it pooches out a little, her butt so tiny. She's going to have a tight little butt like mine, not a big fat butt like her aunts on Shep's side of the family. I see her little breasts the way they are starting up. I see her pubic area where there isn't any hair yet.

She is mine.

I carried her for nine months. I lost my waist for her. My feet grew from size six to seven-and-a-half. I lost my potential for her. I lost my twin boy for her. I could have had twins, but only she lived.

He came out first. He was in my womb. He was born. He stayed awhile and then he died. He had Shep's hazel eyes and red hair like Sidda. He would look up at me and I could see my face in his eyes. He died after four days.

This is how I was tormented. I laid in the hospital bed at St. Cecilia and cried. I did not want to see anyone, not even the Ya-Yas. No one understood. They said it would pass.

Shep said, Vivi, you've got to stop this. Look at our girl, she is perfect. He said, Our baby girl has the most beautiful glittering eyes in this whole hospital.

My twin boy would have made everything work out. He is the one who would have given it all back to me, everything I have lost. And I would have done anything for him. If he would have told me to go to River Street and become a beggar, I would have done it. If he would have said at any time of the night or day, "dance with me," I would have carried him in my arms and danced.

But Sidda is the one who lived. I paid for her with him.

I laid there with the nuns floating in and out and the sounds if their rustling habits and the hospital noises. I did not want the shades open. I cussed at God until He came to me.

Then I said, Will you comfort me now? Will you take me in your arms and hold me?

But God said, The only reason you wanted twins in the first place was to get attention.

I was cheated. Children do not bring you attention. They take it all away.

After that I did not talk about my twin boy to anyone. I kept him hidden inside.

Two weeks later, I was at home with Sidda in her bassinet, and the phone rang. It was an insurance salesman. He said, Don't you want insurance on the twin that lived? You know, Mrs. Walker, she could die too, God forbid.

I could not eat after that. I starved my body back down into a size six, which is where I belong. I drank gin and quinine water to settle my stomach.

Then before Sidda was even old enough to turn over by herself, my father rounded Davis Circle too fast and was killed. Before he ever looked at me and saw who I am! And I didn't know it then, but I was already pregnant with Little Shep.

Part of me spoiled then, and nobody noticed.

All they said was, Vivi Abbott Walker, you look posi-

tively gorgeous after all you've been through. Aren't you glad you have that darling little baby girl? And another angel on the way!

Four children—a husband—a house, dripping god-damn boiling water over the chicory coffee every morning of the world. Everything gets sucked out of me, every ounce of my high school goldenness, every single iota of my college education—gone. The only thing left is the Ya-Yas.

*A*nd now here I am, standing in my missing daughter's room. I can see her navy blue round-toed Keds in the closet. Her stack of books on the nightstand. I can smell her eleven-year-old smell, spicy, and new.

And in an instant I know exactly where my child is.

I fling open her bedroom door and run down the hall.

Caro! I scream, Call the police!

She hands me the phone. The damn police, they treat me like I'm some kind of nut. Calm down, they say, we'll handle this.

I hope you burn in hell! I tell them. Don't you dare treat me like I don't know what I'm talking about! Screw you and the horse you rode in on!

I hang up the phone, light another cigarette, and dial so hard I break a fingernail. The mayor himself answers the phone and I say, Kidd, this is Vivi Abbott Walker.

Then I tell him what I need and he says, You got it, Vivi.

That is the thing about living in a small town. I once dated Kidd Gerard. I broke the man's heart while he was at Auburn, sending me telegrams once a week. I know he'll do what I ask, even though he hasn't kissed me on the lips in twenty-two years. I always tell my two daughters: Don't ever underestimate the power women have over men. And don't ever let them know you have it either.

I make Mother stay with the kids. Then Necie and Caro drive me in Necie's station wagon. They are such good friends to me. They keep lighting me ciggies and Caro has her arm around me saying, Don't worry, Vivi, we'll find her. We will not let anything happen to that child, you hear?

Necie drives that station wagon like a bat out of hell and we beat Kidd there. I take some deep breaths and say a prayer to St. Jude, patron saint of the impossible. Sidda could be roasted to death. She could be suffocated like the millions of children who crawl up into abandoned refrigerators and the door slams shut and they are locked in there for all eternity.

The bookmobile is parked underneath a crepe myrtle behind the library in the gravel parking lot. I get out of the car and take the flashlight I've brought with me and walk over to it. I stand right next to the van and I can still feel the heat of the day on the outside of it. I try the door, but it's locked. I knock loud and hard.

I say, Sidda baby, it's okay. Hold on, honey, we'll take you home before you know it.

If she's not in there, then it's all over. If she's not in there, then she is nowhere and I will kill Shep Walker because I am too chicken to kill myself.

Then Kidd pulls up, looking handsome as ever. He

strides over to me with a huge ring of keys and says, Hey Vivi. What can I do for you this evening? I got the keys to unlock anything you want.

I can't believe the man is flirting with me after all these years, and my daughter almost dead.

I say, Open that bookmobile door, would you, please, Kidd? I think my oldest child is in there.

He does just what I say. I love a man who can take orders. I step inside and it is simply stifling in that van. The air conditioner has been off for hours. *She could be dead, I think. Is that what you want, Vivi Walker? Do you want her dead?*

Sidda? I call out. It's me, baby. It's Mama.

That bookmobile is hot as hell, it's a 475-degree gas oven.

I shine the flashlight around. No air, no Sidda. Once you shut off the air conditioning in a book van and shut the door and windows, it's as good a way as any to commit suicide.

I will not throw up. I will not let the thoughts in my head push me over the edge. I will not have a child of mine kill herself. I will not lose the twin and her too, both without me having any say-so whatever.

I shine the light. I can see the titles on the books. *Look, there is Hemingway, Papa Ernest. Why did he put a bullet through that gorgeous male head of his? Blood all over that thick sexy beard.*

Sidda, I call out, please! Baby, if you're here, please come out, please!

I hear a shuffling.

God, listen to me. If you will let her still be alive, I will give up Bombay gin. Maybe not Tanqueray, but definitely Bombay.

I walk straight to the tiny storage closet in the back and open the door. I follow my instincts. One thing I have is instincts.

There she is—crouched in there, hiding from me.

I bend down to her. I want to kill her.

Then Kidd is at my side. He says, I'll be damned if this is not female intuition.

I say, Sidda, honey, you are carrying this book thing too far.

She is crying. She says, I don't want to go home. You can't make me go home!

I bend down to take her hand and she knocks the flashlight out of my hand. Kidd shines his big torch on her.

I say, Siddalee, get up from there.

She screams, I hate you! You said Daddy was dead.

I want to slap her to death, after all she has put me through.

Kidd says, Young lady, you heard your mother. Now get up out of that closet and stop your foolishness.

Sidda doesn't budge. She stays hunkered down with her arms wrapped around her knees and says, Yall are all sons of bitches.

Well, Kidd has had it so have I. He reaches down and jerks her up to her feet and I say, It's alright, Kidd, it's alright. (But I'm glad somebody has jerked her up. She needs some jerking if you ask me.)

I put my hands on her shoulders and tell her, Listen kiddo, stop being so dramatic right this instant, you hear me? Now let's go get in the car and go home.

The child stares at me like she's about to spit in my face.

Kidd says, Vivi, do you want me to handle this for you?

I say, No. Thank you, Kidd. Excuse us for just a minute, would you please?

I grab Sidda and walk her over to Necie's station wagon. By the time we get there, she's sobbing.

Keep an eye on her, will you, Caro? I say. And don't dare let her out of this car.

I straighten my hair that must look like hell in all this humidity and walk over to Kidd. He's standing by his car with his foot propped on the running board. In spite of myself, that man still gives me goosebumps like he did when he was a quarterback. *You cannot think like that, I tell my shriveled-up insides.*

I give him a little kiss on the cheek and say, Thank you dahling. Everything'll be fine. I've just got a high-strung daughter on my hands, that's all.

He says, Well, I sure hate to see you have to go through this.

I know, Kidd, I tell him—like he has no idea of half of it. Now listen, you and Nona absolutely must come over sometime soon. It has been too long.

Yeah, Vivi, he says. Like he still wants me.

When I get back in the car, Sidda is sitting there shaking and doing her damn hyperventilating trick. She grabs onto me and won't let go. I don't know why she does that, I am not a child psychologist. Her palms are hot and sweaty against my arm. I want to push her away from me. I don't like it when my children get close to me when I'm not in the mood.

We finally get her home, and I draw a bath for her, and hand her one of the Darvons that I always keep around the house for cramps. Then when she's done, I go and lie down in the bed with her. It's cool and dry in her room and the curtains are open with a little sliver of light spilling in from the porch light. We both love it in the summer when it is scorching hot outside, but real cool inside with that huge central air conditioner blasting away.

I kiss her on the forehead. Precious, I tell her, You have got to stop taking things so seriously. Your father came home just like I knew he would. Is that all you were worried about?

She says, Mama, I don't feel like talking, I'm too tired.

I say, Well then, I'll talk and you listen: You can't run away from things, Siddalee. You've got to stay in this house where your life is. Don't you think I want to run off and hide in a bookmobile or join the circus? We all do. But we have responsibilities.

She rolls away from me onto her side. I can feel the little bumps of her seersucker nightgown against my fingers. I stroke her hair and kiss her neck. You are magnificent, I tell her. You are my most beautiful intelligent child. I adore you. Don't ever run away from me again.

I kiss her one more time before I leave the room. I still have guests in the house. It's late, but I fix a round of drinks for everyone. Except for Mother, of course. She has put the other kids to bed and just sits there, pursing those chapped lips, acting like a martyr.

Shep stands behind me, rubbing my shoulders. I

don't even know when he showed back up. He says, Thank you, Viviane. You did good.

You're welcome, I tell him. See? I don't just sit on my butt and eat Ritz crackers.

When the Ya-Yas leave, I take off my makeup and cleanse my face. I rub on my cold cream—I don't care how tired I am, I never go to sleep without doing my cleansing ritual. Then I go and peek into Sidda's room. There she is, propped up like the Queen of Sheba against the pillows, holding her flashlight and reading. Not even trying to hide it. I am so mad I want to slap her. Reading, laying up in bed, relaxing, after all the shit she has put me through!

But I do not say a word. I tiptoe down the hall to the kitchen. I reach up to the pill cabinet and get myself a Darvon too, and swallow it with a jigger of bourbon. That child is not going to get all the attention in this family. I worked hard as hell in this house and I am sick to death of never getting what I want! I swear I could write a book about all the things no one has ever thanked me for.

In summertime the child just lives for the bookmobile. Which is the whole reason why she hid up there and rode downtown and let them lock her up. She thinks books are her best friends and she wanted to be surrounded by them.

I understand. None of this is strange to me. I am her mother, though, and it is my job to teach her that you cannot escape from life. Life is not a book. You can't just set it down on the coffee table and walk away from it when it gets boring or you get tired.

CRUELTY TO ANIMALS
Little Shep, 1964

*B*uggy, my Mama's mama, has got the meanest little lapdog you ever laid eyes on. One of those puny-butt poodles that's nothing but bone and fluff. And to Buggy that dog can't do any wrong. It can pee or poop or tear up the bedspread and Buggy just says, Isn't that just the darlingest thing you have ever seen?

Even though I don't care for yap-butts like that dog, I still think an animal oughta get treated with some respect and not like a nutcase, which is what Buggy has been turning that puff-ball into.

My Daddy says, Buggy is going to drive that animal as crazy as she did her daughter.

See, I'm real fond of dogs myself. *Yard* dogs, that is. We got three of them at Pecan Grove and I'm the one that gets up early in the morning to feed them. They get a cut or scrape, I'm the one that cleans it. We got a Catahoula hound named Jep, who is so dumb that once he ran into a telephone pole and knocked himself out cold while he was chasing my Daddy's truck. We also got Lamar, a German shepherd that Mister Charlie Vanderlick gave us. And we got Jolene, a white collie that Lulu picked out from my cousin's dog Josie's second litter. Josie was a dog famous for her ability to sleep standing up. She got shot with porcupine quills once when Daddy took me and her deer hunting with him in West Texas, and I'm the one that pulled them out of her, one by one. I still got those quills in a pickle jar in my bedroom. I'm saving them for when I'm a vet. Gonna put them in my office to remind me of my first surgery. Because removing those quills was a operation for me, that's for sure. You just try and pull dozens of quills out of a collie. It hurts them something awful, and they're all crying and squirming, but you've gotta pull those quills out or they'll hurt even worse, maybe even get an infection.

You can *have* those lapdogs, though. I'm scared I'll step on them and that'll be all she wrote. Plus, they don't fetch or hunt or roll in the grass with you or anything. They just sit up there on the couch waiting for their favorite soap opera to come on.

My Daddy says, It is just like your Mama's mama to take up with some animal the size of a rat.

Buggy named that poodle "Miss Peppy" and got her this wicker bed with a plaid mattress. Crocheted a green-and-white-striped sweater for the dog to wear in winter, and got one of the Altar Society ladies to make a special bowl with "Miss Peppy" written on the side. Buggy drives all over town in her Fairlane with that dog beside her tearing up the seat covers, and you can see her talking to that animal the whole time. My grandmother always drives with the windows up, whether her air conditioner is working or not. She says it is trashy to drive around in public with rolled-down windows.

And of course, she feeds Miss Peppy canned dog food. That dog has never eaten a table scrap in its life.

My Daddy says, If a dog can't live off table scraps, then it's not a dog. He says, If a dog can't live out in the yard no matter what the season, then it might as well be a goddamn stuffed animal at the Louisiana State Fair.

I bet you the reason Miss Peppy is so nuts is due to the way her head squeezes her brain in, like a fist. I don't blame the dog for being crazy. Dogs are dogs. You teach them to obey, you feed them what's left over from supper, and you pick cockleburrs out of their coats. You don't pull a dog up on the couch with you and talk to it like a human baby and wait for it to talk back to you in plain English. You don't take a creature and breed it so it can't fit inside its own skin, which might be what started Miss Peppy's problem in the first place.

Once when Miss Peppy was in heat, this Shelty down the street from Buggy got her pregnant. When her time came, it was a sad case, let me tell you.

We were all over at Buggy's spending the night because my Daddy was off duck hunting and Mama didn't want to stay at Pecan Grove because of her nightmares. We were all laid up in Buggy's den watching *Saturday Night at the Movies,* eating peanut-butter fudge when that dog went into labor. Buggy had set her up in the utility room with a heater and a transistor radio turned on, and we were reaching a high point in the movie when Miss Peppy started this high, sharp moaning. I ran in there to see what was happening and I tell you—it was truly something awful. I've seen plenty of puppies born at Pecan Grove and at my cousins'. It doesn't scare me. But that dog was being ripped apart. Made me glad I wasn't a girl. We all hovered around, but we couldn't do a single thing to help her.

Buggy got all upset and started lighting some novena candles and Mama yelled, Mother, stop being so sanctimonious!

I said, Hey Mama, Dr. Fitzsimmons would know what to do. He always knows what to do with Daddy's cows.

And Mama yelled out to Buggy, Blow out those damn candles and go warm up the car!

Then I looked up the number, and Mama called Dr. Fitzsimmons' telephone-answering service. I'm going to have me one of those when I'm a vet. And I'll work on large and small animals, just like Dr. Fitzsimmons.

Buggy said, Oh, I'm scared to touch her! I might cause her even more pain.

I scooped Miss Peppy up in her blanket because it didn't look like anyone else was going to make a move.

Dr. Fitzsimmons left a party just to meet us at the clinic, and he worked for two hours while we waited in the lobby that smelled like disinfectant. Mama just smoked cigarettes and Buggy mumbled prayers under her breath.

Then Dr. Fitzsimmons came out with a lab coat over his slacks and said, Mrs. Abbott, Vivi, I'm real sorry. I pulled the bitch through, but couldn't save the litter. I recommend you spay her for her own health.

Buggy stood there sobbing and fingering her rosary and muttered, Don't you *dare* call Miss Peppy names.

Mama said, Thank you for your good work, Dr. Fitzsimmons. We're lucky to have you in this town.

Buggy said, I suppose it's the will of Jesus.

Mama said, Mother, did you hear what Dr. Fitzsimmons said about the hysterectomy?

Yes, my grandmother snapped, Don't talk nasty. Of course I heard. I'm not deaf yet. It will be taken care of. We must think of the safety of the mother first and foremost.

*I*t wasn't too long after Miss Peppy got spayed that Buggy started up with the baby dolls. Her mission in life became to train that dog to treat those dolls like they were her own puppies. We watch Buggy do it all the time. She spends whole afternoons teaching Miss Peppy to carry those baby dolls around in her mouth. She makes the dog drop them real gentle on Buggy's own bed, and then she teaches that animal to pull the covers up over them like they are actual human babies getting tucked in for a nap.

Every time we go over there, Buggy has to show it off. She says, Yall come see what a good mother Miss Peppy is!

And we have to troop into Buggy's bedroom, where she has this prayer kneeler she conned off some nun. The kneeler is facing this Sacred Heart of Jesus bleeding like a stuck pig up there on the wall. There are still a couple stains on it from that time I smeared ketchup on the picture to make it look more real-like. Off to the side of her bed Buggy has a statue of the Blessed

Virgin Mary, with a bunch of flowers that Buggy picks fresh every day.

Just look at what a good mama Miss Peppy is! Buggy says. Can't yall just imagine how proud the Blessed Mother is of her?

And she makes the dog tuck her "babies" under the covers over and over again, and we all have to say, Oh Buggy, that is wonderful, just wonderful.

I whisper to Sidda, Buggy is nuts. She belongs in the same asylum we're gonna drive Mama to. And those dolls are butt-ugly.

Buggy hears me whispering and she says, This is not pretend, yall hear Buggy? This is one hundred percent true. If yall just pretend those are Miss Peppy's babies, she will know. You can't just pretend, you really have to *believe.*

And we all look at each other like, Yeah, right, no wonder this dog is so weird.

If you so much as lean over to touch those baby dolls around Miss Peppy, she will bite your fingers off. Buggy has her believing she has to protect those "babies" from everything. Sometimes I think about calling up Dr. Fitzsimmons and reporting Buggy for cruelty to animals, but Sidda says you can't turn in your own grandmother.

One Saturday Mama and Teensy are heading out to Lafayette to go shopping for the day and we get dropped off at Buggy's. The minute we hit the kitchen door you can hear that dog yipping. You can hear her little toenails tapping against the wood floor while she runs down the hall. Buggy lets those toenails get so long, it's like Miss Peppy is wearing little poodle high heels.

My Daddy told Buggy once, If you don't trim that dog's toenails, someone is going to report you to the ASPCA.

After that, Buggy keeps that poodle away from my Daddy. She doesn't believe in cutting Miss Peppy's toenails, because she says it depresses Miss Peppy. But you better believe she gets scared when my Daddy threatens her with punishment from a big organization. Buggy is terrified of big organizations. She says they're all in cahoots with each other. For instance, she thinks the Communists have infiltrated the NASA space program to ruin the weather so they can destroy the Catholic church. Every time we have a hurricane, she says, See, what did Buggy tell yall?

Anyway, this particular Saturday, Mama is in a hurry to get off to the Lafayette stores, and she just barely sticks her head in the screen door to kiss Buggy and say when she'll be back. Well, as soon as she opens that door, Miss Peppy jumps up on her and tears her stockings to shreds right there on her legs. Without missing a beat, Mama backhands that little dog and it goes flying through the air and lands over by the water heater. I go over to check on her, and she isn't really hurt, just sort of stunned.

Mama says, I'm sorry, Mother, but someone has *got* to teach that animal how to behave.

Buggy clenches her teeth all up and says, Don't you worry about Buggy and her dog. Buggy will stay home with your children and the dog that loves her. You go on and have a good time shopping with your girlfriend. Don't feel guilty about torturing one of God's little creatures.

Buggy always talks about herself like she's some other person. She'll say: Buggy is so tired, or Buggy has to go to the Piggy-Wiggly for some carrot juice. Or Buggy is getting very upset with yall for doing that. Or Buggy and Baby Jesus *both* are getting upset. When she drags Baby Jesus into it, you know you'd better watch out.

So Mama takes off. It's raining and I feel like breaking all of Buggy's stupid little knick-knacks that cover every inch of her house. I hate being stuck in that place with the yappy dog and all those tiny statues of little peasant children, and the Three Wise Men who stay out all year next to the praying-hands planter.

We turn on cartoons and lay down on the rug with pillows to watch *The Road Runner,* my all-time favorite. That whole house smells like dog, even though Buggy burns church incense at least once a day. From the den, I can see into the kitchen. It's clean and everything, but there are matches all over the floor. There are always matches all over Buggy's floors. I don't know if she's too blind to see them, or if she puts them there on purpose. With Buggy, you just never know. One time I tried picking the matches all up for her, but she said, Oh no! Don't pick those up! It'll bring bad luck!

I concentrate on the TV for awhile, but it's so stuffy in there. I say, Buggy, could we please open a window?

She says, No, Miss Peppy has been fighting off a cold.

I stare back at my cartoons. Sidda has one of her library books so she's okay. Lulu's dunking graham crackers into her milk and stuffing as many as she can into her mouth. Baylor is walking around and around the house looking at the photographs on the walls, like he always does. He asks Buggy every single time we go over there, Who is that, Buggy? When was that? Where was that taken? And Buggy is happy to tell him. Baylor thinks that whole hallway is his own private museum.

The Road Runner gets over with, and the only things on the TV are stupid. So me and Sidda and Lulu get out the Sears catalog and start cutting it up. We cut up models and things and glue them back together in different ways. It's a old game of ours—you can play it anywhere, because almost everybody has a old Sears catalog laying around the house. I cut off the head of a man modeling underwear and stick it on a power saw. Sidda cuts off a lady's legs and pastes them coming out of a baby's ears. Whoever makes the weirdest thing wins. We never get tired of that game.

And when we're done, we leave all the scraps of paper and the paste and scissors and everything all over the floor. At Buggy's we never clean up a single thing. We just sit back and watch her do it. We make deliberate messes because we know she'll clean them up. She'll sigh like you're driving nails through her palms, but she always bends over and cleans them up like she's our servant.

So then we have to go and admire Miss Peppy and her babies again before Buggy will fix us any lunch. Finally we get some grilled cheeses and tomato soup,

but Miss Peppy can't take it that we're getting something she isn't, so she pees right on the rug next to
where I have my grilled cheese on a paper towel.

And that is when I get my famous idea.

I don't say one word about that dog peeing right
next to my sandwich. I wait until Buggy is straighten-
ing up after lunch and then I say, Hey yall, let's go in
the grandchildren's room and play.

Buggy says, Little Shep, you sure are being good
today.

I grin and lead Sidda, Lulu, and Baylor down the
hall to the room where we sleep when we spend the
night, and where all our toys are. Once I have them all
in there, I shut the door and tell them, Alright now,
listen to me, hear? Yall want to have some fun?

Yeah! Baylor says.

Uh-huh, Lulu says, chewing a piece of peanut-butter
fudge.

Sidda takes the candy away from her and says,
Mama told me to keep an eye on you. You wouldn't
have your weight problem in the first place if it weren't
for Buggy and her homemade candy.

Shut up, I tell them. Yall listen to me!

Even Sidda listens because she's as bored as the rest
of us. I reach down into the toy chest and pull out two
dolls that Sidda and Lulu have already ripped the hair
off of. One of their favorite things is to rip the hair off
their dolls and throw them up in the chinaberry tree
and laugh at them.

Yall see these dolls? I ask.

Uh-huh, they nod. I am the leader, they're all listening to me.

These are Miss Peppy's new babies, I announce to them.

What? Sidda says.

I repeat, These are the new babies of Miss Peppy, the fart dog!

Little Shep, Sidda says, what are you talking about?

I'm not just talking! I say proudly. I am going to swap these bald-headed rubber dolls for Miss Peppy's babies and see what happens.

Lulu smiles and reaches into her pocket where she has more fudge stashed away. Baylor starts giggling.

Sidda says, Shep, you know how Buggy is about that dog. You're gonna get us all in big trouble. It's a great idea.

I say, Yall leave it up to me. Just leave it all up to old Little Shep.

I wait until Buggy goes outside to collect rainwater like she always does for her house plants. That dog's right behind her, almost peeing on Buggy's shoes. Buggy always says, It is so cute the way Miss Peppy "powders her nose" whenever I'm out in the yard.

I plant Sidda at the sliding-glass door to keep watch, and Lulu and Baylor stay in the hallway to tip me off if the enemy starts to come back inside. As it is, I've got plenty of time. I sneak into Buggy's bedroom, snatch Miss Peppy's babies out from under the covers, and stuff Lulu's old dolls in their place. Then I run into the kitchen and cram those fake dog babies down in the trash can underneath the kitchen sink. Buggy's still outside and I've pulled the old switcheroo off without a single solitary hitch!

I walk over to the rest of the kids and give them the

A-OK sign and say, Check! like I'm a double agent. Alright now, I instruct them: Act normal.

So we get out Sidda's Barbie and Ken dolls and switch their heads. It's great to see old Ken's head on a body with boobs. Sidda always gets a kick out of that. We all do.

Buggy comes back inside with her poot dog and we all say, Oh hi, Buggy! Like we're children from Lourdes or something. She says, Yall are being so sweet. The Baby Jesus is smiling at you right now, I can just feel it.

We keep on playing with the dolls. I get out my troll doll, which is the only doll I have anything to do with on my own. The rest are sissy dolls. My Daddy said my troll doll is a sissy doll too and he won't let me take it in the truck with him. But I still play with it when my Daddy's not around.

We're all staring at each other trying to act like nothing's going on. I am so excited I can't keep my leg from bouncing up and down the way it does when something's up. Sidda is rolling her eyes around like she's in a scary movie, and Baylor keeps licking his lips. He has the longest tongue you ever saw. He can touch his nose with it, easy. Old Buggy's just watering her African violets and Miss Peppy is trailing her around on those high-heel toenails. I start humming "You Are My Sunshine" just so I won't start laughing.

Finally I see Miss Peppy get this thought in her head, and she heads in the direction of the bedroom.

Sidda jabs me in the side and I whisper, Bombs Over Tokyo! They're all looking at me, but I go on brushing my troll doll's hair like life is normal.

Then the barking starts up! Well, it isn't really barking. More like a high yowling that you wouldn't expect from a dog the size of that runt. Buggy drops her watering can and runs straight back into the bedroom, her slippers flapping on her feet. We're all looking at each other—like, Alright! This is it!

Buggy starts shrieking like she'd rehearsed all her life for something like this to happen. Like she'd practiced and practiced, just to be ready to make those sounds.

Jesus, Mary, and Joseph! she screams. Oh, Our Lady of Prompt Succor, come to our aid!

We sit there laughing so hard without making any sound, the way we have to do at Mass when somebody farts. Then Sidda says, Come on, we better go in there and act surprised.

So we all run down the hall and there is Buggy in her room with that dog, both of them looking like they've gone right over the edge. The attic fan is pulling and I can see the curtains getting sucked in, then letting go with the draft. I can hear cartoons still playing on the TV, and Miss Peppy is still making those high-pitched moans like someone's beating her.

What's wrong? I ask, all innocent.

Buggy says, Yall don't even look. It's too terrible. Miss Peppy's babies have been kidnapped and Buggy does not know how!

Then she runs to the open window and looks out, like she might actually catch a doll burglar trying to escape over the hydrangea bushes.

My mouth hurts and my face is starting to develop a twitch from trying not to laugh. Lulu starts to giggle, but Sidda pinches her and she shuts up. Bay just stands there with his mouth open. Sidda comes over and stands in front of me, like she thinks I might be in trouble. No big deal, I whisper. I got things under control.

Buggy gathers Miss Peppy in her arms to try and comfort her. But that dog is in the middle of her own nervous breakdown, and she hauls off with her tiny poodle teeth and bites the inside of Buggy's hand hard enough to draw blood. Well, we're just horrified. We're just fascinated. We are just about to fall out on the floor. I wonder, Will Buggy finally up and get mad at this dog?

No way. She just stands there looking at that poodle with a retarded look of love. She says, Precious little Miss Peppy, no one will never know the pain you are suffering.

Goddamn, I think. I wish my Daddy could see this! He'd know what to say. Then I think, Oh great, what if my grandmother gets rabies and croaks and it's all my fault?

Buggy, I say, Maybe you might want to pour some hydrogen peroxide over that bite.

She looks at me like I'm a real doctor for thinking that up and she goes in the bathroom to open the medicine cabinet, at the same time starting up a holy rosary out loud. She puts Miss Peppy down on the bathroom counter and I swear, the dog keeps *staring* at me. That dog looks so lost standing there next to Buggy's false-teeth container and Five-Day deodorant pads that, for a second, I actually feel sorry for her. It's not her fault she lives in a crazy house.

I say, Buggy, maybe you better go to the doctor. Dog bites aren't good.

She interrupts a "Glory Be" long enough to smile and say, Thank you, blessed child, but you don't have to worry about Buggy. This is not really a bite, but more of a love-nip from Miss Peppy, who is being tested by God this morning.

It gets clear to me that my grandmother is sort of enjoying the whole situation.

She herds us back into her room and makes us kneel down and recite the rest of the rosary with her. Buggy's on the prayer kneeler holding Miss Peppy, who is shaking like Mama does in the mornings. It's hard to concentrate on The Sorrowful Mysteries with those baldheaded dolls still staring up into space from the bed. We just cannot take our eyes off them.

Lulu starts to blurt out something, but I put my hand over her mouth and Sidda says, Lulu, be quiet! We are praying.

Then Lulu bites my hand and we both start giggling, but I try to make it sound like I'm coughing instead. I act like I'm thinking about all of Jesus' suffering so I won't totally lose it. But then Miss Peppy jumps out of Buggy's arms and starts clicking her toenails in the direction of the kitchen.

We rip through nine more Hail Marys before Miss Peppy lets out a series of yips that sound like Nazis are pulling out her teeth. Buggy runs into the kitchen with us close on her heels, and I can't believe the sight in front of my eyes.

The dog is standing there on the linoleum floor with

her "babies" dangling out of her mouth. They are covered with coffee grounds and a banana peel is hanging off one of their arms. That dog has actually nosed open the kitchen cabinet, knocked over the trash can, and fished those dolls out! The poodle starts turning in circles, jerking those dolls up and down so hard it looks like her own head is gonna snap right off and roll across the room. The dog has lost her mind. She's found her babies and lost her mind. We've never in our lives seen an animal act like this. We've seen Mama act like this, but never a dog.

Buggy is red-faced and sobbing, and she turns on us.

Which one of you pagan children did this? she screams. Which one? Who? Who did it? Who has done this cruel thing to Miss Peppy and the Baby Jesus?

We just stand there looking at her. I love the way her eyes bug out and her veins pop when she gets real mad. This is more fun than I thought it would be! It's worth getting in trouble for. Baylor's holding onto Sidda, and Lulu's chewing on her hair as usual. I figure I better be the one to say something.

Buggy, I say, it is a terrible, terrible thing that has happened here and we are real sorry. But we don't know one thing about it.

She says, You should all be shot with a gun! But Buggy will not sin over the likes of you. The Baby Jesus will punish you enough. Yall will burn in hell along with your Baptist father!

Then she locks us in the grandchildren's room for the whole rest of the day so we can pray for forgiveness. We play with all our toys and I make fun of Buggy's face and do a series of Miss Peppy imitations. I make us all lose our breath, we laugh so hard.

When Mama finally gets back, it's already dark. Buggy lets us out and we fly down the hall to greet Mama, climbing all over her. She smells like air conditioning and department stores and she has all kinds of gifts for us. An Etch-a-Sketch for me, two tortoise-shell headbands for Sidda, a wind-up elephant for Bay, and a pogo stick for Lulu. All from Lafayette!

We're starving to death, Mama, Sidda announces.

Yeah, Lulu says, Buggy hasn't fed us since twelve o'clock noon.

All she did was feed that dog, I say.

Mama turns to Buggy and says, Mother, why haven't they been fed?

Buggy reaches down and scoops up Miss Peppy in her arms.

She says, Because your oldest son bit Buggy on the hand and she has a bad fever.

Mama says, Well that is the first time I've ever known Little Shep to bite anybody. Maybe it was just because he was hungry.

Buggy says, It is not funny, Viviane Abbott Walker. It is not one bit funny. I'm just glad it's you and not me who is responsible for the souls of these children.

Don't worry, Mama says, I'll take care of Little Shep when I get him home.

I get a little nervous when she says that, because Mama sure does have her ways.

She kisses Buggy on the cheek and says, Thank you for keeping the little monsters, Mother. Here—I brought you some perfume samples from Godchaux's. And she hands her a bunch of little vials that Buggy already has drawerfuls of.

When we get home, Mama makes us pancakes for supper and she lets me help flip. She doesn't eat anything herself, just fixes a drink and models her new clothes for us.

She says to me, Well, my little cannibal, how do I look? Doesn't this dress look good enough to eat? Is your Mama a living doll or what?

Later, she comes into my bedroom to tuck me in. I say, Mama, I wanna tell you something. I didn't bite Buggy. Really. That dog did.

She holds her cigarette down by the side of my bed. I lean my head over and I can see its red tip burning in the dark.

I know, Little Shep, she says, and she outlines my lips with her fingers. But you have simply got to start behaving when I leave yall with Buggy. Decent babysitters are hard to come by. You're my big man. You understand.

Yes ma'am, I say. *You don't know anything, you old witch,* I think.

When she leaves the room, I just lay there and play back the whole day. Just thinking about all I have accomplished makes me feel great, like I can do anything in the world I want and no one can stop me. I am a born leader.

BEATITUDES
Siddalee, 1963

At Our Lady of Divine Compassion Parochial School, I keep running into trouble because the nuns say Daddy is rich. Which he most certainly is not. For instance, Sister Osberga never lets me be in charge of the record player. She says: Your father is so rich that you'll probably break our record player on purpose just to show he can afford to buy a brand new one. Blessed are the poor, Siddalee Walker, and you are not one of them.

The Divine Compassion nuns are all bent out of shape because my Baptist grandfather, Pap, once owned some land that Bishop Siminaux tried to beg off him for a new church. Daddy says they sicced every fast-talking priest and monsignor they could find on Pap. When Pap finally decided it was too much land to give away to a church he didn't even like, the bishop told him he had blown his one shot at heaven—and that went for his whole family, too. He told Pap this over a big country breakfast my grandmother had prepared for them out on her porch. Daddy loves telling the story of how his mother snatched one of her angel biscuits right out of that bishop's hand and said, You better get yourself up from the devil's table and get offa my porch.

When Daddy was little, he used to sing in the choir at Calvary Baptist, where his Mama organized church suppers. Now he claims he has his own church—The Church of Sunday Drives and TV Football. He says, The old Podnah (which is what he calls God) lives in the cotton fields as much as He does over at Divine Compassion.

Before he could marry Mama, they made Daddy sign an official document promising to raise all of us in the Catholic faith. He also agreed to go to Catholic Instruction every Thursday night for two whole years. But when push came to shove, Daddy refused to join the Catholic Church. He said, Yall are like sheep to the slaughter when it comes to the Penguins (which is what he calls the brides of Christ). Yall can drag me to Mass on Christmas, he says, but other than that, don't swing that damn incense in the direction of my sinuses.

Now I didn't even know about this before we started at Divine Compassion, but at school I'm always singled out because I'm the child of a "Mixed Marriage." That means I'm likely to make the Baby Jesus cry a lot more than a kid with two Catholic parents. From the minute I started first grade with my hair down to my waist and my brand new baby-blue Nifty folder and fat crayons, I have been worrying myself sick about making the Baby Jesus cry.

The nuns have us divided into four groups:

1. Fast and Slow Readers (I am Fast)
2. Talkers and Non-talkers (I am a Talker)
3. Catholic Marriage and Mixed Marriage Kids (yall already know what I am)—and worst of all
4. Children from Broken Homes (the kids whose parents are divorced)

Broken Homes is the most shameful group to be in. But at the same time it gives you more leeway. I am here to tell you that kids from Broken Homes can get away with a lot more than the rest of us can, which is not fair, if you ask me.

You pray for Children from Broken Homes right along with the Public School Kids and Pagan Babies. You can buy a Pagan Baby for eight dollars, and that means you get to name it yourself. We have mayonnaise jars with pictures of Pagan Babies taped on them and the lids have slits to put money in. If the eight dollars comes from the whole class, then we all vote on the name. But if someone just walks in and forks over eight dollars on their own, then they can name the Pagan Baby whatever they want. One time, Little Shep took some money Daddy gave him and named a baby "Orlon," which the nuns didn't think was funny at all. But it was his money, so what could they do? He went around for weeks telling people there was a kid some-where in a pagan country named "Orlon" all because of him. That just cracked him up. Little Shep can sin his butt off and not blink an eye.

Sometimes I wish Little Shep was in my class so he could take up for me. Like when Sister Osberga announced to the whole class that our Mama lets us go to C-rated movies. Which is definitely not true. Every Wednesday when the diocesan newsletter comes out, Mama cuts out the Legion of Decency's list of movies and tapes it to the inside door of the canned-goods cabinet. We have to consult it before making any movie plans whatsoever.

There are A-1, A-2, A-3, A-4, B, and C movies. Walt Disney movies are A-1. If somebody cusses in a movie, it is an A-2. If somebody kisses too long on the lips, it is an A-3. And if unmarried people kiss at all on the lips, it is an A-4. In the B movies, people take the Lord's name in vain while they take off their blouses. And in C movies (like *Cleopatra*), they just sin their lives away in front of anyone who gets to watch.

We only get to see A-1 movies (unless there is something Mama and the Ya-Yas just have to go see and they can't find a baby-sitter). But secretly, I am dying to go to a C movie just once in my life! I love those photos of Liz Taylor with her bosoms and eye makeup. The royal gowns and all her dates with Richard Burton, which Buggy says is just awful.

Buggy says, That poor sweet Debbie Reynolds! Just look how she is forced to suffer, all because Liz stole Eddie away from her in front of the whole world. That Liz didn't even love him, she just wanted to prove that her violet eyes could break up a happy marriage—even if it was a Mixed one. And now the sinner has dropped that poor Jewish boy to carry on with Richard Burton. It just makes me sick to my stomach!

Impure thoughts, impure acts—everywhere I turn, I

stump my toe on impurity. It seems like every thought that comes into my head is impure. I worry that I'm sinning all the time just because of the way my mind works.

Thoughts have a lot of power. Just *thinking* about committing a sin is the same thing as actually doing it. Sister Osberga talks about this in class all the time. She says: If a man plans to kill somebody, but on the way over there he gets hit by a car and dies, then he will die with the sin of murder on his soul. Because he has already killed a man *in his mind.*

In his mind.

I can never get my mind pure. I keep thinking of impure things every minute of the day. They are like rats crawling across the floor of my brain.

So I've started going to Confession every day. There is nothing in the world like that light, pure feeling the second you step out of the confessional. It's such a relief to know that if you croak over right then and there, you'll go straight to Heaven. But the pure feeling wears off quicker and quicker every time. Sometimes I have to turn right around and go straight back into the confessional and confess the sins I committed in my mind in just two minutes!

The priest says, These are little things, stop thinking about them so much. Do not come back here for a whole week. You should go home and ask your parents to take you to a psychologist.

Well, that gives me diarrhea for days. I *need* to go to Confession. Sometimes I just pray to become a leper and get it over with.

I still want to see those nasty movies, though!

But Mama says, You will never so much as set foot in a C movie. Do not ask me again.

We'll be driving in the car and she'll blot some of her blood-red lipstick with a Kleenex.

Why, Mama? I pester her. Why can't I go to a C movie?

Listen to me, she'll say. Sex is for marriage, marriage is sacred. It is a sacrament.

I know, Mama. But why can't I go to see *Butterfield 8?*

But she just lights a cigarette and says, Oh, will you shut up before you drive me to the insane asylum?!

It's a real double whammy—being from a Mixed Marriage and not being poor and holy. It means I have to do much more self-mortification than your regular kid.

Sister Osberga says, Remember: Any pain, discomfort, inconvenience, humiliation that comes your way—*offer it up.* The more you can offer up—the more indulgences you can get—the less time your soul will have to suffer in Purgatory.

I try to commit little acts of self-mortification every day. First of all, lying in bed, I pinch my stomach until it hurts and bruises blue. Then, later, when I have a bad thought, I lift up my blouse and see that bruise and I don't feel so guilty. Second, when I have to go to the bathroom, I hold it for as long as I can. Sometimes this gets me into tight spots, but the way of the penitent is not always easy. If I am feeling particularly bad about something I've done that day, I wait until Lulu is asleep and then I lie down on the bare floor and try to sleep with no covers. Just like St. Therese the Little Flower.

I write down all of these things in my diary and try to figure out at the end of each week how many days I've burned off my time in Purgatory. You've got to rack and stack those indulgences.

I learned how to read way before first grade, thanks to Mama and Aunt Jezie. *Children's Lives of the Saints* was my first book. Buggy gave it to me. St. Martin de Porres, the patron saint of the poor, is the one I really go to for intercession. St. Martin was a barber during the day, but at night he had all kinds of visions. He was the son of a knight and a Negro woman from Peru. And even when all the people started calling him the "Father of Charity," he just called himself "Mulatto Dog."

Every single time I talk about St. Martin, Little Shep starts barking and yelling, I'm a mulatto dog! Woof! Woof!

My all-time favorite, though, is St. Cecilia. She was from a rich family and they made her marry this good-looking pagan. But St. Cecilia had already promised God she would stay a virgin forever, and so she refused to Do It with her husband and actually managed to convert him. So they sentenced her to be suffocated in her bathroom. But she just kept on miraculously breathing. Then a soldier went and tried to chop her head off three times and she would not die! She lay there half-dead for three solid days!

St. Cecilia is one of the things my friend, Marie Williams, and I have in common. We are fascinated by her. Marie and I open the saints book to St. Cecilia's picture and just stare at it for hours. We try to figure out whether St. Cecilia's head was actually still attached to her body while she was lying in that bathroom half-dead, or whether it had sort of rolled off to the side.

*N*ow, as I have said, Daddy is not rich. Oh, sure, we have enough money for Mama to get her hair done once a week, but not at Mr. Julian's, where they serve sherry and where M'lain Chauvin's mother goes. Mama goes to Jeannine at the House of Beauty because she claims Mr. Julian will not use her brand of hairspray. Mama says: Julian is full of shit charging as much as he does, just because he uses hairspray in a pump bottle from France.

Jeannine is a black-haired woman who's a big-time bowler at Bowl-a-Rina out on Highway 17. Mama's appointment is every Friday, before her big grocery shop at the Piggly-Wiggly. Mama is convinced that she doesn't have enough hair. Jeannine sold her this little hairpiece that fits on the back of her head, and every Friday she washes and sets that hairpiece along with Mama's real hair. Then Jeannine sticks it on the back of Mama's head where it stays until she takes it off at night. She puts it in the night-table drawer while she sleeps and it looks like a little strawberry-blonde rat. We are not supposed to talk about it.

On Fridays Mama brings the hairpiece to the beauty shop with her in a plastic bag. And I bring my spend-the-night things to school so I can ride the bus home with Marie Williams and sleep at her house, where everything is all poor and holy.

See, even though the Williams aren't dirt poor, at least they use powdered milk. Marie's father is a garage mechanic and her mother is a housewife named Antoinette, and they don't have a maid or anything. Their house is absolutely cram-packed with kids and canned food and crucifixes. Their yard has one tree in it and a barbed-wire fence and almost no grass, because their mongrel dog is such a rooter. They are real Catholics with a big family, not like Mama and Daddy who stopped after just four. (Five, if you count my twin that died.)

They have seven children in a two-bedroom house. All six of the girls sleep in three sets of bunk beds in one room, and their brother sleeps on the fold-out couch in the living room. He waits until everyone's finished watching TV to unfold his bed. Since it is so crowded at their house, Marie sleeps in a sleeping bag on the floor when I spend the night and I sleep in her top bunk above her sister Bernadette.

I am so jealous of the fact that they all got named after saints. Do you think Mama gave a damn about saints' names when it came to us? No. I ask you: Who ever heard of a Saint Siddalee? Who ever heard of a Saint Lulu? When I bug Mama about it, she just says, Most of those saints' names are just too Italian-sounding for my personal taste.

On Friday evenings, the Williams sit around a crowded dinette table in their tiny kitchen. The older girls help their mother prepare the tuna loaf or other poor people's food.

Afterwards, I always go home and beg Mama to use powdered milk. She sometimes buys some to indulge me, but there's no way tuna loaf will ever pollute her kitchen. My parents are steak-and-baked-potatoes people, and that smell of Lea & Perrins steak sauce sprinkled on near-raw meat drifts out from under the broiler at least five nights a week. Daddy raises his own cattle, so after dinner we're all expected to say, Umm, good meat, Daddy! Like it's his own flesh we've just eaten instead of a dead cow's. On Fridays when we can't eat meat, Mama cooks red snapper or fried shrimp. But her idea of a meal does not include tuna loaf.

All I want is the Williams' macaroni and day-old bread, and the way Marie's mother makes things last, and her father wearing those green overalls, and the brother Jude with his old *Popular Mechanics* magazines.

Oh, their bathroom is so heavenly. It smells like cedar, and they have these huge bottles of the cheapest shampoo and creme rinse like I always see at Kress. They use Sweetheart soap and they have those kind of towels that come free inside of jumbo boxes of laundry detergent. Even with all the people who use that bathroom, it's always clean. Mrs. Williams has a hand-written sign by the sink that says: "Did you clean up after yourself?"

Sometimes I lock myself in there, just to stare at all the poor people's stuff in their cabinets. Gigantic industrial-sized bottles of aspirin—and they never use toothpaste, only baking soda in huge boxes. There is a picture of the Holy Family next to the sink mirror, with Jesus, Mary, and Joseph standing behind a gate. I do a few genuflections there in the bathroom and murmur a quick prayer before one of the little girls starts knocking on the door needing to get in and pee. I feel lighter and purer every time I step out of the Williams' bathroom. It's almost as good as going to Confession. I swear, if the Pope himself came to Thornton on a surprise visit, he'd drive straight over to the Williams' house and not be disappointed.

On Saturday mornings when it's cold outside, Mrs. Williams makes a huge pot of oatmeal. Each of us gets up and ladles some into a cup, then we crawl back into bed to eat it because the house hasn't warmed up yet. They don't have heat in the bedrooms, so it's much warmer under the covers. But your toes freeze off from walking barefoot to the kitchen and back. If Mama ever found out I was this cold, she would stop me right away from ever visiting them again. But as it is, I knock off days in Purgatory right and left, just by spending the night in that wood frame house.

Marie and I lie in the top bunk in the morning and pretend to be missionaries, and we sing "Dominique" like the Singing Nun. We discuss how we'll be missionary nurses instead of nuns, because in Africa what they really need is medical help. Plus, we don't want face warts with stiff hairs sticking out like Sister Osberga.

At the Williams' house, every single bit of food is rationed. If you take more than your share, it's against the rules. I know that, because it was one of the first things Marie explained to me when I started spending the night over there. I love it! It feels like we're all pulling through a war together by not being pigs.

But one Friday night at dinner when they are passing around the plate of day-old sliced white bread, I swear I get possessed by Lucifer. I know that there's only enough bread for each person to have one slice. But that does not stop me from reaching out and grabbing two pieces so fast that nobody notices. I hold the pieces together so they look like only one. I smear one of them with margarine and put the other one in my lap.

The blue plastic bread plate gets handed all the way around the table, and when it stops in front of Mrs. Williams, there is not one single solitary slice left for her.

I stare down into my spaghetti and tomato sauce as Mrs. Williams asks, Who helped themselves to two pieces of bread?

I start sweating. I begin balling that second piece of bread up in my palm so it fits there like a sticky little glob of Play-Doh.

Each of the Williams children looks up at their mother with these totally innocent eyes. Mrs. Williams calls the roll, to find out who the greedy one is. Marie? Bernadette? Kathy? Theresa? Monica? Jude?

She leaves out Mr. Williams and the baby girl who is still in a high chair.

I'm so thrilled with what I've put into motion that I can hardly sit still. I don't know how I can ever confess this! It feels great, like something I was born to do. I play with my food and steal little glances at the holy family's drama.

Finally Mrs. Williams settles on Jude. Leave the table, Jude, she says.

But Mama, he protests, I only took one piece, I promise!

Please leave the table until you can learn not to take more than your share, she tells him.

It's not fair—he starts to say, but Mr. Williams interrupts, You heard what your mother said, Son.

And Jude gets up from the table without saying another word.

I have never seen a boy take something like that. All humble, like Jesus when he was unjustly accused. And all because of me!

After dinner I say to Mrs. Williams, Thank you for the lovely meal. May I please be excused now?

Then I go into the bathroom and flush that balled-up bread down the toilet. Later that evening I teach Marie and Bernadette the dance number to "Personality" that I've been learning in dance class. I tell them, I don't see how yall can stand living here—there's not any room to tap dance at all.

The next day, Mama comes to pick me up on her way home from one of the Ya-Ya *bourrée* games. Her hair is particularly poofy, with the hairpiece done in this cascade of waves. She has that anything-can-happen Saturday afternoon look and her arm is propped on the partially rolled-down window with a cigarette dangling between her fingers. Mrs. Williams comes out of the house, wiping her hands on a dishtowel, and walks to the end of the driveway to be polite. Marie and I hug goodbye and I climb in beside Mama, with her plastic tumbler of vodka and grapefruit juice sitting on the seat between us.

Mrs. Williams says, Oh Mrs. Walker, your hair always looks so pretty.

Mama smiles generously. Thank you, dahling, she purrs. You don't know what I go through to get it like this! I only have three hairs on my entire head, you know—the whole thing is done with mirrors.

Mama loves to put herself down when she's feeling all superior to someone. It's how you can tell something is coming. She lifts up her sunglasses and then French-inhales while she stares at Mrs. Williams' hair. This is the first time I notice how oily and stringy it is. It has no luster to it whatsoever. It looks like the kind of hair that if you sniffed it, it would just smell too human to bear.

Mama says, You know, Antoinette, you really ought to get yourself on over to the House of Beauty. Talk to Jeannine. She's my girl. Tell her I sent you. Would do you a world of good! You really shouldn't let yourself go like that.

I cannot believe my ears! Mama telling a poor holy woman that her hair is ugly!

Mrs. Williams rubs her hands on the dishtowel like they've got something on them. She takes a tiny step back from the car and stares down at the grass growing through the cracks in the driveway.

Then she clears her throat and says, I wish I could. But I . . . we . . . we just can't afford it.

Don't be ridiculous, Antoinette! Mama exclaims. You can't afford *not* to!

Then Mama puts the car into reverse and slowly backs out into the street. Idling the motor for a minute, she instructs me, Tell Mrs. Williams what a delightful time you had, Sidda.

I cannot bear to look at Mrs. Williams with her

hands hanging at her sides. Marie is standing beside her, and for a second I have this clear vision that when Marie grows up she will look exactly like her mother.

I say, Thank you, Mrs. Williams. I could not have had a more enjoyable time.

But what I'm really thinking is, I'll have to do penance for my mother's sins—along with my own—*for the rest of my life.*

Mama points the car toward home and I turn on the car radio because I do not want to talk to her.

She takes a sip of her drink and says, Did yall have fun? What'd yall do?

I tell her we pretended to be Connie Stevens. I don't mention a word about our missionary plans. Mama reaches into her purse and hands me a piece of gum. I put it on the seat beside me.

She keeps driving along for a minute or two before she says, Listen to me, Siddalee, and listen good: There is *no excuse* to let your looks go, no matter how poor you are. Cleanliness might be next to godliness, but honey let me tell you, ugliness will get you nowhere.

Yes Ma'am, I say. And I stare out the windshield of the T-Bird.

*W*ell, after that, I am just too ashamed to set foot in the Williams' house. Marie asks me to spend the night and I just have to tell her: No thank you. Even though it breaks my heart in two.

A couple of months go by and I'm at Bordelon's Drugstore, with Mama waiting out in the car for me while I run in to pick up some of her nerve medicine. And who do I see over by the vaporizers but Mrs. Antoinette Williams! At first I don't even recognize her because she has lost weight and she has this new haircut. I think about running and hiding, but she spots me and walks right over.

Siddalee, she says, how are you? We sure have missed you over at our house.

You have? I think.

I say, You look so different, Mrs. Williams. I mean—you just look so pretty.

She says, Well, I have your mother to thank for that, Siddalee. She is the one who inspired me to start taking care of myself. Your mother is a good lady. Don't you ever let anyone tell you different.

I can't think of a thing to say, except Thank you.

She says, Don't be a stranger to our house now. You're welcome anytime you want.

Then she walks away down the aisle and I pick up Mama's medicine. When the druggist rings up the bill, I sign for it on Daddy's charge account. Then I walk out of the store. I feel light and good. I feel like I've just come out of Confession, even though I've only been in a drugstore, not a Catholic church. Even though Mrs. Williams is a regular person, not a priest or a nun or a saint.

THE ELF AND THE FAIRY
Siddalee, 1963

*O*ur Lady of Divine Compassion Parochial School is surrounded by sycamore trees. In the fall those big leaves turn yellow and the scorching days of summer are almost over, and you can start breathing again. I walk every school day underneath those trees to the music building, which is between Divine Compassion and Holy Names Academy, where the high school girls walk and talk in their blue-and-white straight skirts and starched blouses. I can hear them at choir practice while I'm walking along with my music folder under my arm. I love the high school girls, especially the ones with bubble hair-dos. But mainly I love getting out of regular classes to take piano. It's the calmest part of my day. I get so tired of everyone—from my classmates to my brothers and sister to my mother—making so much *noise* all the time. I take my quiet wherever I can find it.

On lesson days, I knock on Sister Philomena's frosted-glass door. When she says, Do come in, I open the door and say, Good afternoon, Sister. She is a big nun with a wide face who quotes the Bible a lot. She always seems glad to see me. I'm working on my recital piece, "The Elf and the Fairy," which is considered quite a difficult composition for fourth grade.

At first Sister Philomena asks me, Siddalee, are you certain that you want to choose such an advanced piece for your recital?

Yes Sister, I assure her. I love that piece. I can handle it, I promise you.

This is my big chance to take something hard and do it right.

The first time Sister Philomena plays "The Elf and the Fairy" for me, I close my eyes and go somewhere else. To a place in another state that doesn't have all the hot white light of Louisiana. There are waterfalls there and the air is so sweet and easy to breathe. There are actually fairies darting around, and when you see them you can't tell if they are working or playing—it's all the same thing to them. My grandmother Buggy talks to fairies frequently. She calls me on the phone and tells me about her conversations with them. Fairies aren't strange to me at all. They're sort of like midget guardian angels with a good sense of humor.

I am determined to take myself to that same magic place by learning my recital piece perfectly. I practice for hours and hours, alone in the tiny practice room in the music building. That room is like a monk's cell and I enjoy it—just me, the piano, and one window where the afternoon light comes in and tries to make me sleepy. Sometimes I am tempted just to lie on the floor and take a nap, but Sister Philomena says: God will not allow us to be overwhelmed by temptation, but with it

He will provide a way of escape so that we will be able to endure it. I play those notes over and over, until it feels like I can climb up inside them and live there. Piano practice is the best way I know to feel organized.

It's just impossible to practice at home because Little Shep and Lulu do nothing but make fun of me. They run around the piano like wild Indians, screeching out their imitations of opera singers like hyenas. It is kind of a family hobby, to make fun of opera singers. Mama taught Lulu to sing in pidgin Italian, "Ahhh! Spitonya! Ahhh! Pickaya-boogers!" and other nasty high-pitched phrases, and that is now Lulu's specialty for our family skits. Playing the piano is right up there with opera singing for Little Shep and Lulu in terms of being something to make fun of.

The other problem with trying to practice at home is that you never know when the place is going to be filled with the Ya-Yas. They roar up in their station wagons and Cadillacs to drink and play *bourrée*. After they play and scream and cheat and drink and smoke, they always start singing songs about men.

They moan out how fish have to swim and birds have to fly and so they have to love one man till they die.

You just cannot concentrate with all their moaning going on. But when I complain to Mama, she says, Don't get dramatic with me, Little Miss Sarah Bernhardt.

So I make a bargain with Baby Jesus: If I play "The Elf and the Fairy" perfectly at my recital, He will forgive me for pinching Lulu in church just to make her cry. If I play the composition flawlessly, Baby Jesus might also forgive me for some other things that I can't quite name but always feel guilty for anyway.

I work harder and harder on the piece, picturing those notes while I try to fall asleep at night. My fingers strike the mattress until it feels like the bed is vibrating. I get all my memory work, fingering, timing, and phrasing down. All I have left to do are the final polishing touches.

But the week before the recital, Mama goes to a big Ya-Ya party out at Little Spring Creek and cuts her foot up something awful on a broken Coke bottle. The other Ya-Yas take her to the nearest emergency room and get the wound sewn up, but the cut is so deep she has to use crutches to get around. We have never seen Mama crippled like this before and it is kind of scary.

The night after Mama's injury, Lulu and I are already in bed. I've sharpened my pencils and laid out my clothes for school the next day. They sit next to my book sack where my books, papers, and art supplies are arranged all neat. I can never fall asleep until everything is organized and ready to go at the foot of my bed.

When I first hear the screaming from my parents' room, I think it's hurt dogs or something. I bolt up and dash down the hall. I can feel my bare feet squeak on the shiny wood floors. When I get to the entrance of Mama's long narrow dressing room, Lulu, Little Shep, and Baylor are already there. How did they get there so fast before me? Daddy is standing next to the chaise longue in his socks and boxer shorts. He has a toothbrush in his hand. Mama has on her pink nightgown with the lace, and the way its gathers fall, you can't hardly tell she's using crutches. I can smell the night-cream on her face. In one hand she has one of the squatty crystal glasses she drinks out of at night, the ones with heavy bottoms that don't tip over.

They are already in the middle of it.

Mama says, You redneck bastard, don't you dare make those kinds of insinuations to me!

Daddy says, Insinuations, hell! I said you're a god-damn drunk and I'll say it again! Why do you think you almost cut your fool foot off?

Even though he hasn't touched her, Mama looks like Daddy has split her up for kindling. Her expression changes and she goes for him, slapping him hard in the face.

They stand there yelling like the four of us are invisible. One closet door is open and I can see Mama's ice-blue crepe sheath hanging with a laundry bag over it.

Daddy lets Mama slap him, then he knocks the glass out of her other hand. The glass falls to the floor and breaks, ice going everywhere, and you can smell bourbon in the dressing room along with Mama's rose sachets that hang in the closet.

Mama braces one of her arms against the wall and raises the fist of her other hand and punches Daddy in the stomach.

As if *you* can talk, you pathetic excuse for a man! she yells. You cowardly dirt-farming loser!

This is not happening I think. *I am not in this room.*

Then she goes to hit him again, but he pushes her away—not hard, but like she's a duck trying to bite him. It throws her off-balance and she falls down. Those crutches just fly out from under her.

This is the first time in our lives we've ever heard one of them call the other a drunk. It is like dynamite. It's bigger than even seeing her hit him, or the way he pushed her. Just his saying that word "drunk" changes everything, even changes the air in the room.

I don't cry because I can't breathe. Lulu starts eating her hair, like she does whenever she gets upset. Little Shep and Baylor are mute, and Baylor is shaking. He looks so much like a little bird to me.

Daddy looks down at Mama on the floor and then he looks at us. But we won't look at him. He says to Mama, You are not fit to raise these children. Then he turns and walks out of the room.

I help Mama up on her crutches. She is shaking and crying and she says, We are getting out of this hellhole. Yall go get your school clothes.

When we stand there frozen, she yells, Don't just stand there like ignoramuses. Yall heard me, go get your damn school things!

I race to my room where I have my brown-and-gold dress with the drifting leaves laid on the chair. I scoop it up, along with my slip, panties, socks, and cordovan tassel loafers. These loafers are my all-time favorite shoes, hand-me-downs from my teenage cousin and broken-in just right. When I wear them, I feel like a cheerleader who writes poetry, like I have a guaranteed good future.

Lulu says, Sidda, can I bring my turtle?

I say, Shut up, Lulu!

Then I grab my book sack, take my little sister by the hand, and fly down the hall to the kitchen door. As I run, I can see the couch, the TV set, and the piano from the corner of my eye. All our familiar things look foreign to me, and for just a second I can't remember where I am or what I have done in my life before right now.

Mama is already in the car with nothing but her nightgown, crutches, and purse. She's smoking and leaning on the horn, cussing at Daddy, who is nowhere in sight. I'm so frenzied, I drop my book sack, and all my papers fly everywhere. Crayons roll under the car.

One of my loafers falls on the concrete and I reach down to get it, but Mama yells, Sidda, get in the god-damn car!

Then she backs the car out of the long driveway and speeds down the gravel road—away from the house. We are all keyed up. We are quivering with fear and excitement at leaving the house so late on a school night.

We quiz her, Where're we going, Mama? Where're we going?

We're going to Buggy's, she explains and I breathe with relief to hear she has some kind of plan. Maybe this isn't so bad after all, I think. Maybe she's got this all mapped out. Maybe I'm being delivered into the life I was meant for. I love spending the night at my grandmother's old house near City Park. You get to stay up late there and walk to school. It's like a little vacation, if you don't mind her dog and kneeling to pray all the time.

But halfway down the road lined with old pecan trees that leads away from our house, Mama slams on the brakes and turns the car around.

I'm not losing every single thing I deserve because

that bastard claims I run out on him! she yells. We're going back! That sonovabitch is not going to get rid of me this goddamn easy!

She squeals the car back under the carport. I walk toward the end of the driveway to catch my breath. But Mama yells at me and I walk back into the house that is all quiet except for the sound of the air conditioner that Mama leaves running till Halloween. I don't let myself look at the furniture like I did on the way out. I go in the bathroom and run cold water on a washrag and put it on my forehead, like you're supposed to do when you're upset. Then I sit in my bed with my flashlight and try to straighten out my school things, which have gotten all messed up in the big getaway.

I don't sleep that night and I keep having a hard time getting my breath. I wish I had a fan blowing straight on me so I could get some air into my body.

The next day at school, my head hurts and the back of my eyes burn. It's Friday, the day for my last piano lesson before my recital. Sister Philomena asks me to rehearse every move—the way I'm supposed to lift my hands to the keyboard before beginning the performance, the exact way I should gracefully rest them in my lap after the piece is over, my perfectly rehearsed curtsy. I try to picture smiling faces applauding for me, but all I can think of is how jumbled up all my school papers are, and how there are some important things missing from the night before that I can't seem to find.

When I play for Sister Philomena, I don't miss any notes, but my timing is way off.

She says, Siddalee, be sure to give yourself some

quiet practice time this weekend. And on Sunday, go to Holy Communion. Offer the recital up to the Baby Jesus and everything will be fine. He will give His angels charge concerning you to guard you in all your ways.

But there's no chance to practice on Saturday. The day is devoted to converting our schoolroom into Mama's new bedroom. Daddy is nowhere in sight. Mama and Chaney rip down the blackboards from the walls. They haul out our desks, our toy boxes, and the tall shelves with the set of *World Books.* In their place, Mama moves in a Hollywood bed she gets delivered from Holden's Fine Furniture, along with a matching nightstand and a new portable TV set. Before, no one was even allowed to smoke in that room because it was just for children. It was all ours. But now it is Mama's new bedroom, and she has her silver and crystal ashtray with "Ya-Yas, 1960" engraved on the side right there on her new night table.

On the day of the recital, I'm real tired but still sure of myself. I *really* know "The Elf and the Fairy." Those notes won't abandon me in my powder blue dressy dress and patent leather shoes, with my hair rolled into a French twist, Mama's favorite style. I fast my three hours before Communion. But at Mass, the Sacred Host sticks to the roof of my mouth and makes me nauseated. I feel like spitting up on the floor, but a mortal sin like that could easily take away my power of speech and make me grow a harelip to boot.

That Sunday afternoon the Divine Compassion auditorium is filled with mothers and fathers and aunts and grandmothers and the smell of floral arrangements and floor varnish.

Mama hugs me tightly and whispers, I adore you!

I join the music students in the front row. I perch on my folding chair with my feet crossed at the ankles and off to one side like we're supposed to do. I watch the other students, one by one, rise from their seats, climb the steps to the high stage, and plunk out their recital pieces. Each one of them looks so afraid. I almost pity them. They're so insecure, so ill-composed. I feel utterly calm; I do not even feel like a child.

When it's my turn, I sit down at the piano. My hands are steady, my hair is clean, my heart is true. But the moment I hit the first note, somebody else's hands—wild, shaking, and ignorant—take over. At first I'm only kind of curious and dizzy. It takes me eight entire measures to realize that I am the one producing the crazy frantic noise. I am confused, because part of me can actually hear myself playing the music impeccably. But the other part of me knows that the only thing left of "The Elf and the Fairy" is the phrasing. The rest is ugly, unrelated notes that crash through the thick air in that gymnasium. Inside myself, I can hear all the beauty, but my body can't respond. *And I don't even consider just giving up.* I keep on playing because I *have* to. And because I truly believe that I will finally discover the right notes and lead the audience into my elf and fairy world, where peaceful out-of-state light glimmers and cleanses and redeems.

I cannot stop myself. I attack the keyboard for the exact length of time it would've taken me to perform the piece like it's written. But not once do I manage to hit a note that sounds anything like the music I have spent months rehearsing.

When I finish, I am sweating all over. I stand up from the piano in a trance and curtsy like I've practiced a hundred times in front of the mirror. I look out into the audience. Even the other children are silent and wide-eyed. All the mothers are wiping tears from their eyes. I hate them all. Afterward they walk by me and stare at me. Later that afternoon, some of the mothers call Mama to see how I am "taking it."

The next day at school nobody makes fun of me. In fact, they are nicer than usual, which feels worse. I don't want anything to do with them. That afternoon, instead of going to my music lesson, I sneak out behind the parish hall where nobody can see me. I take one of Mama's cigarette lighters out of my uniform pocket and I light the sheet music of "The Elf and the Fairy" on fire. I just flip open that little lighter and hold the flame under the notes. I think about setting all the grass back there on fire as well, but that would cause more trouble than I feel up to. I just burn up all those elf and fairy chords and stomp on the runaway sparks.

Just as I'm finishing up, I hear somebody over by the walkway calling out my name. It's Sister Philomena. She sounds like she is scared that I'm lost. I remember how clean and neat her music room is, how when she plays the piano it makes me feel like everything is in the right place for at least a while. I think about running to her and burying my head in her rustling black habit. For some reason I think that if I do that, she will reach down and touch my face with her

long cool fingers that know how to move across a keyboard with total control.

I don't run to her, though. I hide behind the concrete steps until she stops calling out my name and finally goes away.

All I think then is, Don't you dare call out my name
ever again. *You don't even know who I am.*

THE PRINCESS OF GIMMEE
Lulu, 1967

I am—bar none—your best shoplifter in the town of Thornton, Louisiana. I would go so far as to say in all of Garnet Parish. Maybe even in the entire great state of Louisiana. But to be perfectly truthful, I haven't spent enough time in New Orleans, our biggest city, to say that is definitely true. But I bet if you gave me one good weekend down there on Canal Street, I could ace out anybody in that city when it comes to five-finger discounts. I'm not bragging, I'm telling it like it is. I have learned to reach out and take what I want for my own self. I don't have to listen to Mama anymore saying: Gimmee Gimmee Gimmee every time I ask her for something. Gimmee Gimmee Gimmee, she says, that's all you are, Tallulah Abbott Walker, is Gimmee.

Mama named me for Tallulah Bankhead. My Daddy told her, No you will not name a daughter of mine for a woman who claims she is "pure as the driven slush." But Mama told him she was the one who had thrown up and carried me for nine solid months and she would name me after whoever she damn well pleased.

I will tell you this: Saint Siddalee the Goody-Goody does not have one iota of trouble using all the stuff I steal for her. Every time I fork over something, she says: Lulu, you are sinning your butt off. But you should just see her whipping out that mascara-wand like there's no tomorrow. I've run all over town kyping things for her, putting my reputation on the line. For the past year it has been me and me alone keeping her in Bonne Bell White-White which she loves-loves-loves to put under her eyebrows. I've brought her Yardley eyeliner, eye-shadow, and oatmeal soap that costs a fortune. And I've also brought her the Yardley Slicker Lip Gloss, which Mama says is not half as good as plain old Vaseline. Mama also says that oatmeal soap is not half as good as plain old Camay with the quarter-ounce of cold cream. Sidda claims Mama says all this just so she won't have to spend money on my big sister's beauty.

When Sidda read in *Seventeen* that Yardley was the only makeup to use, I had to make the jump up from stealing at Woolworth's to your more expensive stores. Now see, I had it *down* at Woolworth's. I know those bins and shelves inside and out. I know just how to browse, looking like an innocent child who wouldn't steal a No. 2 pencil, even if you gave her the chance. I am not dumb. I always buy me something—like a magazine—and sit at the lunch counter and drink a Coke and act very natural. I pay for my Coke and then I just wander around, looking. You have to always buy something. That throws them off the track. I buy some little what-not and then I stuff my gifts in my pockets or my purse. (Rule Numero Uno: You never set foot in a store with a big purse. It's the first thing they look for! You got to have you a classy little purse that nobody would ever think you'd use to stash stolen goods in.)

I walk right up to the cash register and say, Good afternoon, ma'am, how you doing? Then they say back, Fine, how you? And I say—just like Mama—Marvelous, couldn't be better. Then I pay for my what-not with my allowance, counting out the nickels and quarters. And they just smile at me and give me a piece of Super-Bubble because I'm so cute. My insides might be shaking like Mama's hands in the morning, but on the outside I am cool as a cucumber! Once I get out of the store, I run around the corner to the covered bus stop where all the colored maids wait. Then I take out all my free stolen goodies and examine them and I feel like a million dollars! I love it! I get so excited I can hardly stand it. One time I was so happy that I asked somebody's maid if she wanted a compact I'd just stolen. I said, Go ahead, take it. It's a gift. But she said, No thank you, I already got me one.

I never plan what I'm going to take. I just go browsing and see what catches my eye. Sometimes it will be something real stupid, like a tiny tube of Prell shampoo. But my favorite things are lingerie and makeup. I can take what I want for free because I am so good! The fuddy-duddy salesladies just look at me and smile and I steal them blind right from under their noses!

At Woolworth's I get all my Maybelline eyelash curlers and Sable Brown and Sky-Blue eyeshadow and Max Factor Brownish Black mascara-wands that I give to Sidda. And I get my lipsticks and any color fingernail polish a person could want.

I've brought Mama home five different shades of red

nail polish. I am the one responsible for introducing her to Aladdin's Fire when she had been using only Rich Girl Red on her toenails for years and years. When I gave it to her she said, Oh Lulu-Cakes, you shouldn't have gone and spent all your allowance on me!

So I said, Well Mama, maybe you could think about raising my allowance a little.

And do you know, that is exactly what she did! Right there on the spot. Which of course meant she raised Sidda's, Little Shep's, and Baylor's too. Even-Steven is what Mama says. I take care of myself. I take care of all of them, in my way.

I went right out after that and stole Mama a Ronson cigarette lighter that flips up with a sharp little click. She just adores that lighter. Every time she uses it, she says to the Ya-Yas, Yall know Lulu gave this to me?

And Caro and Necie and sometimes Teensy say, Oh, isn't that the sweetest?

And I stand there and smile and suck in their cigarette smoke, which I crave. I have my own stash of cigarettes that me and my best friend Amy smoke anytime we feel like it. We do it at her house because her mother is never home. She is having an affair with a world-history professor at LSU-Thornton. We saw them kissing in the parking lot behind St. Cecilia's Hospital one time when we were riding our bikes. Amy's mother was sitting there in her station wagon wearing her Ladies Auxiliary volunteer uniform, kissing on that professor like all get-out! Amy said you could tell they were tongue-kissing because of the way their heads moved. Your head moves different when you tongue-kiss because of the suction. I haven't tongue-kissed yet, but Amy has. She says it's not all it's cracked up to be, that sometimes it can make you gag. But I think it must have something going for it, since the Penguins say it's a mortal sin.

So. I had been making-do at Woolworth's. Then Sidda discovers from *Seventeen* that the darling things I've been bringing her are cheap cosmetics that only trailer-trash would wear. She says: Don't bother bringing me any more of that tacky junk. I would rather look homely than cheap. From here on out, it's Yardley for me, or nothing at all.

Mind you, she read this from a *Seventeen* that I stole for her. The big fat Back-to-School issue that almost got me nabbed, but that I managed to get away with due to the baggy shorts I was wearing that day. (And to the fact that I am just plain superior at what I do.) Like I said, it was that *Seventeen* that caused me to widen my horizons.

I had to make the jump all the way up to Wayland's department store! Their cosmetics counter is on the first floor near the glass doors off the street. The second you walk in there, you get a whiff of the newest perfume. And there is Rosalyn, the cosmetics lady, in her white smock just waiting to pounce on some rich lady and rub makeup all over her face and squeal: It's you! Oh, it is so *you!*

Mama uses Daddy's charge account at Wayland's, so I have been known there since the day I was born. Which is very dangerous in one way and very helpful in another. It means I don't look too suspicious just taking my time, but if I ever did get caught, Mama would probably belt-whip the skin off me.

I wait until Rosalyn is busy contouring some old fat-butt's cheeks, and then I steal only one or two Yardley things at a time. Well, maybe three or four. I cup them in my hand—don't even spend the time to put them in my pocket—just put them in my hand and walk out of the store. The first time I did it I almost wet my pants! Stealing from Wayland's! Wayland's, where every time Mama walks in with the Ya-Yas she says *Hello dahling* to all the salesladies, like she is the queen and they are her servants. Wayland's, where Mama blows cigarette smoke right into the shoe salesman's face, and asks him, Honey, would you mind running upstairs and getting me a cold Coke because my throat is just parched?

Yeah, I was nervous the first few times—but after that, it got to be a good kind of nervous. Finally I got so good that I actually stepped over to the Wayland's jewelry counter and picked myself up a pair of Monet earrings in the shape of seashells! I love them! They are so rich-looking! They go with the diamond dinner-ring I won playing Bingo with Buggy at Our Lady of Divine Compassion on Las Vegas Night. My grandmother was so jealous she could have spit, but she just bit on her old chapped-up lips. Tough. I'm the one that won that ring. Won it fair and square and nobody can say a thing about it. They didn't have any rules saying that a child could not win a diamond dinner-ring. But after my big win, they put an age limit on the more expensive prizes. That is just like the Catholics, is what my Daddy said.

I wear that ring all the time, everywhere. I don't even take it off to bathe. Mama would snatch it up and sell it for the money and swear it got sucked in the vacuum cleaner. I am not dumb. My diamond dinner-ring is worth something. It might come in handy if I ever decide I need to make a quick getaway out of this place.

I steal for myself and for the people who deserve gifts in my book. You take my best friend Amy. She would love to steal, but she is just not brave enough. We stand in front of her mirror and practice being models. Some-times I let her wear some of the stuff I've stolen in exchange for letting me hide it over at her house. Her mother never goes in her room—only their maid, who isn't like Willetta at all, but more like plain hired help. My very very favorite thing that I have stolen so far is an aqua chiffon nightgown with spaghetti straps. It is so beautiful, and so European! I put it on in the dress-ing room at Wayland's, then I tucked it into my jeans, pulled my LSU sweatshirt on over it, and just walked out of the store! Right out onto Cypress Street! Can you imagine?! I am the best! Me and Amy take turns trying it on and practicing runway modeling and turns. That nightgown cost $20 and I got it for free!

I have to keep it over at Amy's because Mama would know for sure that something was up and whip the hell out of me, which I am not about to let happen. I know what that woman can do once she gets started. I am too good at this to let anything slip through the cracks, let me tell you. I cover my tracks. You have to.

It's the small things I keep at home. Like the little satin bikini panties with the butterflies on them. I hand-wash them myself and dry them in my closet at night. Then I slip them on and wear them to school.

Only I know how gorgeous and sexy my lingerie is under that dumb-ass Divine Compassion uniform. I just love how those panties poof out in the back! As far as I'm concerned, my own mother does not pay enough attention to lingerie. She just wears plain old white panties. If she got in a car wreck and died with them on, she wouldn't have to be exactly humiliated. But still, she could do so much better. After all, she is a Ya-Ya.

I love getting presents for everybody. It's so easy I can't believe it! For Baylor and Little Shep, I go to Central Louisiana Sporting Goods. I walk in there and I buy me a bandana and maybe a package of new Ping-Pong balls. Then I walk over to the bin where they keep the pellets for my brothers' Benjamin pump guns and I snatch up as many of those little round green cans as I can. Then I pay for my stuff and say real sweet to Mister Couvillion who has worked there for a million years: How you doing, Mister Couvillion, how's your hunting? He hunts out at the duck camp with Daddy sometimes. If he only knew that I was lightening his pellet load any time I feel like it!

Little Shep thanks me for the pellets. He says, Hey Lulu, didn't know you cared. And then he treats me real nice for about two days afterward.

After giving Baylor pellets a couple of times, he says to me: You know, Lulu, if you really want to give me a present, could you make it something other than pellets? I have pellets. I don't even know why Daddy gave me a stupid gun.

I say, Well what *do* you want, Bay?

And do you know what he says?! My little brother

says, I want that antique globe of the world at Miss Hanaway's antique store.

Oh sure! Even I couldn't pull off stealing a globe of the goddamn world! What would I do? Stick it under my blouse and pretend I'm pregnant? My little brother always has peculiar ideas about what he wants. He is not as easy to satisfy as Little Shep. I am telling you!

At first the boys don't realize that I'm stealing their presents. When they finally catch on, all they say is: Boy Lulu, if you get caught you're really gonna get it. But they don't tell.

Sidda's not going to tell either. She doesn't even want to know where I get all her stuff. She pretends everything just appears. She goes to Confession and tells Pig-Face the priest all about her eighty-four-thousand impure things, and then she turns the other way when I dump her stolen stash on the bed. She acts like it's magic.

Oh God, my favorite, my absolute favorite spot in the world to steal things is the Pro Shop at the Garnet Parish Golf and Country Club! We don't belong because my Daddy says they're all a bunch of whiny babies. But Amy's family belongs and her mother plays tennis there three times a week. Me and Amy go out there with her to swim, and we eat in the dining room, where we can charge whatever we want to her daddy. We order club sandwiches, french fries and pecan pie à la mode, ice tea and just everything. And Amy just signs her name on the check.

But what I really go out there for is the Pro Shop. There is this darling hunk working in there who is a senior, and Amy goes and flirts her butt off with him.

That girl might be too scared to steal, but she is really good with boys, I don't care what age. She says it's not important that you put out, but that you act like you would if you felt like it. While she is batting her eyes at the senior hunk, I browse around and steal my brains out. I adore stealing from the country club! I go into the dressing room and pull on three different sizes of tennis shorts under my wrap-around skirt and then I walk out past Amy and the senior hunk and say, Meet you out by the pool, Amy.

Later, she meets me in the ladies lounge with the rattan chaise longue and I show her all my prizes. She says, Really boss, Lulu.

When I get home, I give Sidda, Little Shep, and Baylor their shorts, and they just ooh and ahh, especially Little Shep who plays tennis at City Park with his friends. He's playing in the city tournaments and everything. Mama says he takes after her. She was captain of the tennis team at Thornton High, which she won't let anybody forget. She says it's a sin and a shame that my Daddy deprives Little Shep of being a member of the country club, where he could really perfect his serve.

Those people at the Garnet Parish Golf and Country Club Pro Shop deserve being stolen from. My Daddy says they are a bunch of lazy bums who sit around and live off other people's money and have been snobs all their lives. My Daddy says they were born with silver spoons shoved up their asses and have never grown anything in their born days. Mama tells him, Shep, I wish you wouldn't talk like that around the children. And he says, Viviane, what I'm saying is mild compared to the garbage that spews out of your mouth when you're drinking.

At the Pro Shop I have also gotten two sport shirts and ten packages of golf balls—even though nobody in our family plays golf. Me and Little Shep like to cut those golf balls open, like you're not supposed to do because they'll explode and put your eye out. It's real fun. It's like there's a little prize inside that you have to work to get at. First off, you have to cut off the white outside plastic part of the ball. That's the hardest part and the most dangerous. It's better if you use a saw instead of a knife, but either way, the actual cutting could cause you to lose two or three fingers and go through life a cripple. But getting the outside of the ball off is really neat. Almost as good as peeling off a sunburn. Then comes the best part—because under the hide is a long skinny rubber band and that the center is wrapped up in. It's like rubber-band spaghetti and it must be a mile long when you unwind it! Then you finally get down to this marble-sized little ball. It takes a lot of work to get to it, but it is really worth it! One time when I stole the most expensive balls, they turned out to have this kind of goo at the center. Baylor got scared because he thought it would burn his skin off. And all he was doing was watching. I don't know where he gets the thoughts in his head.

Anyway, my Daddy is the one I would really like to get something good for. Just surprise him with something out of this world and have him scoop me up and say: Lulu-Cakes, you're my sweet patootie!

But what are you gonna get my Daddy? I got him a couple boxes of 22-caliber bullets once, but big fat deal.

He has eighty-four thousand of them already. He hardly even noticed when I gave them to him. He *is* a tough customer.

Finally it came to me, though.

So I get myself over to The Cowboy Store of Thornton on the double. I have to ride a city bus to get out there—which Mama would kill me for if she found out because only white trash ride buses. But I've got to get there!

I walk in, and it smells all like tack and leather and harnesses and saddle soap. The floors are old wood ones that squeak when you take a step. It's kind of like being in a cleaned-up barn or something. There are two salesladies who look almost just alike, except one is strawberry blonde and the other is black-haired. They're both wearing cowgirl pants and shirts and boots. I smile at them and I'm relieved to see that they don't know me from Adam. Mama and us never shop there, only my Daddy. Mama says The Cowboy Store is too country. So I am a total stranger in there. I browse around looking for something for Daddy, and the only thing that really gets me going is this straw cowboy hat that he could wear in the fields. I finger it and try it on. It's way too big for me, so I figure it will fit him fine. It smells like hay and when I hold it up and look through it, I can see light through the straw weave. I think: *This is the hat that could really stop the hot sun from beating down on my Daddy, from burning him up and wearing him out.*

Now, a cowboy hat is not your easiest thing to steal. I mean you might as well try to walk off with that antique globe that Baylor wants! You've got to be a true ace, which I luckily happen to be. I go up to the counter and buy some saddle soap that Daddy uses on his boots. Then I wander around, watching the two ladies close and waiting for them to turn their backs. Those salesladies are stuffed into their cowgirl pants like that Italian fennel sausage my Daddy buys from D'Stefanos. I like the way they look, their hair all like Loretta Lynn and the way they walk is kind of half-sexy, half-horsy. They both have on real pointy boots and bright blue eyeshadow, which I can definitely tell you is straight out of the discount off-brand bin at Woolworth's. If there's one thing I know, it's my cosmetics. If Mama saw them, she would sneer her face off. But Mama isn't anywhere around.

Finally the phone rings and one of them picks it up. She's got that twangy voice like the people who live year-round at Spring Creek where we go in the summer. The other lady takes out an emery board and starts filing her nails. I'm the only customer in the whole place.

This is my chance! And I reach up and pull that straw cowboy hat down off the shelf. I stick it in front of my stomach and walk straight out of that store.

I am sweating like a field hand. This is the best heist I have ever pulled off! The perfect gift for my Daddy! Finally. The kind of thing he really *needs*. Those seed company caps he wears don't do shit to protect him from the sun.

I'm dizzy and my blood is pumping so hard, and I'm trying to remember where to go to catch the bus. I pause for a minute to catch my breath.

And that is what trips me up.

The lady with the blonde hair comes running out on the porch of the store where there are saddles hanging all along the railing. She runs down the steps yelling, Hey you! Little Girl! Little Girl!

I act like I don't hear her. I think about running. But running is so dumb! Running is the kind of chicken-ass thing Sidda would do! I don't need to run, I think. I can handle this.

I turn around to the lady and say, Yes Ma'am? so sweet that you'd want to adopt me in a split second if you heard me.

And she comes right up to me, with her butt in those tight pants and she says: If you're fixin to run off with that hat, you got another think comin, girly-girl.

I look down at the hat all ashamed-like, to give myself a chance to work up some tears.

Then I look up at her—right straight in the eyes—and say: I'm sorry. I really am. I apologize.

The whole time I'm saying this I am sobbing my eyes out.

Don't you give me no boo-hoo act, she says. Who are your parents? I'm fixin to go inside and call them up right now. You're lucky I don't call the Louisiana State Police.

I wipe a tear from my eyes and try to talk just like her.

I don't have no parents, I say. They was killed in a car wreck just five-and-a-half months after I was born. I was getting the hat for my brother. He works driving a tractor over in Bunkie. He's sixteen. He takes care of me.

Then I work myself up into a state, until I actually

feel like I am an orphan who lives with her only relative in a shack on the edge of a cotton field. I don't stop crying until the lady puts her arm around me and says, Let's us go on back inside. It's too darn hot out here.

Back in the store, she says, Well, Verna, I caught up with our little sneak thief.

Verna glares at me and I squeeze out another round of tears for her. The blonde-haired one whispers to Verna, Both her parents are dead: car crash when she was an infant.

Then Verna looks at me real kind-like. I can't believe it!

The two of them stand there for a minute with their hands on their hips. And finally Verna says, Well Maxine, what are we goin to do with her?

Maxine says, Well, we could throw her in the Angola State Prison for life. And then she pauses and gives me this long look.

Or, she continues, we could get her an Orange Crush. Do you like Orange Crushes? she asks me.

Oh yes ma'am I say, Orange Crush is my very favorite cold drink. I adore Orange Crush.

And Maxine goes in the back and opens an icebox and brings me out an Orange Crush in a tall cold bottle.

Sit yourself down on that stool and drink it, she says.

I do what she says.

Alright now, Verna asks me, what's your name?

Corina, I lie. "Corina, Corina, Where You Been So Long?" is my Daddy's favorite song in the world. He sings it in the truck when we ride back in the fields and he hums it while he's shaving in his bathroom.

Corina what? Maxine asks.

Axel, I tell them. Corina Axel, tasting the name in my mouth. My Mama and Daddy were Axels from Greenville, Mississippi. Yall might of heard the name.

No, honey, Verna says, I don't reckon I have. But I'm sure they were real fine people.

She says it like she doesn't want to hurt my feelings.

Then I get quiet, like I figure I better. Best to just sit there and let them feel sorry for me. Mama always says it's running my mouth so much that gets me in trouble to begin with.

You say you live with your brother? Maxine asks. She starts up with her emery board again, so I figure they're not going to turn me over to the cops.

Yes ma'am, I say. He tries to take good care of me. He quit school to support us. He gets real sunburned in the field and don't have no straw hat, just this old felt one that's too hot to wear in the summer. I was getting the hat for him. I'm awful sorry.

I am actually becoming Corina Axel! And I like her too. She is pitiful and plucky at the same time—the kind of kid people always want to help out.

My brother's name's Bucky, I lie to them.

Verna reaches into her shirt pocket and shakes a Viceroy out of the pack. She reaches under the counter and pulls out a big box of kitchen matches, strikes one, and lights her cigarette. Très tacky, Mama and the Ya-Yas would say.

My Mama used to smoke that exact same brand, I tell Verna, forgetting for a second that I was five and a half months old when she died.

I thought you was only an infant when your Mama passed on, Maxine says.

These ladies are sharp, I think. You better watch what you say, Lulu!

My brother Bucky told me, I continue. Bucky has told me every single thing he can remember about our Mama. Mentally calculating his age, I said, He was about five when they died. He remembers what she smelled like and everything.

Then I thought: Shut up! Don't push your luck. But I can't stop myself.

Ummm, this Orange Crush sure is good, I tell them. I don't get to have cold drinks very often. Me and Bucky can only afford ice water.

I roll my eyes around the store like I have never been in such a fine establishment.

That sure is an awful pretty belt buckle you're wearing, I compliment Maxine.

Mama would drop dead before she would let a belt buckle of a man and woman square dancing onto her waist. She would melt that thing down for scrap metal just to keep it from offending her eyes. I can feel myself starting to really like Verna and Maxine. They are A-OK in my book. They're my kind of folks.

Thank you, Corina, Maxine says. My husband gave me this belt buckle for our tenth anniversary.

Well, it sure is pretty. You're lucky to have a husband like that. I sure wish I could of known my daddy.

Then Maxine gets all soft and turns to Verna, and they pass a signal between them with their eyes. I'm thinking: They are either going to reach for the phone and call the state police and I'm going to need Perry Mason quick, or they are going to let me right off the hook.

Verna nods to Maxine and the two of them stand a little closer together. They look kind of like sisters off that show *Louisiana Hayride,* but wilder. They're both leaning over a display case filled with horseshoe cufflinks and fancy spurs and lariats.

Tell you what, Verna finally says, How 'bout we give you that hat? You can hand it to Bucky and tell him it came from two of his admirers.

Maxine flicks her ash on the floor and says, Tell him he's doing a fine job rearin' you up all by hisself. Even if you do have some sticky fingers.

I know I ought to feel guilty, but I don't. I am Corina Axel. I am an orphan. My Mama and my Daddy are dead.

I start crying again, but this time they're not crocodile tears. They're real tears from my dry heart.

I can't believe yall are being so nice to me, I tell them. No one has ever been this nice to me in my whole entire life. *I want to stay here and live with yall,* I think to myself.

And they come and put their arms around me.

It's like a fairy tale or something. When they hold me, I really haul off crying. Not the kind of tears that just turn on and off like a faucet, but tears that I don't know where they come from, like they've been there on the edge waiting for a long time. I feel my hand reach up to pull at my hair the way I used to do when I was little. I want real bad to yank out two or three hairs and eat them, because that always used to calm me down.

But Maxine takes my hand and says, Aw honey, don't pull on your hair. You've got the prettiest blonde hair in the world. I wish I had me a little girl with hair pretty as yours.

The way she says "wish" it comes out sounding like "wursh."

I put my hand back in my lap and curl my fingers together. At first Maxine and Verna looked like cartoon sisters, but now I see how different they are from each other. Maxine smells like "Evening in Paris" cologne, but Verna smells more like pine straw. And Verna is a little older. She's got a mole on her cheek. Not a mole like the nuns, with hair sticking out of it, but a mole that's almost a beauty mark.

I let them hug me for a while. When I'm finally able to stop crying, I say: Thank you, Verna. Thank you, Maxine. Thank you both very much.

The bell on the door tinkles then and a man walks into the store. His boots hit the wooden floor hard and heavy and he brings field dust inside with him. I pray he doesn't know my Daddy.

Verna breaks away to help the man and Maxine says, Well, Miss Priss, I certainly hope your brother enjoys the new hat you bought for him. If it doesn't fit perfect, you bring it on back and we'll get him the right size, okay?

Yes ma'am, I tell her. Thank you again.

Then she puts the hat in a box for me. She whispers: You take care of yourself now, you hear? And watch those sticky fingers. Not everybody in the world is me and Maxine, you know what I mean?

Yes ma'am, I do. I know what you mean.

And I walk out the door. Outside the light is all hot and white, like when you step out of the Paramount after a good movie in the middle of the day and you get all blinded. I feel dizzy again and it takes me a long time to find the bus stop. When I finally do, I go and get me a window seat and crack open the window and let the air blow on me.

I give the hat to my Daddy that night when he gets home. Here, Daddy, I tell him, I got a present for you.

But when he tries it on, it just perches up there on his head like a stupid little Shriner fez or something.

Walker men have got big heads, Lulu, he says. Don't you know that by now? We come from a long line of big heads. Maybe you oughta just give this thing to Little Shep. It's more likely to fit him.

So I give it to my brother and he likes it good enough. But it was a gift for my Daddy, not for my brother. And that makes me real tired.

Later in my room, I write a letter to Maxine and Verna at The Cowboy Store. I disguise my handwriting and leave off my return address. I write:

Dear Maxine and Verna,

My brother Bucky and me want to thank you a whole bunch for the hat. It keeps the sun off his face in the fields and fits him just fine. We both want to tell you what good people you are. Please don't yall ever change.

Your friend,
Corina Axel

At night in my bed when everyone else is asleep, I lay there and feel sad. *I can't go back and exchange that hat for the right size. I can't go see Verna and Maxine again. I've used them up and now I can't have them any more. Maybe it's true what Mama says: All I am is Gimmee Gimmee Gimmee, and after a while people get sick of me.*

Well, Mama ought to know. She is the *Queen* of Gimmee. Where do you think I learned every single thing I know?

HAIR OF THE DOG
Siddalee, 1965

*I*t's Saturday morning and we are all riding over to the Hotsy-Totsy Room with Mama and Caro. We have to get Mama's high-heel from under the *porte cachère* where she forgot it the night before.

Little Shep, Lulu, Baylor, and I are packed into the back seat of the T-Bird like sardines, and Mama and Caro have the air conditioner cranked up full-blast. Caro spent the night with us at Pecan Grove, even though Mama originally started out the night with Daddy, who ended up not coming home at all. When Mama and Caro woke the whole house up coming in, I took one of Mama's Nytols that I had stashed in my nightstand and went back to sleep. But Lulu must have stayed up all night. When I got up, she looked all dazed and she had another picked-at red spot on her head.

I said, Jesus, Lulu, have you been at it again? I don't see how anybody can actually eat their own hair.

She said, Siddy, I *try* not to. Really.

I know, I said, and rubbed a dab of Vaseline on the spot. Now don't pick at it anymore today, you hear me?

In the front seat of the car, Caro and Mama are wearing sunglasses, even though it's overcast outside. I put on my sunglasses too. We just pull up in front of the Hotsy-Totsy Room, and without the car hardly coming to a stop, Caro opens the door and scoops up Mama's ice blue sling-back pump, and we drive off.

The Hotsy-Totsy Room is the only cocktail dance lounge of its kind in Thornton and it is very popular because of the Ya-Yas and their friends. It's a stucco building with sparkles built into it. Seashells are set in the concrete driveway, and at night, twinkly lights shine in the bushes. Every time Mama and Daddy walk in there, the band stops whatever they're doing and plays "Moon River," Mama and Daddy's favorite song.

After we pick up the high-heel, Mama pulls out onto the service road and says, Sidda, reach into that ice chest and get Caro and me those cold rags, will you?

I hand them the rags and they each put one on their forehead.

What's wrong with yall's heads, Mama? Little Shep asks.

We don't know, Mama says.

We both caught one of those little bugs that's going around, Caro explains. And they both give a little laugh.

Mama turns to Caro and says, I don't know about you, girl, but I'm sick as a dog.

Make that two dogs, Caro mumbles. Drive a little smoother, will you?

Well, I've got those damn little floaties in front of my eyes, Mama says. They don't make for the best driving I've ever done in my life.

Well, says Caro, we have got to stay on the move. I cannot bear the thought of seeing either one of those men we married until I feel a little more up to snuff.

Plus, Mama says, pressing her finger to her right temple, I don't want the party to end. It's hell this morning, but it was heaven last night. I haven't danced like that since high school.

You finally had some decent dance partners again, Vivi—that's why.

Mama says, Little pitchers have big ears.

I stare out the window and act like I'm not listening to every word that comes out of their mouths.

Hell, Caro says, you know damn well Shep has never been a dancer. The man might be able to grow cotton, but he's a slew-footed clod on the dance floor.

Mama giggles and says, He tries.

That's about the extent of it, Caro says, he *tries.*

Well, it didn't slow me down any, Mama brags.

That's an understatement, Caro laughs. We were magnificent! We danced with every man in the place at least twice.

Yeah, Mama says, until we wore them out or teed off their wives and had to start dancing with each other. Hell, Chick's the only male who can keep up with us. I knew I should've married him instead of letting Teensy have him.

He was too short for you in high school, Vivi, and he's too short for you now, Caro says.

Well, he still could grow, Mama says and laughs.

Anyway, it was glorious, Caro says. Just like the old days. And of course, those diet pills didn't hurt.

Not one bit, Mama says. Then she turns around and

looks at the four of us. How yall doing, spooks? Yall hungry?

Yes ma'am, we all say.

Hold on then, Mama says, We'll get something in your pitiful stomachs before you know it.

We didn't eat any breakfast or anything. Mama didn't even try to fix my hair like she does every morning. My hair is almost down to my waist, and if it isn't done in a certain way it just drives Mama to the insane asylum. She says with all my hair I could easily look like poor white trash or a Pentecostal if I'm not careful. This morning, though, she completely forgets about my hair, and I'm glad, because the way she usually whips it around feels like she really is trying to jerk me bald-headed. She always says, That's the price you have to pay for beauty, Siddalee.

The thing is, Caro says, Shep gets so burned up when the Ya-Yas get together. It makes me want to kill him, the way he talked to you last night. Saying: "You have never known how to act in public, Vivi." Caro says this in a voice like Daddy's.

Well, Mama says, Shep was raised different than we were.

That's no excuse for him to drive off and spend the night at the goddamn duck camp, Caro says. If Chick hadn't driven us home, then I don't know what we would've done. It's not like Thornton is New York City when it comes to taxicabs at four A.M.

Then she just snorts like she does not have the energy to go any further.

Don't you have a pillow anywhere in this car? she

asks Mama. Mama lets Caro boss her around and criticize her like nobody else ever can.

Caro holds her wet rag in front of the air-conditioner vent, then lays it over her whole face and leans
back against the door.

Mama drives real slow and careful—until she comes
to an intersection and then she speeds across real fast,
stepping on the gas like she's afraid someone will slam
into her. Then she slows down again and crawls the car
along the street until she comes to the next intersection.
We stop and fill up the car at Roland's Texaco and then
Mama drives us in fits and starts over to Ship-Shape
Donuts.

She leaves the car running, hands me ten dollars,
and says, Go get whatever yall want. Get us two huge
coffees, black.

They stay in the car and we run in and get a dozen
donuts and some cinnamon rolls and Lulu gets four of
her rum balls. She hordes those rum balls and eats them
on the sly. We all get Cokes too, even though Daddy
says that having a cold drink before twelve noon is "a
whore's breakfast."

Back in the car, those donuts are so soft and squashy
and sweet, all warm out of the oven, and we sit in the
back seat of the T-Bird and just eat and eat. Ooh, all
that sugar and those Cokes on crushed ice just go down
so good.

Mama looks in the rear-view mirror and says, Lulu,
put that donut back in the bag right this instant.

Lulu says, Oh Mama, why?

Mama says, Just do what I say. Trust me, you will
live to regret that donut if you eat it. I am only trying

to save you from growing up to be a lard-ass like the women on your daddy's side of the family.

Do you think a cigarette will kill me? she asks Caro.

I would not touch a ciggie with a ten-foot pole, Caro says. Not until I swallow a hair of the dog that bit me.

Mama sighs, Thank God I have the Ya-Yas to tell me what to do.

Where in the hell are we going next? Caro asks.

Mama says, Who cares? Let's bomb over to Chick and Teensy's and see if they're up yet. I hope they feel just as bad as we do.

Fine, Caro says, just fine. And she settles back with the cold air blowing on her.

Mama pulls the car out onto the almost empty street. Where is everybody? It feels like we're in a sort of Twilight Zone town.

Little Shep pulls out his Etch-a-Sketch and Lulu says, Let me play!

Little Shep says, Shut up, Porky.

She starts to cry and I say, Yall cut that out. Mama doesn't feel good.

Lulu sits there sucking on a strand of her hair and I give her a look like: You remember what I told you, Baldy.

I pull *Nancy Drew and the Mystery of Lilac Inn* out of my purse and try to forget where I am. The car is so crowded there isn't even enough room for us to hardly sit, let alone stash any of our stuff. So we have to squinch in together and it is horrible being that crammed in. Mama and Daddy had a big fight over Mama getting the T-Bird because it's only built to seat four. But Mama says if she's going to haul us all over the place, she's going to do it in the car of her choice. When the six of us have to go somewhere together as a whole family, Daddy just follows behind in his truck.

After four or five blocks, Mama says, I simply *cannot* drive another inch. Caro, you have *got* to take over, the floaties are killing me.

Caro groans, You think I've got it any better? When are these kids going to start being good for something? Let one of them drive.

We should be so lucky, Mama says, and starts to slide toward the passenger seat. They climb over each other, because neither one of them is about to step outside into the heat. Caro gets in the driver's seat and Mama props her foot up on the dash and complains: If we didn't have kids we could have cars with tinted windows. We're martyrs, that's what we are: martyrs to the cause.

Caro laughs. She says, Blaine is probably still sound asleep and I bet the boys are tearing my house to shreds. Let them. I'm sick of that rat-trap anyway.

And they both laugh and turn on the radio to some Easy Listening. The Ya-Yas love Easy Listening whenever they catch one of their bugs.

At Teensy and Chick's we pull into the driveway and pile out of the car. Mama raps on the kitchen door like shave-and-a haircut, two bits! She says, They damn well better have a pitcher of Bloody Marys ready.

Ruffin, who is my age, answers the door. He still has on his cowboy pajamas.

Mama says, Hi, Ruff, where're your Mama and Daddy?

Ruffin crosses his arms and says, They're still asleep. Yall better not wake them up or they'll kill you.

Caro says, Good boy! Then she and Mama push past him into the kitchen. We trail in behind them.

I say, Hi, Ruffin.

He says, Yall better get out of here, I mean it. Yall better not make any noise.

All over the kitchen counters there are those tiny cereal boxes you can eat right out of and you can smell burnt toast in the air.

Ruffin says, Really, Vivi, if you wake them up they're gonna be really mad. They don't feel good.

Well honey, Mama says, *we don't either,* and we want some company. Now take all the kids and yall go play in traffic.

Ruffin stands there looking stupid and hurt.

Mama gives him a hug and says, Ruff dahling, I'm just *kidding!* Now yall go watch some TV.

Ruffin mumbles, Our antenna is broken.

Mama ignores him, and says to Caro, Plan 27-B (which is their code for: move on, no matter what). The two of them head back to Teensy and Chick's bedroom. The door is shut and you can hear their big window air conditioner blasting away inside.

Ruffin gives one last warning: I mean it, they're not going to like this.

But Mama and Caro burst into Chick and Teensy's room and just jump in the bed with them, and yell: Get up! Yall think yall can sleep all day while we're awake suffering?! Get up!

We stand at the door and watch. Teensy's nightclub

dress is on the chair next to the bed, and she has on this poofy peignoir. Teensy props herself up in bed and stares at Mama and Caro like they are Ubangis. It looks like there are pieces of red thread stuck to her eyeballs.

You damn fools! she says. Get out of here. Yall think because I'm the only Ya-Ya with a fun husband you can come in here and wake me up like this?

Chick just rolls over without opening his eyes. He kind of waves his hand like he's swatting flies. Chick is real little and wiry and cute, kind of like a horse jockey. He is sort of an honorary male Ya-Ya. When his hand reaches out, you can see his silk pajama sleeve. I never realized grown men actually slept in pajamas except in movies. Daddy always sleeps in his boxer shorts.

Come on Teensy! Mama says. Come on Chick! Don't yall want to get up and play? We drove all the way over here just to commiserate.

The hell yall did, Teensy growls, and turns her pillow over to the cool side. Yall came over here because you're scared to death to face Blaine and Shep. I can't *believe* some of the stunts yall pulled last night. Yall were out of control, even for Ya-Yas.

We didn't do anything you wouldn't have done if you hadn't married Chick, Mama says.

Teensy says, Yall are terrible, now get out of here. Go find somebody else to torture.

Mama and Caro just keep lying on the bed like they think she is kidding.

I'm serious, Teensy yells. Yall go on. Chick and I are going to sleep till three, then get up and have eggs Benedict. Hit the road.

Party-poopers! Caro says.

What a bunch of spooks, Mama says. Then Mama and Caro both climb out of the bed and start to lead us out to the car, but not without checking the liquor cabinets first.

Where is your mama's vodka? Caro asks Ruffin.

I don't know, Ruffin says, she hides it.

Oh well, Mama says, and gives Ruffin a kiss on the forehead. Then she opens the kitchen door and we all walk out again into the hot gray day and climb into the hot stuffy car.

Mama and Caro look at each other and Caro says, Those SOBs. I was *counting* on them for a Bloody.

Mama says, Well, we can have one of the beers out of the cooler.

I will die before I drink any of that alligator piss, Caro says. I need a real drink.

Mama looks at Caro and says, *Abra!*

Caro winks at her and says, *Cadabra!*

Then Caro guns the car in the direction of Davis Street, which means the Abracadabra Liquor store.

Usually we go to the Abracadabra at night when Mama and Daddy run out of something or need to stock up. They go inside and leave us in the back of Daddy's pickup. It's always dark all around us, with the only light coming from the blazing fluorescent lights inside the store and the sign that hangs out front.

The Abracadabra sign is huge pastel-colored neon about the size of a Brahma bull. You just can't help but be in awe of it. At the top of the sign is an angel with a skull for a face. Its neon wings pulsate so fast that it looks like the angel is panicked, like it's trying to get away from something. When the bottom of the angel flicks back and forth, it looks like a serpent tail stabbing the night air. Underneath the angel, the name "Abraca-dabra" is spelled out with the kind of little white bulbs that movie stars have on their dressers. Below that, the words "Liquor, Party Foods, Ice, and Gifts" pulse in green, pink, yellow, and blue. Just the letters in those words are scary to look at, like they have a mysterious power that nothing can control. That panicked angel lights up the four of us in the back of Daddy's truck and makes us easy targets for all those things that hide in the dark. If there are stars in the sky, you can't even see them because that sign blinds your eyes to anything else.

The place isn't nearly so spooky during the day. We pull up to the drive-up window and Mama and Caro order a fifth of Smirnoff and a bunch of V-8 juice from a guy with a transistor radio playing the colored music station. Daddy never lets us listen to that station. The Ya-Yas love it though.

Mama says, Just put that on Shep Walker's account, dahling.

Then she turns around to us and says, Yall want any-thing?

Yeah, I say, some Fritos.

What did you say? Mama asks me.

I correct myself: *Yes ma'am,* we would love some Fri-tos. Thank you for asking.

That's better, Mama says. Throw in a couple bags of Frito-Lays, would you, Tony?

The man says, We ain't got no Fritos, just pigskins.

Okay then, pigskins, Mama tells him and he flips three bags of pigskins into the back seat. I am not about to touch them. Eating the skin of dead pigs fried in their own bacon grease is something I will not do, even if I'm starving to death on a desert island.

Of course, Lulu snorks them right down and Little Shep says, Hey Porky, why don't you just inhale them through your snout?!

It's not that Lulu is really all that fat. She just has a round little face and cheeks that make her look chubbier than she is. Still, it's a habit for everyone to pick on her for being a little fatty. You can upset her with it every time, so we tease her just because it's so much fun.

Mama and Caro mix up some drinks in Dixie cups, then we head out again. Mama lights up a cigarette and things are looking better. It's cool in the car and the cigarette smoke smells familiar.

Then, out of the blue, Caro pulls over to the side of the road and slams on the brakes, opens the door, leans her head out, and throws up on the street. Son of a bitch, she says. Son of a goddamn bitch!

Mama says, You poor baby. You alright?

Oh I'm fine. Never been better. It's your damn cigarette. I told you, I cannot handle smoke until I've had the chance to get a drink down.

I'm so sorry, babydoll, Mama says, and she takes her wet cloth and dabs Caro's face with it.

You want a Lifesaver to take the taste out? Should I take you home?

God no, Caro says. You just drive. I'll be fine, once I get down a drink or two. And don't you dare light up another ciggie or I will strangle you with my bare hands.

So Mama gets behind the wheel and she says, I just hope the floaties don't cause me to run this damn T-Bird into the ditch. She sits there for a minute idling the motor, sipping her Bloody Mary. Then she says— like it's the most original idea she's ever had and she should get an award for it: I've got it! We'll drive out to Lucille's! She's always ready for a party!

Caro is mixing another drink, mumbling, These Dixie cups are so damn tiny.

Well Caro, Mama asks, what do you think?

Inspired, Vivi dahling, simply inspired. Drive on.

*Y*ou can tell they're both starting to feel a little better as we drive down the tree-lined state highway to Natchitoches. Miss Lucille lives alone up on Cane River in this huge antebellum house. She divorced her husband and took him for every cent he had. She's older than the Ya-Yas and they all worship her. She's sort of their living idol. Miss Lucille was once a very famous horse-woman until she was thrown by her favorite horse. And she just quit riding after that. She told everyone it wasn't that she was hurt or anything, it was just the way that horse had betrayed her.

Sometimes she just shows up in Thornton in her chocolate brown Cadillac to do some shopping, and a whole party will start up just because she is in town. Mama and the Ya-Yas have known her for years—ever since they were in New Orleans one weekend on a shopping trip and they met her one night at the Carousel Room in the Monteleone Hotel. They just fell in love with her, and all of them ended up riding the train back together, and they have been friends ever since.

Miss Lucille's house is a huge place at the end of this long drive of oak trees with trailing Spanish moss all over them. The house has eight big white columns across the front and this deep veranda upstairs and down. It's the kind of gracious old home that the Ya-Yas adore visiting, but you couldn't *give* them a place like that because there isn't any central air-conditioning or a dishwasher.

We pull up the long drive, with Mama blowing the horn like she always does. All of us have our eyes glued to the windows to catch a glimpse of Miss Lucille naked. Miss Lucille is an artist now and she always works on her sculptures while she's buck naked. We can barely see her throw on her kimono and tie the sash before the T-Bird comes to a stop in her circular drive.

She runs out shouting at the top of her lungs. Vivi! Caro! *Petits monstres!* Hey!

Miss Lucille always shouts. It isn't that she is hard-of-hearing, she just loves to talk loud, Mama says. Around her you have to shout back, or there just isn't any conversation. Sometimes the way she yells, you don't know whether she is really really happy to see you, or whether she is mad at you for invading her privacy.

Lucille, dahling! Mama shouts back, although you can see her wince like it's killing her head.

They all hug each other like it's been fifty years since they've gotten together.

Miss Lucille uses a long cigarette holder and smokes like Marlene Dietrich. Every time you watch her take a puff, you think you're in Europe. Her hair is gray everywhere, except in front where it's bright red. And she has these large hands that look like a pretty man's. Mama and the Ya-Yas love playing *bourrée* with her because she's such a superior cheater. They claim they learned everything they know about cheating from her.

She says, Well, what are we drinking? G&Ts?

We follow her through the house and she stops to put on an Edith Piaf record on the stereo. Then we go into the big kitchen, where she mixes up a huge pitcher of gin and tonic like it is lemonade. Miss Lucille has five golden retrievers that lounge around inside that house, and they yelp and growl when we (accidentally) step on their tails. Those dogs just go with Miss Lucille's house, like they're mink coats or something draped across the furniture.

Baylor stares around the house, peeking in every room we pass, like he always does. He says, I'm gonna have me a house just like this when I grow up.

Miss Lucille hands Mama and Caro their G&Ts, and then says to Bay, Well, Handsome, are you still going to come live with me as soon as you turn eighteen?

When she winks at him, he goes over and holds onto Mama's leg. But Mama says, Bay, honey, don't hang all over me, please. Not today.

Lulu says, Miss Lucille, can I go upstairs and take a nap? She does this every single time we come here. She has a thing about those bedrooms.

Miss Lucille has fans set up everywhere you turn, and it makes you almost forget how hot and sticky it is without air-conditioning.

Caro says, You *must* show us what you've been working on, 'Cille.

Love to, Miss Lucille says, absolutely love to.

They always ask to see her sculptures. But whenever I ask Mama about Miss Lucille, Mama says, Honey, Lucille is more an artist in her *mind* than anything else. (Mama also says you're not a real artist unless you live in New York City.)

Miss Lucille takes us on a tour of her sculptures, which are all over the house and out on the veranda. Every single one she points to, she says, Of course it's *unfinished.* You can see that for yourself.

One particular sculpture scares me to death. Miss Lucille calls it "The Sleeping Bitch." It has been at her house for as long as I can remember. It is a woman taking a nap. Her whole body looks relaxed except for her face—which looks like it's witnessing something so horrible her eyes could burn up. Her mouth looks like she's trying to scream, but can't get any sound out. It always reminds me of a dream I have where I'm grunting and sweating, but I can't squeeze out one single sound. Every time I see that sculpture there is something ever so slightly different about it, like Miss Lucille works on it for about five minutes a month.

After we view the art, the ladies settle in the canvas butterfly chairs out on the veranda, and Little Shep and me go out in the yard to play. Over beyond the cedars are millions of crepe myrtle trees and during the summer they're all rose-colored. I like the way all that rose color looks against those black cedars, and sometimes I kind of relax my eyes so that it all blends together. Little Shep and me have this game we play, where his name is Barry and mine is Jennifer. Whenever we use those names, we feel great. It doesn't matter what we're doing, as long as we do it as Barry and Jennifer. We're playing "Barry and Jennifer in the Civil War" behind the crepe myrtles, and it is so hot, you just know the Yankees are coming. Then, out of nowhere, we get one of those afternoon rains that cools things off and makes the air smell fresh.

We stand out there and let ourselves get soaking wet. The sun is starting to peek out from behind that scum of gray sky, and light trickles down through the cedars. The rain stops as quick as it comes, and we're standing in a real clean spot and we both know it.

Little Shep says in a fake accent, Jennifer, shall we go back to the big house?

I say, Oh yes, Barry, let's.

And we hold each other's hands, like we never do when we're our real selves. My hair is hanging down heavy on my shoulders and when the water drips, it tickles and feels good on my skin.

We walk back to the veranda and Mama eyes me like she's never seen me before, like she's studying me. I pull my halter-top down where it's slid up a little. I don't know why she is looking at me like that. I haven't done anything.

Without taking her eyes off me, she announces, Siddalee, you are too grown-up to have all that hair hanging down to your butt!

Then she grinds out her cigarette in a crystal ashtray that is full of butts and says to Caro, Why don't you give Sidda one of your haircuts? It's something that's long overdue.

Caro is famous for cutting hair, not like a real beautician but just when she feels like it. She cut her own hair in all these different angles and she looks sort of like a skinny Ingrid Bergman. She gets up and lifts my hair off my neck and twists it softly in her hand. I have always been a sucker for anyone who wants to touch my head, as long as they're not pulling at it the way Mama does.

It's so thick, Caro says. This is just too much hair. Don't you get tired of the weight of it, Sidda?

I have never gotten tired from my hair before, but I say, Yes ma'am, I do. I just get exhausted sometimes.

I adore having them all look at my hair. They all get into the act. Miss Lucille runs and gets some yellow-handled kitchen scissors and a brush and hand mirror. They sit me on a stool on the veranda and Caro starts cutting. I close my eyes and just listen to the scissors and the dripping of the rain off the magnolia leaves and the sound of Mama's cigarette lighter when she snaps it open. It's so quiet, you can even hear the tiny *whiff* sounds my hair makes when it hits the brick veranda floor. I sit there and feel all their eyes focused just on me. Caro lifts my hair and snips and touches my head. And I kind of float away from the veranda into the trees.

When I open my eyes, fifteen inches of my hair is on the brick floor.

Caro hands me the mirror and says, *Viola!*

When I look at myself, I resemble the pictures of Heidi's friend Peter. I don't even look like a girl. My chest closes up. I feel all naked. I feel like they've cut off my legs or my arms, not just my hair.

You are magnificent! Mama says, and jumps up from her chair to examine me. She ruffles her hands through my hair and I can feel her fingernails against my scalp. My head is so bare, it's like she could push her fingernails down into my skull if she wanted and leave permanent dents. Her cigarette smoke curls around me and I can smell the lime in her drink.

You have never looked better! she pronounces. My God, you are gorgeous! Caro, you are an artist.

Then she says, Little Shep, go find a broom and trash can and sweep up this mess! And she gestures to my cut-off hair like it's dog poop under our feet.

Caro winks at me and says, Sidda, get ready dahling, the boys are gonna really come sniffing around now.

Miss Lucille doesn't say anything. She just stares at me like she wants to ask a question.

Do you like it, Miss Lucille? I ask her.

What does it matter what I think? she says. What does it matter what anybody thinks about anything?

I look down at my reddish-brown hair lying on the bricks. The bricks and my hair are about the same color. I can feel tiny bits of hair sticking to my skin, like they don't want to let go of my body. I get up and stand in front of the fan and lift up the back of my shirt to try and let the hair blow off me. My hair has been long since I was a real little girl, and without it I feel cockeyed and dizzy. Like losing the weight of my hair has thrown me off-balance. I was used to how I had looked for so long and how my hair felt when I reached up to roll it between my fingers. When I was alone, I used to hold a clump of my hair and just smell it. And that would make me feel good because it was my smell and it made me feel more *there.*

I stand by the fan and try to get used to the new me. *Why did I lie and say I was tired of my hair? When really, it was the main thing about me that I loved?* I ruin everything, I think. I ruin it all. I feel like crying, but I can't. I brought this all on myself.

Baylor, who was sitting on the steps watching the whole thing, gets up and does something that surprises me. He bends down and picks up a lock of my hair and puts it in his pocket. He looks at it and smells it and puts it in his pocket.

Mama watches him and says, My youngest has always been a little strange.

Miss Lucille says, I see nothing strange about him whatsoever. And she walks into her house and comes back out with an envelope that she hands to Baylor. Here, she says. You can keep it in this.

Thank you, Miss Lucille, he says very seriously.

Then he reaches into his pocket, takes out my hair, and places it in the gray envelope that has "Lucille Romaine, Cane River, Natchitoches, Louisiana" embossed on it.

I say, Bay, why are you doing that?

He mumbles, It's not really for me. It's for someone else.

And I say to my little brother, Where do you *come* from?

The sun is setting by then. Miss Lucille lights some mosquito torches and the smell drifts through the air, covering up all the other smells. She turns on the veranda lamps and hands Mama and Caro some Six-Twelve to rub on.

Miss Lucille says, Here, Vivi, let me rub some on your back. That's where those damn things always get me, right under my bra.

And she sticks her hand under Mama's shirt and smears on some insect repellent, and then they get out the cards so they can really start having a party.

*N*ot too long afterward, Lulu comes down the stairs from her nap. I'm hungry, she says. I'm starving. When she sees me, she seems confused, like she isn't completely sure who I am.

There is never anything to eat at Miss Lucille's, so we just go into her kitchen and scrounge around till we find some crackers and anchovy paste and a little left-over tonic. The whole time Little Shep and Baylor and Lulu keep staring at my hair.

Finally Little Shep says, Sidda, you look like a mop.

Baylor says, Siddy, can we put your hair back on?

It gets dark and it looks like nobody is going anywhere. So the four of us watch TV for a long time in Miss Lucille's den. Finally we get tired and turn it off and fall asleep on the couch and chairs.

I don't know how long we doze, but I'm the first one to smell it. I yell, Yall get up! Something's burning!

We all run out to the veranda and we find the ladies screaming and screaming, going crazy everywhere because the trash can filled with my hair is on fire. Mama is standing there with an empty ashtray in her hand.

Caro says, You fool! You should never have emptied that! I hadn't stubbed my ciggie out yet.

Well, Mama says, I was getting sick of looking at all those damn dead butts.

The three of them just stand there staring at the blazing trash can, amazed—like it is more than they can ever cope with.

I can taste anchovy in my mouth, and I wish I could brush my teeth. The smell of my hair on fire is awful. I did not know that something cut off of me could really smell that bad.

Little Shep runs into the kitchen and comes back with a decanter full of water. He dumps it into the can and the fire goes out. Just like that.

Miss Lucille says, Oh it is so good to have a man around the house! Now let's all just take a couple of Bufferin, spray a little perfume out here, and everything will be fine.

We spend the night at Miss Lucille's without even calling Daddy. I wake up real early the next morning before anybody else opens their eyes. My hands shoot straight up to my head where my hair used to be. *I miss it. I want it back.* I don't look in any of the mirrors. I rub my hands across my scalp. My hair feels more like a hat than hair. Like it is a bird's head, not my own.

I walk out into the yard and there is still dew on the grass, although you can tell the day will be another scorcher. I go out behind the cedars and over by the crepe myrtles. I stand there for a minute, feeling far away from everything because it's still so early. Then I lie down on the grass. It's cool and damp, and it itches and feels good at the same time. I can see the sky above me just coming to light, and the fringes of the cedars and all the pink of the crepe myrtles. There aren't any bugs or mosquitoes, nothing to bite me. I lie on my back in the grass for a long time and then I turn over and lie on my stomach. My heart starts pounding, my breath gets real tight, and I get all afraid.

But I can feel the ground underneath me. And I tell myself: The earth is holding me up. I am lighter than I was before. My hair is like grass planted on the top of my head. If I can just wait long enough, maybe it will grow back in some other season.

Part

TWO

☙

WILLETTA'S WITNESS
Willetta, 1990

*M*iz Vivi started gettin holy on us after her and Mister Big Shep done had the big fight. I knew somethin was goin on that night, when me and Chaney was settin out on the porch. It was back when Chaney still smoke those devil L&Ms—fore I give him the ultratomato. Fore I tole him: You drink and smoke anymore round here, you can find your ten-cent self another bed to sleep in, you hear me, peckawood?

We was settin out on the porch when Miz Vivi fly out that brick house with all them four chilren. Yellin, packin them in that pinky-gray T-Bird, revvin up that motor, scratchin out the driveway in the dark of night, headin up the road to town.

Where she goin? I ax Chaney. It must be ten o'clock at night. Them chilren got school tomorrow.

He say, Letta, mind your own bidness.

I tell him, Those chilren *is* my bidness.

He say, Oh, keep still. White people act like that sometime. Maybe she gonna go buy her some cigarettes.

Ain't no stores open now, I tell him. This was back

when stores still closed up at five o'clock. You want somethin late at night, you just wait for it.

Oooh, I wanted to sass Chaney somethin bad! Tell him, Oh I forgot, Mister King-Know-It-All, you know everything there is bout white people!

But I helt my tongue that time. Chaney a good man, he just tryin to roll with the punches. That my Chaney's motto: You got to roll with the punches.

So I walk myself down the lane, act like I just lookin up at the sky. And fore I know it, Miz Vivi just roarin right back into the driveway like her hair on fire. Musta turned round right at the end of Pecan Road. Herdin all four of them chilren back in the house.

It was a starry night and Siddy was standin there on the edge of the driveway holdin somethin in her hand, just cryin and cryin. Had on that white sweater with the dogs on it her cousin hand her down. I bet I knowed just the nightie she had on underneath it, cause I done Cloroxed, line-dried, and folded it in her drawer just that afternoon. I knowed every pair of little panties that child had. I could see her cause the carport light was still on. I don't reckon she could see me, standin at the edge of the field in all that darkness. But I was there.

I woulda gone to her, only I be scart what her Mama gonna do. People be stickin they nose up in Miz Viviane Walker's bidness, she cut it right off. I seen her do it to them chilren's aunts, seen her do it later to Miz Necie when she got on her bout the drinkin in the mornin.

Then like I tell you, Miz Vivi stick her head out the kitchen door, and yell, You get your butt in this house,

Siddalee Walker, before I give you something to cry *about!*

And I hear that tone in her voice, all full-up with bein mad at I-don't-know-what-all. At things happened fore her chilren was even born. I seen her when Mister Big Shep first brung her out to Pecan Grove and they was courtin. Oooooh, she was pretty! Tiny little waist, all that curly hair and those hats. But she was mad even back then. I could smell it like when a hurricane be movin in.

When I witness how that woman treat her chilren, I start gettin myself over to that brick house earlier than she want me, just so I can check on my Siddy.

Miz Vivi be up in that front room sayin to her little daughter, Shut up and stand still! I'm not letting you go to Divine Compassion with your hair looking like a Two-Bit-Suze!

And Siddy wasn't but what—six, seven years old—standin in front of that armoire mirror. And Miz Vivi jerkin on her long red hair so hard, she like to pull it out in clumps right off the child's head. That child squirm and her Mama slap her, say: You're just tender-headed! You damn redheads are too tender-headed!

Well, I had me two little nappy-headed girl chilren of my own and they was just as tender-headed as Siddy, and nary a one of them got no red hair! No ma'am, Miz Vivi be jerkin her child around just to make her cry. Just to be mean. She jealous of that girl's hair, always has been. Her own hair got all thin-like after she had them four babies—five, countin the twin that the Lord done took. She used to get her head fixed at Mister Julian's over by the City Park, but he quit usin her hairspray. Say it cause cancer. So she switch to Miz Jeannine, who she just love-love-love, but you know that don't last long. Miz Vivi in love with you one day and drop you like a hot potato the next.

I say, Miz Vivi, you got your hands full tryin to get these chilren off to school in the mornin. Lemme fix Miz Siddy's hair.

Her hands be all shaky, but she say, You don't know a damn thing about hair, Letta. Now go do the breakfast dishes, then start on that hand-washing.

And Siddy be catchin my eye in the mirror like she tryin to thank me, but there ain't one single thing I can do to stop her head from hurtin fore she catch her bus up to the nuns' school. Don't you know I was feelin it all in my heart, watchin, just standin there watchin? Wantin to tell that woman: That ain't how you raise no child!

But I work for Miz Vivi. Me and Chaney live on their place. I had my own two chilren to think bout. Their clothes, their hair ribbons, their teefes.

The mornin after Miz Vivi done took off in the T-Bird and roared back, she tell me first thing: Letta, you get in Mister Big Shep's room and haul out every single thing of mine. I'm not sleeping with that sonovabitch again as long as I live! Not if he's dying of a heart attack and holding out a million dollar bill in his hand.

Well, she done said this sort of thing to me before, when we done went and ripped all the gold "HIS" monograms off they anniversary bath towels and writ SHITHEAD on them with Magic Markers. That was the time he took off wild-turkey huntin in Texas just when she was throwin that big fortieth birthday party for Miz Teensy. She had done hired a little combo and all, and set up men to tend bar and park cars and what all. And Mister Big Shep he up and left to go shootin turkeys. We done ruint all his towels, then she had me hang them in the bathroom right where he'd walk in and spot them.

Then me and her went in the deep freeze with a freezer marker and scrawled "CRAP" all over his frozen duck and deer meat he done put up. That was a shame cause you couldn't even see the date when that game was kilt.

When that man got home, he give all that meat to Chaney and me. Us thawed it out and had a big cook-up! Our people thought we done hit the jackpot!

Everybody be settin round the table smilin, sayin, Oooh, this the best "crap" I *ever* ate!

Yeah, uh-huh, when Miz Vivi ain't callin Mister Big Shep her Lover-Man, she callin him Poor Excuse. That what she say: He a damn poor excuse for a man.

But it sho look like she mean bidness with this bedroom move. I had to move out all her lingerie and makeup from the dresser and all her pretty what-nots she done collected from all over. And she say: Letta, you can take that picture of Mister Shep and me at Pat O'Brien's and stuff it where the sun don't shine.

I like to say, Don't you be talkin like that to me.

But of course I don't say nothin nohow. If it's one thing I learnt in this life, it's to bite my tongue when I got to, and yell when I don't.

*C*haney and me been livin at Pecan Grove all the time since we done been married. He been here even fore

that, workin for Mister Big Shep and his daddy, Mister
Baylor Senior. We used to live in them two-room shot-
gun houses on the bayou. Fallin-down steps. Newspaper on the walls. You had to walk through the
bedroom to get to the kitchen. Yeah, uh-huh, and that
outhouse! Wooo Lordy, havin to sprinkle that lime
around, and all them flies, and it be stinkin to high
heaven! And me havin to get myself out there in the
middle of the night when I was carryin Ruby and Pearl
and peein all the time. Uh-huh, that's where we live
when I first come here from my Mama's house. Then
Mister Big Shep he moved us outta them houses and
put us in these new little white houses with the indoor
plumbin and the attic fan and my good-size kitchen
you can set down in. Oh yeah, Chaney be workin with
Mister Big Shep every day of God's world. And me up
to the brick house cleanin and cookin and carin for
them chilren ever since Siddy done left her Mama's
belly. I'm the one drove Miz Vivi to St. Cecilia's to
have Little Shep cause Mister Big Shep was out at the
duck camp. But the times I try to say somethin in that
house, seem like it just make things worse. So I bite my
tongue till it like to bleed.

*I*t took Miz Vivi a couple weeks to get all the way
holy, after she start goin down talkin to that pig-face
priest—the one what wore that big fat emerald ring.
That man look like a mean cat to me is all I have to say.
I don't care whether he a man of God or not. Times he
come over and track mud all over my clean tile floor
right after I done finish my moppin. Couldn't even be
bothered to wipe his feet on the mat, like the mud on

his shoes was the mud of Christ and we be lucky to have some of it. Mister Big Shep don't even do that! I had to stop myself from takin a broom to that priest and whompin him upside the leg.

But Miz Vivi be talkin to him every day and readin the book he give her on the life of the saints. We don't have that book at the Good Shepherd Temple where my daughter Pearl sing in the choir. (That Pearl got the sweetest voice in the world. She my jewel. She my little Mahalia Jackson Jr.) I never laid my eyes on that book till that pig-face priest brung it into the brick house. I open it one day when I was in Miz Vivi's room dustin and I like to get sick to my stomach. Pictures up in there of a man with all his insides gettin pulled out by a wheel! And a blind woman holdin her eyeballs up on a plate like she be offerin you a snack! This the kind of trash that man bring into the house. Like the Walker family ain't got enough trouble already.

Then Miz Vivi start her goin to Mass every mornin and actin like she be prayin all day long. Makin up her lists of what be a sin and what not be a sin. And she all the time be linin it up for you. Like to wear me out!

She say, Letta, it's a sin for you to wear that wig Chaney got you because it makes you vain.

Now, I done love that wig! I axed Chaney to buy it for me at Kress cause it got them shiny swirls in the front that do just right. You just slip it on and walk out the house, look like you straight out the magazines.

And she tell me it a sin the way I watch my stories on the TV while I fold the clothes.

I tole her, I gotta keep up with Julie and Doug on *Days of Our Lives!* They be up to somethin new all the time. One day he singin to her, call her Beautiful Lady Love, and the next day she be throwin him out the house cause he still be wantin Hope, his old wife. Even though Hope got her amnesium livin in another city, and done forgot all bout him. I done been watchin that story for years and years—and then Miz Vivi come and tell me it all filled with impurity and what-have-you.

But what really got me is when she done start up listin sins for the chilren. Her baby Baylor only four years old and she tellin him it a sin if he make any smackin noise at all when he be eatin his food. That child already got trouble swallerin. I seen it with my own eyes. I fix that boy a little ham sandwich and a Coke, and when he try to swaller, that bread get stuck up in his throat. He try workin it down, but his little throat so tight he just have to spit that food out. He look up at me like he in trouble and say, Letta, may I please be excused?

Like to break my heart into a million pieces right there on that breakfast room floor. Only thing he can get down is smashed bananas with cream and I feed him more of that than a child oughta eat.

Can't a woman see what she doin to her own blood chilren is what I wanna know.

Then Miz Vivi done gone and perclaimed it a sin for Miz Lulu to set up in front of the bathroom mirror with her candy cigarettes pretendin she at a cocktail party. And that girl start eatin on her hair again, somethin I ain't never seen in a child before or since.

Miz Vivi tole Mister Little Shep he can't go near his cowboy boots cause they sinful footwear. Well, I got my own thought bout what kind of church say boots be sinful. Don't you get me started.

All in all, though, Siddy be the one takin the holy bidness the worst. Cause she always tryin to do like her Mama anyway. Siddy start listin what is a sin for her own self—don't even wait for her Mama to do it! She just find somethin she enjoy, then she decide it gotta be a sin and she start feelin all bad bout it.

She tell me, Letta I can't go outside and play on the pecan tree swing anymore, because I am putting that swing before God and that is a mortal sin.

I be thinkin, *Maybe they got a different God than mine.*

I say, Miz Siddy, babygirl, that ain't no sin. That just swingin under the Lord's blue sky.

But she say, No, I can't swing anymore. And she set inside the house and look out the den windows while Miz Vivi up in her bedroom (what used to be the chilren's schoolroom) fingerin them prayer beads.

Sometimes Siddy be cryin in her room off by herself and I go in and ax her, Baby, what is wrong?

And she say, I'm asking God to forgive me for thinkin unkind thoughts.

That brick house is gotta be the saddest place in the state of Louisiana, I tell Chaney when I get home. That place ain't nothin but a big air-condition house of sadness.

And would you believe, Miz Vivi done got that pigface priest to bring her one of them prayer kneelers into her new bedroom where them chilren used to have they desks and blackboards? And she brought her a white statue of that Virgin Mary. Two more things for me to dust. Then Miz Vivi she gone to the Catholic bookstore and bought herself a big old huge picture of that same Mary, with them eyes followin you all over the place. I don't care where you standin in that bedroom—that old virgin be lookin at you. They not the eyes I want followin me, nuh-uh. I gets to where I shut my eyes every time I passes that picture. I just do my dustin and vacuumin and get myself out.

And Miz Vivi quit her singin like she always used to do. Used to, she be beltin out: Oh what a beautiful mornin it was! And she be singin how she got to love one man till she die! All them tunes what she used to love. Oh, she'd sing those songs all the time puttin on her makeup or layin out dressy dresses for Siddy and Lulu to wear to birthday parties. She loved to sing, that woman did.

She clear her throat, say Damn filthy cigarettes! Then she sing some more.

Also Miz Vivi even quit playin *bourrée* with her Ya-Yas for two-three months. She say Mister Big Shep forbid her to have anything to do with them, but I think she done made it all up in her head. I think she punishin herself cause she don't have faith that the good Lord gonna hold her up. She don't know nothin bout the Lord of mercy.

Ain't nothin the same round that house since she done cut her foot all bad, got on them crutches and had that fight with Mister Big Shep. I didn't see the fight, but I was in that house the next mornin, and I been round them two long enough to know how they can do each other.

Somehow hittin the Jack Daniels bottle still ain't no sin in that house, though. Used to be, Miz Vivi wouldn't start up till three o'clock just fore the chilren come home from the bus stop. But then she start makin herself them little what-they-call "Mimosas" first thing in the mornin. She pour it in a cup so I think she drinkin coffee. I got news for her: You don't have no ice cubes chinkin the side of no coffee cup. Chink-chink-chink, that the sound in that house. Chink-chink-chink and the sound of that big old central air condition whirrin all the time. By the time I get to my stories, she already done had her a few. Not so no one else can tell, but I know how her voice dip down and get all relaxed the way it do when she drinkin. Oh yeah, she might quit a few days here and there, but she gain one or two pounds, then she get right back on the sauce. She say her drinkin keep her weight down. She say she the same size six she was in high school. And if she get fat, she gonna pay the Ya-Yas to shoot her. But she still announcin to everyone she ain't touched a drop of whiskey since Mardi Gras. Uh-huh. I keep my lips zipped, is what I do.

See, one time I gone to her when she was in the den settin on the window seat with her saints book. Chaney done laid a fire for her, even though it wasn't cold outside. She cranks up that central air condition and I don't care if it's ninety degrees outside, she announces to everyone that she *need* a fire. That's what Miz Vivi always say when she be wantin somethin: I *need* it.

She look calm-like, so I says: Miz Vivi, I been workin for you more than ten years and you know I wouldn't do nothin to hurt this family.

I know that, Willetta, she say.

And I tell her, I don't mean no disrespect to the Walkers. Yall been good to me and my family. But somethin bad wrong goin on in this house, Miz Vivi.

She drag on her cigarette and say: Oh, don't I know, Letta, don't I know. There is more sin in this house than anyone will ever be forgiven for.

Well I don't know bout that, I tell her, but your chilren is gettin mighty shook up the way you and Mister Big Shep be carryin on. Can't you two say I'm sorry and let bygones be bygone?

She don't move from the window seat, just look out the window like she gonna get a answer from the sky. Then she look at me all blank-face like I be a stranger. Look at me like we hadn't been in that house together six days a week for ten—goin on eleven years. Like we ain't cleaned up those chilren together when they been throwin up from the flu.

She look at me like I'm a nigger offa the street and she say: Willetta, you are a maid in this house. You are not a confessor, you are not a friend. You are a *maid.* Do not ever give me advice about how to handle my life again as long as you live. Do I make myself clear?

Yas'm, I tell her. You real clear. You clear as can be.

And then I gone outside and hung sheets on the line. It was a good day for laundry, lots of wind and not too cloudy.

I swore to keep my mouth shut after that, never open it up again. All I could do was stand on the edge of that driveway and watch, try to let them chilren know I was there, even if it was only with my prayers.

Specially Siddy. She start up with her asthma and

three–four times Chaney and me had to take her up to St. Cecilia's. She get it at night after Miz Vivi and Mister Big Shep done passed out from drinkin. I thank God they was out, cause if they was to try and drive in the shape they was in, that girl wouldn't need no oxygen, cause she woulda been dead in a car wreck. Baylor the one who call us up. I taught him our number soon as he could count—3-3-9-0. I get him to sing with me and show him the numbers on the dial phone. That was way fore you had your push-button emergency. He call, so me and Chaney go up to the house to get Siddy. She be wheezin and holdin her chest and that long red hair all tangled up in her face and she be holdin onto me. And I say: Just take it easy, babygirl, you gonna be alright.

I put her in the truck between Chaney and me and all I can do is rub her back, see can I get her to calm down. Half the time she got red belt whelps on her ankles and legs. And Lord, I don't wanna even think what kinda marks she got under her little nightie. But those doctors at St. Cecilia, they don't say nothin bout them marks. They know she Mister Big Shep's and Miz Vivi's child. They just hook her up on the oxygen and give her a shot. Ain't nobody in this town gonna say nothin to nobody bout the way they raise they chilren.

Back home in bed I lay up next to Chaney. I be cryin and he say, Letta you doin all you can.

My own two girls, Pearl and Ruby, already in they bed asleep, breathin regular. They my little ones, but I spend more time rearin the Walker chilren than I do my own babies, and that is the good Lord's truth. Times I had to leave them by theyselves with

102-degree fever cause Miz Vivi be havin one of her dinner parties. Walkin up to that brick house to help serve court bouillon, when my babies be coughin and layin at home with hot little foreheads. Make me wanna hit that white woman.

And where is Mister Big Shep most all the time after the big fight? Out at the duck camp, leavin Chaney and the rest of the workers to run Pecan Grove. Chaney say, Bossman don't know his crops from a hole in the ground these days. He don't look out, he gonna lose ever'thing he done put in the ground.

Well, ain't none of us want that to happen. All of us eatin the same gumbo round here, one way or the other.

This is how Miz Vivi done gone too far with the holy thing. She left me stayin with the chilren and gone off to a retreat in Arkansas with that pig-face priest and a bunch of other Catholic women, nary a one of them a Ya-Ya. She come back after three days, had lost six or seven pounds, and her hands was shakin like Mexican jumpin beans. Tellin me she hadn't touched a drop since she reached the Mississippi state line. Somethin bout her eyes make me wish she *had* been drinkin, cause I ain't never seen her look that het up.

She say, Letta you go on home. I'm back now. I'll take care of my chilren.

They was in the den watchin the TV. Little Shep had his little plastic gun thing what make his nametags that he put on everything. That boy love puttin his name on things. Siddy had on her false fingernails that she love. Lulu eatin her Oreos, settin up next to her big sister on the couch. Baylor, he holdin that old doll of Lulu's with the bald head. They all loungin, all laid up. Don't even get up to greet they Mama. Not cause they bad, just cause they be relaxin.

I shoulda never left out the house that day. I had a bad feelin up in my joints. But you can't look back. Good Lord didn't mean for us to hate ourself. He made us to love ourself like He do, with wide open arms.

I gone on home like she tell me. Chaney was in the rocker and Pearl and Ruby was plaitin each other's hair, stickin in the little plastic barrettes I done bought them at Kress. Chaney had started some collards and corn-bread the way we like on Sunday evenins. I been lucky, cause they's most men won't lift a finger to help you out round the house.

I gone in and drew me a bath with my Calgon and was soakin when Chaney yell out: Letta! Come on out to the porch!

What in Sam Hill is goin on? I say. Ain't no rest for the weary.

I grab my robe and run out to the porch and Chaney point to the Walker yard and say, Look over there!

I done heard them chilren screamin fore my eye even seen what was goin on. All four of my babies lined up against the wall of that brick house and every one of them buck naked. Miz Vivi out there with a belt, whuppin them like horses. And them just standin against the red brick. Yellin and cryin and screamin, but not even tryin to get away from her. Standin there, lettin her beat the livin daylights outta them like there be some big invisible wall round them. Why they not runnin away?! I shoulda taught them to run!

Me and Chaney watch it all, and what we supposed to do? We got jobs and a place to live and Miz Vivi is Mister Big Shep's wife. She a white woman, she can do whatever she want.

I hear Siddy's voice over the others. She be screamin, Mama don't hit Baylor! Don't hit him, Mama, please!

And I say to Chaney, You think I gonna stand out here and watch the chilren I raised get beat to death?!

He say, You wanna lose what jobs we got? You got somewhere else for us to live, niggerwoman?

I look at him and say, The Good Lord provideth. You call me niggerwoman again, you gonna end up with a voice higher than Ruby's.

Chaney go and set on the porch steps, he ain't movin. Say, Ain't my bidness.

Pearl and Ruby come out on the porch. They watchin, too. Chaney look at them. He look up at me. I head over to his truck and the girls start trailin along.

Chaney he stand up and say: Pearl, Ruby, yall go on back inside.

Then he finally move hisself (like I knowed he would). He get behind the wheel and we fly down the lane, Sunday dust blowin every whicha way, settlin on my skin still wet from my bath.

I be prayin out loud: Heavenly Father, you gotta guide our hands—you gotta guide our feet—please tell us what to do in these white people's yard.

Chaney don't even use they driveway, he pull straight up on the lawn where she beatin on them. And that truck hardly come to a halt fore I jump out, run over to Miz Vivi, say, Stop it, you hear?! Stop that! You leave them chilren alone!

And she turn like she plannin to whup up on me, too. She swing out with that belt and hit me round my elbow. But I got on my robe, where them chilren ain't wearin a stitch.

Chaney he reach up and grab that belt outta her hand, say: Miz Viviane, you gotta stop behavin like this.

And she go for him tryin to slap and kick him. You filthy nigger, she yell, don't you dare touch me! I will have your black ass fired off this place before you can spit!

But Chaney he a big strong man and he grab her hands and hold them together, and she still kickin and yellin, but she not doin no more harm to anyone. Them babies all cryin, they bleedin, and Siddy—oh Siddy, she done wet all over herself! Lulu be eatin on her hair like she do. Little Shep tryin to act like nothin done happened, like he a little bitty daddy. Like he got important bidness to tend to somewhere else. And Baylor be all blue-faced from holdin his breath.

I get holt of him and say, Breathe now, baby, breathe.

Sweet Jesus, I seen they whole lives in front of them, how they would be when they was grown. I seen it all just by lookin at them right that minute in that yard. And it done froze my blood.

I put them in the truck and Chaney let go of Miz Vivi. He jump in with us and he drive down the lane to our house. I be thinkin, Maybe Miz Vivi might come after us. But she just stay standin in that yard, lookin out at the fields like we never been nowhere round.

It was the first time I seen the truth: That woman ain't just a drunk, she crazy as a Betsy bug.

I call up Miz Buggy, Miz Vivi's Mama, tell her she better come on over. And then I wash the blood off them chilren's little white bodies, tryin to be careful as I can round what that belt done did to them. Take my what-they-call "burn plant" and pat on some of its juice, all the time prayin: Lord, Lord, come down and help these little ones.

I put them in some of Pearl and Ruby's clothes, even though Little Shep he starts to cryin and cryin, say: I don't want to look like a sissy! I can't wear these! I want my clothes! He don't stop cryin, now he worse off than any of them.

I set them down round the kitchen table and I don't know what is gonna happen next. My own two girls starin at them Walker chilren with they mouths hangin open.

I say, Ruby and Pearl, babies, yall close yall mouths fore they get full up with flies.

Ruby say to Siddy, You look funny in my dress.

I say, Shush, Ruby! Don't you go makin fun of this child right now!

I be thinkin: What in the good Lord's world gonna happen to us all at Pecan Grove? Mister Big Shep fire us, I don't know where we gonna go. It ain't easy to find jobs like we got in 1963 Louisiana.

Siddy's false fingernails hangin off and she gnawin on her own bit-down nails and she ax me: Letta, is it a sin for us to be over here when Mama is over there by herself?

I pull her to me, tryin to be careful cause I know her

skin be raw. I tell her, I don't wanna hear you worryin yourself no more bout what be a sin, you hear me, babygirl?

I stand up and tell all them, Just set there. Letta gonna fix yall some cornbread and milk.

My own daughters be holdin onto me over by the stove actin like they scart of white chilren in our house. I forget that I knows these Walkers inside out, but my own chilren ain't hardly never been round them. Pearl, she finally go get her and Ruby's colorin book and the coffee can of Crayola pieces and put them on the table. Baylor he start to colorin. He cryin out the side of his eyes but colorin all the same.

Miz Buggy finally come and get them. She say: Now Letta and Chaney, I don't want a word of this to go any further than this house, yall hear me? Miz Viviane is just upset with all she has on her mind. Miz Viviane has just been pushed too far by that Baptist husband of hers! Don't you ever repeat any of this.

I tells her, Yas'm.

And she take off to her house up by City Park with them chilren in her Fairlane. And I ain't never forgot it, not even when I looked down at that old woman in her casket: She ain't never thought to send back my own two babies' clothes what I had dressed them four Walker chilren in. What did she do with them clothes? Turn them into dustrags? I still wish I knowed. This is somethin what haunt me when I pray, somethin I can't forgive.

That evenin I took myself to our prayer service at Good Shepherd Temple and my church sisters come up and was so sweet to me. My best girlfriend Lucinda hugged me to her like she do, with that big self of hers that's shorter than me by a foot, but full and brown and smell like warm biscuits. I just let her hug me there in the back of church and I could hear them all singin. I got me a good church home. They look out for you when you in need.

*M*ister Big Shep he never fired us, never said nothin at all. He come round the next week with a mess of ducks already cleaned for me and Chaney to eat. Then later he give Chaney his gold El Camino. Said he was gettin hisself a new Ford anyway and wanted Chaney to have the El Camino. So we had us two vehicles that coulda took us anywhere we wanted to go. We coulda drove off Pecan Grove, straight outta the heart of Louisiana, to some other state and never come back.

But even though I ain't a big one for countin sins, leavin outta here woulda been a sin in my book. Cause some people God give to you to look out after, and that just be how it is. I got to keep my gaze on them chilren till the day I die. Too many things can happen in the blink of a eye, and that's why I count my blessings every single day.

That's why I tole my girls, that's why I tell my grandchilren: Don't ever worry bout bein holy, baby-child. Just keep your eyes wide open except when you sleep. Then let the Lord's mighty vision see you through the night.

SNUGGLING
Little Shep, 1990

*M*ama didn't fool me.

Oh yeah, she tried. Saying, I'm going to shrivel up and blow away if you don't give me some snuggles.

I believed her at first. Thought she was actually gonna kick the bucket if I didn't snuggle with her right when she wanted. I thought, She'll die and they'll say it was my fault. They'll say: He killed his mother because he wouldn't hug and kiss her like she wanted. He wouldn't let her rub that cold-cream face against his. Wouldn't let that cotton nightgown float around him, smelling like her skin.

I still can't take the smell of cold cream on a woman. Just a whiff is enough to start up one of the migraines. First thing I noticed when my wife, Kane, and I got together was how clean her face smells when she gets in bed. She never uses any cream at all. Washes her face with plain old soap and puts maybe a dab of baby oil around her eyes, that's it.

I give her three pair of silk pajamas for her birthday every year. Before we got married, I told her, Please don't ever wear a cotton nightgown around me and I promise I won't pick my nose at the table. And Kane said, You got a deal, Shep.

*M*ama acted like it was all normal, you know, like it was her right. I'm not sure what all she did with Sidda and the others—I just know what she did with me. They moved Baylor out of my room when I was in third grade. They added onto the house so we could each have our own private cell. No wonder she wanted to have us all in separate rooms. That way there wouldn't be but one at a time to witness what she was up to.

My room was right across the hall from the bathroom next to Sidda's. I would lay in my bed at night and hear Mama doing her nightly whatever in the bathroom. The woman spent hours on her face. I could tell exactly when she was finished because of the way she'd tap her toothbrush against the sink and then clear her throat. God, I hated those sounds.

Then she'd pad down the hall and say, Good night, Mister Walker, and Daddy would grunt something back, if he was even home. After that, she'd go into Sidda's room. I didn't want to, but sometimes I couldn't help but hear them. My hearing was already bad in my left ear by then. It took the doctors a while to diagnose it, but finally they said, You've lost eighty-three percent of the hearing in your left ear. Claimed it was from early exposure to guns and loud farm equipment. I could of told them exactly what it was, though: I made the hearing go out of that ear because it's the one that faced the wall when I tried to sleep. I got tired of hearing all the shit you had to listen to in that house.

If Sidda convinced Mama she was already sleeping or if the bitch hadn't gotten enough, the old lady would come into my room. And then it would start up.

I would kill someone before I let that kind of shit happen to Kurt or Dorey. Kane and me never let them sleep with us. Not even when they were tiny. I never crawl into bed with either one of my children. I've been careful from the beginning to watch how I hug them, kiss them, touch them.

Kane had to talk me into helping bathe them, she had to tell me it was okay. One evening I stood in the doorway and watched her while she lathered them up in the tub, their little ducks and boats floating in the water. Kurt's hair all slicked back and Dorey's chubby little arms. It was all warm and misty in the bathroom and Kane had her sleeves rolled up and her hair in a ponytail. She just looked so damn competent, so damn normal. But I didn't want to go near the kids while they were naked. Finally Kane got up and put a washcloth in my hand.

She said, Shep, it's alright! Go bathe your children, you're not going to break them!

Kane only knows part of what went on at Pecan Grove. Sometimes I'd like to tell her more, but you just never do know how people are gonna react to things.

What was so sickening was the way Mama'd root herself down under the covers and say, Let's snuggle. I need to snuggle.

Any time my mother wanted anything, she'd say, I *need* it. Then she expected people to give it to her. Like it was her fucking right. Like the right to water or food or air.

She'd sucker me into it by saying: Little Shep, let me tickle your back.

Well, I was a goner whenever anybody tickled my back. It worked like a drug on me. How in the world I kept on letting myself fall for it, though, I can't explain. She'd start out tickling my back with her fingernails the way I craved. And just when I'd be drifting off, she'd start kissing me and her hand would start wandering.

Hell, it makes me want to puke just thinking about it. I wonder how it was for the rest of them. Was it just the same? Did she do the same thing with Baylor?

I know there was that one time out at the duck camp when Baylor and I had a little too much to drink and we got to talking about sex. Now he has got some problems. After he'd had four or five scotches that evening, he told me: Bro', most of the time I can't even get it up. When I do, I just want to do it and get it over with. You tell anyone I just said that and I'll call you a bald-faced liar.

I told him, Hell, Kane wouldn't stand for that kind of stuff. She laid down the law to me about no drinking at home, and I flat-out had to toe the line. If I acted like that in bed, she'd kick my butt out of the house.

Baylor lit a cigarette and looked at me. We were sitting out on the porch and I was cleaning my fingernails with my pocketknife.

He said, You clean your nails just like the old man. Said it to me like it was an insult.

Yeah, little brother, I said. But at least I still want to get it on.

Yeah, he said, except when you're knocked out with a migraine.

Baylor can be pretty damn depressing sometimes. Before that conversation ended, he told me he was actually thinking about getting hormone shots. A Walker man actually talking about hormone shots.

*A*nyway, here's what finally did it for me. I got a crush on Bibi Crowell. God, she was the prettiest girl in sixth grade. Hair down to her waist, with these pink ribbons laced through it. Cute little nose and long eyelashes. That girl was born flirting. I adored her. I would of done anything for Bibi Crowell.

At the Catholic Youth dances when we danced together, just smelling her was as good as Christmas. I'd be wearing an oxford-cloth shirt, cords, and matching socks. Clean ears and a dab of Canoe. Ready for action, man. People will never understand how sexy those Catholic Youth dances could be. Hormones zinging all over that parish hall! We'd try to get our bodies as close as possible before the Nazi chaperons came around, pulling us apart from each other, saying, Let's see some daylight between you two!

Every boy in the whole place drooled to dance with Bibi Crowell. I had to wait my turn. But then one night—I remember it was around in November, before the holidays, in sixth grade—she turned down Pres Davis for a slow song. Flat out told him no.

So I stepped up and asked her to dance with me, and she said yes!

Man, Pres was a buddy of mine, and I still felt like king of the world. It felt so goddamn powerful to have her choose me.

Later that night Mister Gremillion dropped me off at home. He was always taking us home from things at night—Mama wouldn't drive across the highway after dark, and the old man was nowhere to be found. It was around ten o'clock. Sidda was spending the night out, and Lulu and Baylor were in the den watching the TV, with a fire going, eating oatmeal cookies. I stoked the logs up a little and laid down with them in front of the fire and watched whatever was on the screen. But all I saw was Bibi's face. All I could smell was her fresh sweetness. I wanted to tell someone what had happened to me, but I didn't have the words for it. Everything I laid my eyes on looked good, that whole house looked good, even my little brother and sister looked less weird than they usually did.

We polished off the cookies and turned off the TV. I went to my room, got undressed, and climbed in bed. I could smell the Tide on my pillowcase and feel how it was sort of crackly from drying on the line outside. Bibi Crowell had chosen me, and man, life was sweet. I laid back in my bed and smiled at the ceiling.

Mama came out of her hole after I'd been in bed for fifteen minutes or so. She walked in and sat on my bed. I made myself be perfectly still so she'd think I was already asleep.

How was the dance, Little Shep? she said, like I was about five years old.

I thought, Not tonight, Mama. Not tonight.

She said, Now don't you try and play possum with me. I know you're not asleep.

I rolled over and looked at her. She had on that pink cotton nightgown with the tiny flowers embroidered on the collar. I could make out those gargantuan breasts of hers hanging underneath. I know those breasts and I hate them.

She looked at me and whispered, Give me a hug, Little Shep. Give me a hug and a kiss.

Automatically I sat up and hugged her. She squeezed back real hard and I could feel those breasts against my chest. I felt like throwing up, and then the tingling at my temples that comes just before a headache starts up. Out of nowhere I thought: *I hate her. I hate her guts.* The thought was sharp as a piece of glass. It felt great. Made me excited, like doing a cut-away off the high dive for the first time. I broke the hug and laid back down. The bitch stared at my chest.

She said, My God, before long you'll be getting hair on this chest.

Then she reached down and started to rub her hand across one of my nipples.

She said, You are so beautiful, Shep. Sometimes I can hardly believe you're mine.

Then all the thoughts went out of my head. It was simply my body doing exactly what it wanted to. I clamped my hand over her claw. At first she thought I was being affectionate, that I actually wanted to hold her fucking hand. But then when she tried to move her fingers, to continue her rubbing, I tightened my grasp over her hand as hard as I could. At first she looked confused. Then she giggled. I kept squeezing as tight as I could, like I had one of those fist-grip exercisers in my hand. I stared straight at her.

She tried her whining like a little girl. Little Shep, she said, Let go of my hand. Pretty please.

I squeezed even harder. I was hurting her, I could tell.

She said, Quit it! That's too rough.

I said, Then get off of my bed, Mother. Go back to your own bed. Get out of my room and don't ever come back here unless I say you can.

Man, I couldn't believe I was saying that! Something just got into me. I'd thought it before, somewhere in the back of my mind, but I'd never said anything like that out loud. It was the power of Bibi Crowell. It was the tiny little bit of down on Bibi's cheek. That light little dusting of soft blonde hair on her skin, like on a peach. Like the sun had kissed her and left this little blonde fuzz behind. I'd deliberately brushed my cheek against hers during "Eleanor Rigby" so I could feel it.

Mama said, Don't you ever speak that way to me again as long as you live, Shepley Abbott Walker.

I let go of her hand and got up out of the bed. She looked at me in shock. All I had on was my Jockeys. I opened my bedroom door and said, Get out.

Daddy wasn't home yet. Lulu and Baylor were already asleep. Sidda was gone. No one could hear us. I was twelve fucking years old. At first Mama didn't budge from the bed, but when she did, she moved quick. She lunged for me and landed a punch against my rib cage.

I didn't hit her back. If I'd of hit her once, I would of never stopped. I would of killed her, I would of gone all the way.

She swung her hand back and smacked me hard in the face. Man, I didn't even feel it. It was like I had something protecting me. The slap threw her off-balance long enough for me to get out of the room.

I didn't go far. Just down the hall to the kitchen. I opened the refrigerator and poured a glass of orange juice, like I was somebody else's kid in some other house. I could see the refrigerator light spilling on the tile floor. Just come in here, you bitch, I was thinking, just try one more thing with me. I could hear her going into the bathroom. Great, she's taking a pee before she gets out the belt.

Then—I couldn't fucking believe the timing—the old man's truck pulled up. I could hear the gravel crunch and the way the sound changed the minute the tires hit the concrete driveway. I stood there with the refrigerator door open, staring at a plate of fried chicken covered with wax paper.

The old man stumbled in, drunked-up as usual. I could smell the Jack Daniels and cigarette smoke on him. I heard Mama open the bathroom door. She must of heard the old man too, because she went straight into her bedroom and slammed the door. I could hear her jam in the lock button all the way down the hall.

I said, Hey Daddy, you want some juice? Man, I knew the bastard didn't want any juice, I just couldn't think of anything else to say. I was tired. I'd done enough for one night.

For once he didn't start anything. He just said, Son, you oughta be asleep by now.

Yessir, I said, that's where I'm headed.

$\mathcal{B}$ack in my room, I could still smell my mother. I opened the window and turned my pillow over to the cool side.

Yessir, I should of said, *Why don't you kick in the door of the blue bedroom that used to be our schoolroom and screw your wife so good she's exhausted, laying back with a stupid silly grin on her face? Why don't the two of yall have a car wreck off a cliff in Acapulco?*

I made my bed up and slept on top of the covers. I didn't sleep on those sheets again till Willetta washed them. And I dreamed about Bibi Crowell.

God, Bibi Crowell was perfect. I love my wife, but she's no Bibi Crowell. Bibi Crowell was a sixth-grade goddess. I still dream about her. She was my protector in my room in that brick house on the bayou. That stinking bayou of thick brown water that didn't move. Stagnant water that was full of shit you couldn't see, couldn't guess at, didn't even want to know about.

CATFISH DREAMS
Baylor, 1990

1.

*U*sed to be, when Sidda'd call collect from New York City and ask me what I think I'm doing living back in Thornton, I'd tell her: It's simple, I moved back here because I'm a lemming. Because moving back to their hometown is what lemmings do. I'd tell her, I moved back here because Thornton is such an exciting, progressive, multicultural metropolis bursting with endless potential for everyone, regardless of gender, creed, or color. I moved back here so I could be close to the Pecan Grove Mental Farm. I moved back here because every person in this town knows who my grandfather was, and I don't want to live like a fucking cockroach in a place like New York City. I moved back here because Willetta can help raise my twins. I moved back here because I'm going to make six figures this year. I'm the first person in our goddamn sicko family to become a lawyer and I like rubbing their noses in it. And every single day when I go for lunch at the Theodore Hotel, they know who I am. And they bring me my *Baton Rouge Daily Advocate* folded up just right and set it next to my pink linen napkin.

But now I tell her: Because there's nothing in the world that compares to the goings-on in the "Gret Stet of Loosiana," like the Cajuns call it. This is a place apart. Man, politics and theater simmer in the same pot here, and the gumbo that results is mixed up with the past in a way that I've been hooked on since the day I was born. Where else are you going to find a place that's one-third black, one-third Cajun, and one-third Bible Belt Baptist? And Thornton's right smack in the middle of it! I mean, if Louisiana's shaped like a boot, then Thornton is the instep. We're the dividing line between the South Louisiana liberal Catholics and the North Louisiana conservative Baptists. So we party like South Louisiana and wake up with the guilt hangovers of North Louisiana. I love it and I hate it and I couldn't leave it if I tried.

You just name me one other state in the Union that had "The Kingfish," Huey Long, who would have become president if you ask me—if that damn dentist hadn't shot him down in the State Capitol Building. You name me one other state that had a Governor Earl Long getting off planes wearing paper bags over his head so the media wouldn't recognize him with Miss Blaze Starr. Hell, the *New Orleans Times-Picayune* reporters used to say, Governor, why are you wearing a paper sack on your head again? And do you think it was easy for the man to act as governor while he was in a Texas mental institution?! Another thing: You just try and name me one other state that's had a governor who's also in the Country Music Hall of Fame. Shit, Jimmie Davis can *still* flat-out sing "You Are My Sunshine."

And I need not even mention that we are the only state who can boast that we have a former Ku Klux Klan leader as one of our state representatives.

And I moved back here because of catfish!

Our honorable bigot of a mayor, Wascomb Belvedere, has proclaimed that it's high time Thornton became Financially Revitalized. Now this is truly a novel idea, given the fact that this burg has been in a slump ever since the Reconstruction.

According to Belvedere, the whole key to our new prosperity is going to be—catfish. Yeah, baby, *catfish*. The mayor claims catfish have a brand new image now. Tells anyone who will listen that when fried catfish was served at the Williamsburg Summit Conference back in 1983, there wasn't a single scrap left on anybody's plates. He predicts catfish will become as trendy as blackened redfish, coveted by four-star restaurants from coast to coast. Uh-huh, those trailer-trash fish are gonna swim uptown and Thornton isn't gonna be caught napping when they arrive.

Now we're talking the lowlife fish that I was raised to believe was a lazy man's fish, a poor man's fish, a black man's fish. Mean old feline-looking bottom fish with whiskers. Some of them so butt-ugly they look like their heads got smashed in a car door. Chaney used to work the banks for them with a cane pole, sinker, and worms.

Before Chaney's little brother Lincoln was sent to get his jaw blown off to keep the world safe for multinational corporations, he used to tell us stories about a cousin of his who caught a catfish big as a car. He'd get all excited and stutter, Fish was b-b-b-big as a Ch-Ch-Chevrolet!

Willetta used to batter and fry those catfish up and serve them swimming in catsup, with hush puppies and coleslaw. Man, that was their idea of a party. Mama wouldn't allow catfish in our house, but I ate them down the lane at Chaney and Willetta's, and that meat was as white and flaky and tender as it gets.

Well, His Honor the Mayor closes down City Park Pool, where Mama used to teach Red Cross swimming classes if her hangover wasn't too bad. Belvedere has big plans to convert the pool into the Thornton Municipal Catfish Farm. He calls it Catfish Plan for Revitalization—or "CPR." The man comes on the radio a hundred times a day with this corny-ass public service announcement and says, "CPR is a kind of resuscitation for the whole community."

People all over town are getting this crazy flash of hope in their eyes. The guys down at Rotier's where Daddy drinks get a swagger in their walks when they discuss the Rebirth of Thornton. Even the old man himself has a "Thornton: The Catfish Miracle" bumper sticker plastered on the back of his Suburban.

The mayor and his people go and drain all the old water from the City Park Pool, and fill it with new. Then they put together this big ceremony for the dumping of the first load of fish. They actually spend taxpayers' money to build bleachers so people can witness this historic event in comfort. Everyone starts calling the mayor "Catfish" Belvedere, and he plays it to the hilt. The fearless leader shows up at the ceremony with a huge pair of scissors with handles shaped like catfish. He snips a ribbon in half, and hundreds of cat-fish pour from a holding tank into the pool. About two hundred Thorntonians are there and they give the fish a standing ovation.

As for the reception afterward, well, it rivals any-thing you could experience at Gallatoire's in New Orleans. The head of the LSU-Thornton Home Ec Department was commissioned to create all the uptown catfish recipes she could come up with, and let me tell you, you have never lived until you have eaten catfish amandine.

Oh yeah. Things are really changing. There hasn't been this much excitement in Thornton since Ardoin's Potato Chip Factory opened in 1959. I was little, but I remember it clearly. I don't forget anything. Every time Thorntonians ripped open a bag of chips back then, they said: These potato chips are made right here in our very own town! Like it was a fucking miracle. You learn to take your thrills where you can find them in a dump like this.

Well, the whole town goes ape-shit over the damn catfish. It's on the local news every single evening. When people from out of town come to visit, Thorn-tonians take them over there and make them pose for pictures in front of the hurricane fence that rings the pool. Yep, we're gonna make millions trucking those fish to processing plants where they'll get shipped all over the country. I tell Sidda she could possibly even end up with a Thornton-raised catfish on her plate right up there in midtown Manhattan! Then she can brag about where she's from. What pride, what rich ancestry, we children of catfish!

This catfish enterprise is assuming mythic propor-
tions. The old man actually said he thought Charles
Kuralt should do a show on Thornton's Catfish Miracle. Said he thought the rest of the country would enjoy
seeing "how one little old town pulled itself out of the
swamp without sucking one single dollar from the fed-
eral guv'ment." You know something's really cooking
when the old man gets that positive.

2.

Something's gone wrong. Every damn time I go by
the Municipal Catfish Farm now, there are more dead
fish. They're floating belly-up, their eyes bulging like
they're looking for some message in the Louisiana sky.
But nobody talks about it. The mayor's office says,
There are just a few sick ones that need to be weeded
out. But every single day, more of those fish are dead.
The stench of dead fish is getting so bad I can hardly
stand it.

One night I wake up in a cold sweat from one of the
drowning dreams. Mama and Daddy and all of us are
fishing in a small boat back in the canal that borders
Pecan Grove. The boat turns over and the canal becomes the ocean. Everybody's going under. Dead fish
are so thick in the water, it's like soup. I try holding
onto the fish like life preservers, but Sidda yells: Bay,
don't! Dive under! Dive under with me! There's an air
pocket down here, dive under!

I wake before I dive under. Melissa's so used to my
nightmares, my thrashing around doesn't even wake

her up. I walk into my study and light a cigarette. We're five miles from the damn City Park Catfish Pond, and I can smell those dead fish in my study.

Melissa wakes up and comes to the door. You okay, sweetie? she asks me.

You smell it? I ask her.

Smell what, Baylor? she asks.

The dead fish.

No, she says. It's just another nightmare, Bay. Come on back to bed.

I'm going to stay up and work for a little while, I tell her. Then I get up and give her a kiss.

Thank you, she says.

For what? I ask her.

For the kiss. You never usually kiss me after a nightmare.

I sit in my study and smoke cigarettes.

Work, eat, smoke, sleep, scream at claims adjusters, take depositions in podunk parishes, try not to drink so much, try not to smoke, keep playing with the twins, try to make love to Melissa. Barbecue, plant a hibiscus in the yard, try not to go crazy.

Sidda says that sometimes she'll just be going along, and then—out of nowhere—she'll smell the exact odor of the inside of Mama's purse when we were little. She says it makes her chest close up and she has trouble breathing. She says she feels like she's a veteran of a war that doesn't have a name.

I miss Sidda. Melissa doesn't even notice the absurdity of this Gret Stet. Neither does anybody else I know. I'll try to catch someone's eye at a political function when I see something wacko going on, and they don't even pick up on it. Sidda and I always caught each other's eyes when we witnessed that nutsoid shit, and later we'd crack each other up, doing imitations of what we'd seen.

I liked it when I had Sidda around. I remember when just the two of us lived together at LSU. In that big old stucco garage apartment by the lake. Must've been a thousand oak trees surrounding that place, and all those camellia bushes. I always loved the way the apartment smelled inside. Like citrus and linseed oil. Those old hardwood floors.

All I did that semester was read. I read *Lanterns on the Levee* by William Alexander Percy. All about the Great Flood of 1927. Man, that Mississippi broke free and flooded 26,000 square miles of land, drove about 700,000 people from their homes, and killed 214. I listened to Randy Newman's *Good Ole Boys* album about a thousand times, listened to him sing "Louisiana." That song still breaks my heart into slivers on the floor. I read and re-read *The Moviegoer,* by Walker Percy, the finest writer to come out of this state. His daddy's cousin was the same Percy who wrote *Lanterns on the Levee,* and Walker was raised by the man. Shit, no wonder old Walker could write like he did. That river was in his blood. I cried like a baby when he died this year. I mean, Walker Percy fucking knew about being haunted. He knew about being honorable. I'm not talking bogus Southern Gentleman honor. I'm talking honor that doesn't wash away.

I quit going to classes. I ate vanilla wafers and drank Dr. Peppers all that semester, and all it did was rain. People were going to classes in pirogues. LSU went nuts. They pulled couches out of the fraternity houses and just sat out in the rain and drank gin. Half the school was drunk the whole time.

Sidda cried all that fall. I put my underwear on my head and danced around the apartment like a chicken to cheer her up. We stayed up all night and watched old black-and-white movies on TV. We cooked red beans and rice and drank strong coffee in that old light green kitchen. That natural gas heater with the blue flames licking smelled like old Louisiana, and we had a floor lamp with a tasseled shade in the kitchen. All the time it rained, we felt like we were back in 1927.

We have been through some shit, Sidda and me. Back to when we all still lived at Pecan Grove, and Mama and Daddy passed out every single Thanksgiving before dinner was even on the table. All those holiday decanters of Jack Daniels—they'd make trips to the Abracadabra and buy them special, instead of just pulling a fifth out of the case in the storeroom. Lulu and Little Shep would go hide in their rooms, but Sidda and me wanted a real holiday. We'd carve up that turkey by ourselves and eat Mama's cornbread dressing and sweet potato fluff. Then we'd lay down on the rug in front of the fireplace with the comforter pulled up over us and watch whatever was on TV. Sometimes we'd make up songs about the Pecan Grove Mental Ward and sing them to the tune of "The Beverly Hillbillies." I remember the time Mama got going on the Mimosas and let the damn turkey burn to a crisp. That poor turkey was carbonized. Mama and Daddy were already back in their rooms when it started smoking. We were almost asphyxiated until we opened up all the windows in the den and got out Pap's old industrial fan from the storeroom. It was freezing in the house, and Sidda and me laid up in the den and sang. It's a grand legacy. Fourteen fucking carat.

I tell Sidda: You're the only one I can talk about it with.

She says, I know, Baylor. That's what scares me.

*S*idda spends all her money on therapy. She's seeing this guy now who costs eighty-five bucks an hour. I tell her she oughta sue the Pecan Grove perpetrators for punitive damages, have them foot the bill.

Man, somebody's going to get rich off all the shit we took growing up. Sidda just has to keep dwelling on the past. I try to tell her to just fucking forget about it, like I do. She says I dwell on it too, but I just won't admit it.

Sometimes she'll call up crying her brains out, and I know immediately that she's tried to talk to Mama and Daddy. I tell her, Get off it, Sidd! Just leave it alone. They'll never change. They're drunks. They're goners. Don't talk to them about anything but the weather and what's on sale at Wayland's. Don't ever call them after five o'clock Louisiana time because they're knee-deep in the swamp of cocktail hour by then. Look, if you need to keep seeing the shrinks, fine, I'll even send you money. But don't put yourself on a goddamn spit. Our parents are dead, okay?

My children are my salvation. Jeff and Caitlin are incredible. Having twins is the best thing that's ever happened to me. When they were born, it was like the fucking Holy Spirit or something coming down on me.

It's the one and only time I have ever felt that alive. I live for that boy and girl. Playing with them is the only time I don't feel like someone's trying to screw me up against the wall. I love how their hair smells after it's washed. I never thought I'd smell something that clean in my whole life. Caitlin kind of looks like Sidd, with that big forehead and huge eyes. I can't believe how damn much they take in! You have to be careful what you do and say, because the next thing you know they're trying to imitate it. I walk in from work and they act like it's Christmas just to see me. And they are funny.

Jeff will go, Da! and it sounds like "Daddy." But then Caitlin will take it as a command to dance and she'll start wiggling her little butt and flailing her arms till she loses her balance and falls down. Then they both crack up and I scoop them up in my arms and say, Where did yall come from?

They're talking in this language all their own now. Jeff will say something totally incomprehensible and it will totally crack Caitlin up. Man, all those kids do is sit around all day while I'm miserable at the office and crack jokes for each other. They've got it made. Caitlin even laughs out loud in her sleep. I can hear her from our room. Sometimes I'll walk in there, that little heart-shaped night-light Sidda sent will be glowing in the dark, and I'll just stand there and watch Cait while she sleeps. If she starts giggling it'll get me laughing too. Or sometimes it'll make me cry. Man, I'd give anything to laugh in my sleep.

I'm going to make a lot of money. I mean a *lot*. Caitlin and Jeff are going to have everything. I'm going to send them to the best schools, get them out of this hole before they get stuck.

My alleged parents are crazy as ever. I brought the twins over there the other day and Mama and Daddy were already smashed at four-fucking-thirty in the afternoon. I stayed all of five minutes, then put the twins back in their car seats. Daddy was cussing, and Mama kept ranting about how she could have been happy *if only she'd been born Jewish!* It's the same old shit. I'm going to make so much money I'll forget I was ever their child. I won't need a damn thing from them, ever.

The only thing is, I hate being a goddamn fucking lawyer. The twins are the only ones I sing and dance for anymore. Sometimes when I'm down at the courthouse and the floor has just been waxed and I hear my heels clicking against the tile, I just long to break into a tap dance right on the spot. The kind of shit Mama used to do just to shake people up. I just want to do something silly, you know. But you can't.

I hate being a lawyer every minute of the goddamn day. I hate being a parasite and I hate never making anything new. I hate this whole business of making money off of people when they're hurting, when they're at their worst.

But even though being a lawyer sucks, it sure beats the hell out of farming. I decided when I was twelve years old I couldn't put up with that kind of life. Sweating out in those dusty fields, getting your hands filthy, getting sunburned so bad it hurts to turn over in bed at night. I used to sit out on that tractor working for Daddy in the summers and think, I will kill myself if I have to do this for the rest of my life.

I'm going to endure this mental anguish till I'm forty-two, and then I'm retiring to write books like Walker Percy. That man is my hero. He started out being a doctor, but he got TB. He laid up and read Camus and Kierkegaard and all those guys and figured out the whole thing was so absurd he had to become a writer. He moved to Covington, Louisiana, and never practiced medicine again. Man, he could take all those words like "honor" and "gentlemen" and show you how fucking empty they are, but how underneath the emptiness there's something else, something that's real, not just some dream about the Old South. Something about loving the land and people and being lonely. Something about putting one foot in front of the other, in spite of the fact that the whole thing is probably already doomed from the beginning.

When I'm forty-two, I'm quitting law and I'm going to have a little studio out behind the house. I'm writing a novel called *After the Hurricane*. I don't have the plot worked out, but that's definitely going to be the title.

One time I lost the autographed first edition of *The Moviegoer* by Walker Percy that Sidda bought for me when we were at LSU. I searched all over and couldn't find it anywhere. It used to be in my office over by the twins' pictures. But it was gone. It was lost. I needed that book. I needed to hold that book in my hands. So I called Sidda, and she made me chant the St. Anthony Prayer for Lost Objects with her. I'm sitting there in my law office with the senior partners walking by, and I'm on the WATS line going: St. Anthony, St. Anthony, won't you please look around? Something has been lost and must be found.

Sidda says that prayer always works for her. Says she started taking it seriously when she lived in Cambridge and had such a bitch of a time finding parking spaces. She said if I kept saying it over and over, the book would turn up.

And it did.

Sometimes I think my sister has magic.

One time Sidda called me from a pay phone in the Actor's Equity Lounge. I can't breathe, she said. I need to know whether it happened or whether I'm crazy. Did Mama come and get in bed with us, after she belt-whipped us? Did she? Did she lay there and hug us and tell us she'd shrivel up and die if we didn't hug her back? I just got through auditioning hundreds of desperate actors for seven solid hours, and I can't tell what's real from what I'm making up.

You think too much about the family, I told her. Do you have to examine every single thing? Some things just happened and that's it. But in answer to your question: Yes. It happened. You didn't make it up, it all happened. If it makes you feel any better, you're not crazy. You've got a one-track mind, but you're not crazy.

That is so pathetic, Sidda says.

It's what you come from, I tell her.

3.

One morning all the catfish vanish from the City Park Pool. Overnight. It's like the whole thing never happened, like it had been a catfish dream, from another town in another state. At first a few people try to ask questions. I mean, we're talking taxpayers' money, after all. But all the damn mayor's office will say is: No comment, no comment. Like they think they're the White House.

Jesus Christ, the reason the fish died is because the dumb-asses didn't have the pool treated for chlorine residue before they put the fish in there! They poisoned the fish that were supposed to save their town. Hell, Chaney's the one who pointed it out to me. Said, Bottomfish don't like chemicals, no.

So folks just drop the whole thing. They walk around like it's their own fault the damn fish died. When you drive by the grain co-op you can see four or five pickups with their bumpers almost scraped clean of the "Thornton: The Catfish Miracle" stickers. But nobody says a word. It's just like everything else in this place: Something bad happens, you better shut up and feel guilty.

Then the mayor ups and goes nuts. Everybody still calls him "Catfish," but they say it like it's a pocket-knife they can nick out little pieces of him with. He starts commandeering patrol cars for his own personal use. Just jumps behind the wheel and screeches off with the lights flashing and siren screaming.

Over at the Walk-on-In Cafe, he arrests a woman on her way to a bridal shower because he claims her pant-suit's illegal. Melvin Jeansonne, the chief of police, tries to reason with him.

But Catfish says, Mel, listen here, buddy. I got me this ring, see, and it gives me special powers. It tells me just exactly how to clean up this town.

Old Melvin looks down at Wascomb Belvedere's

ring and all he sees is a Thornton High School class ring from 1942.

I hear about this at the Theodore Hotel when I have lunch. I've got people all over town reporting these things to me because they know I'm interested. Well, more than interested. I guess obsessed is the word. I laugh about it every day, but sometimes I wonder if the man has something growing on his brain or something.

All Mama and Daddy say is, Oh don't pay any attention to Wascomb. He's been crazy since high school.

Anyway, this is what does Catfish in. I hear it at Sammy D'Stefano's downtown grocery, where we get that good Italian fennel sausage. (Around Thornton, Sammy's grocery is called "Little City Hall," because so much gossip circulates there.) It seems the illustrious mayor drives out to The Bayou Room, that old cinderblock dive on Highway 17 where they have striptease shows. Goes in there and coerces two of the dancers into his squad car. Then he makes them speak into his "microphone," which is actually the car cigarette lighter. He makes them state their names, addresses, make and model of their cars, and also their shoe sizes. Then he tells them to shut up and listen to WCCR, The Christian Radio Voice of Central Louisiana.

During a commercial break for glow-in-the-dark Bibles, Catfish explains how he gets coded messages over the radio that help him "purify" the town of Thornton. When he finally lets the ladies out of the car, they complain, but decide not to press any charges. They tell everybody that the worst part was having to listen to all that radio preaching.

The City Council gets all mortified and they give Catfish a big reprimand, but he tells them to go mind their own business. But the *Thornton Daily Monitor* gets in on the act and plasters all kinds of pictures of Catfish on the front page. Now Thornton is the laughing-stock of the state, if it wasn't already before.

When I tell Sidda about it, she says, Baylor, you are drowning in this gossip. The poor man sounds like he's mentally ill. And when I tell her, Well maybe he oughta see your shrink, she bites my head off. Tells me not to dare turn her attempts to recover from our family into one of my cynical jokes. She tells me at least she is trying to come to grips with our childhood.

I say, What happened to your sense of humor? You used to have a great sense of humor. Excuse me for living, like Mama used to say.

Shit, Mama needed to be excused for living. One time she tried to slap me because I called her a Nazi, but I ducked so fast that her hand hit the doorframe and she broke her damn wrist. It's so lovely to consider what she would've done to my jaw. The woman's wrist had to be in a cast for six solid weeks. It was great, I loved it. Sidda was cool, the way she came home from college and autographed it with this tiny swastika hidden in the date.

Sometimes when I'm supposed to be working on a brief, I'll stare at pictures of Wascomb Belvedere in the paper, and before I know it a whole hour has gone by. I'm bad as Sidda, dwelling on things, just dwelling on them. If I'm not thinking about Catfish, I'm thinking about my children. All day long.

4.

*W*ell, Catfish finally gets nabbed. He's laying rubber on Cypress Street in the middle of the night and a young cop stops him. Makes him get out of the car and try to walk a straight line, which the mayor fails to do in a big way. The officer cites him for DWI, and then calls his wife Hazelinda to get out of bed and come get him.

When Hazelinda arrives on the scene with her all-weather coat flung over her nightgown she says, Wassy Belvedere, you have pushed this thing too far, you have just gone too far this time.

The next day Catfish schedules a press conference. He up and gets K-Dixie-BS television up to his office and then proceeds to claim he wasn't drunk, but simply could not walk straight due to a bunion on his foot. Then he actually takes off his boot and sock and sticks his big ugly foot right up in front of the camera.

I think it was the sight of that bunion that made me feel like deep-sixing. I take off early from the office, get me a oyster po'boy and a Dr. Pepper and drive out to the Walker graveyard out near Lecompte. Pap is buried there. Also Sidda's twin. I sit in the car and eat my sandwich and think about living and dying and going crazy.

I decide to reach down and call Sidda on the car phone.

She says, Bay, it's nothing short of psychic that you called at this very moment! I was just going to call you with my good news! I got a job directing a very important contemporary Czechoslovakian play!

Great, I tell her. I didn't know you spoke any Eastern European languages.

She says, It's a translation, stupid.

Does it pay? I ask.

No, she says, but it's in Manhattan.

Terrific, Sidda, really. Listen now, don't forget your little brother when you're famous. I'll hang around the stage door in a old worn-out seersucker suit and hit up on the producers to let me sing some of my impromptu blues.

So how are you, Bay? I mean, really.

Well, to tell you the truth, Sidda, I'm parked on the edge of the graveyard. Sometimes this town wears me out. The other evening after work I drove down the bayou road out where Pap and Daddy used to farm near the Dutchmen. Do you know where I mean? To where those live oaks cover the road like a cathedral? And I had to pull the car over for a minute because my chest was pounding so hard. Something just came over me. At first I thought it was a heart attack, but then it passed.

I sat there on the side of the road and stared into those old trees and I thought to myself, These are the same trees I stared at when I was four years old.

I tell my big sister, I am entombed here. I will not get out of this town until I die.

5.

Mayors disappear around here faster than catfish. Somebody somewhere removes Catfish from office— and before we know it, Crowell Jeffers is the new mayor. Ex-state senator with blond hair. His family owns that restored plantation home just outside of town on the way to the old cotton gin. He went to Princeton, has perfect fingernails and no accent. The kind of guy Daddy always mispronounces words around.

It's not in the *Monitor,* but Johnny Rizzo who has the newspaper stand on River Street told me that Hazelinda took Catfish up to Shreveport for some mental help. I've got to hand it to the lady, she manages to hold this press conference for her husband on TV and it takes me by surprise. She says: My husband and your ex-mayor, Mr. Wascomb Belvedere, is very tired. He will need to rest for a long time because he is mixed up and just worn out.

Jesus, there's something so damn eloquent about her speech that it depresses the hell out of me. I have to leave the office before lunch. Drive on out to Pecan Grove to take a look at Daddy's rice. Chaney's out there, and we chew the fat for a while.

Chaney says, How you be doin, Doctor-Lawyer?

For some reason Chaney saw those words on my law school diploma and he always says them like a title— like Bishop or Captain or Judge. Somehow just seeing Chaney, the way he holds that denim cap of his in his hand, makes me feel like things are more solid.

A few weeks later, Catfish sends this letter to Mayor Jeffers' office. Written on this big sheet of butcher paper, folded up to fit into a regular envelope. Handwriting like a six-year-old's in different colors and he's drawn a bunch of fish on it.

The letter says: Dear Thornton I am sorry about the fish forever.

Well, Jeffers and his cronies frame the thing all handsome and hang it in the hall with a brass plaque underneath that says "No Comment" like the clippings from small-town newspapers that *The New Yorker* magazine likes to make fun of.

When I tell Sidda the end of the story, she says, What's really bothering you, Bay? This has you real depressed.

Me? I say. Depressed? You've got to be kidding. Man, I'm the original smiley-face golden boy down here. I love it that you lose your fucking accent and sit up there and laugh at Thornton.

She says, If you feel so bad about Thornton, why don't you run for political office? Try and change that insane place or at least work on your own feelings about it, instead of being such a cynic.

If I'm a cynic, I tell her, then I'm a goddamn well-paid cynic, which is more than I can say for you, Ms. Thrift Shop, USA! And no, I won't consider running for office. I've got my hands full as it is with my practice and my family.

My sister sounds like she's trying not to cry. Baylor, she says, it makes me so sad to hear how hurt you are. It's not just all those dead catfish and that poor crazy mayor, is it? I mean, it's everything, huh?

I don't know what the hell you're talking about, I tell her.

Bay, she says, you're the one who told me I didn't make it up. It all happened.

Well, I don't see you down here trying to change things! I tell her. I don't see you down here witnessing our parents becoming the highest insurance risks on record. You're the one that escaped two thousand miles away from where you grew up. I'm the one who lives and works here day in and day out. I can't save this place, goddamnit! I'm not fucking Jonas Salk. You're the one who never comes home and who still gets sick with the flu wanting to make this town well. *You're* the one who can't get Thornton out of your mind—even in the middle of millions of people who will let you be any fucking person you want!

Sidda doesn't speak for a while. Then she says, You're right, Baylor. I'm fighting the Thornton Flu. It's not easy.

I'm trying not to cry myself. I tell her, I know. We must have inherited one of those "bugs" that Mama and the Ya-Yas always got on the morning after.

Then we both kind of laugh a little because the whole thing truly is funny. Not funny ha-ha, but funny tired. Funny sad.

6.

I haven't talked to Sidda in a couple of months now. I've been working my butt off as usual, and in between I play with the twins. They run across the yard, singing and dancing. Sometimes when you laugh at them, they just stare at you, like you're the one who's crazy.

I sit on the deck and watch them and smoke a cigarette. Sometimes I remember when I was little and Mama used to make me wear these hand-me-down shoes of Little Shep's. God, they were ugly-ass shoes. Scuffed-up turd-brown with the toes all crinkled up from Shep's altar-boy genuflecting. I looked like a fucking goon. All the rest of them used to think it was so funny, the way those shoes stuck out from under my pants. Sidda and Little Shep and Lulu would point and laugh their heads off.

If I was feeling brave, I'd say, Yall shut up and leave me alone! But most of the time I would just stand there with my hands in my pockets, trapped.

When the levee breaks, I'm gonna drown. I'm gonna drown in poisoned water.

I'd wish I could tell my big sister: Please just give me a break. I'm younger than you. You were already dialing the telephone when they first brought me home from the hospital.

E-Z BOY WAR
Big Shep, 1991

I watch all the news from my E-Z Boy lounger. I got the chair by the windows back in my room. Originally put it back there so I could hear the TV over the kids' screaming and carrying on at the other end of the house. Now that they're all gone, I guess I've gotten used to sitting up by myself and watching what's going on in the world.

They started another war. I was down at the grain co-op last week and Charlie Vanderlick told me his grandson was in a Marine assault unit in the Gulf. Not our Gulf of Mexico, the one farther east.

Then, after a Levee Board meeting out at LSU-Thornton, I saw some graffiti on the wall in the men's room that said "18 males per gallon."

Goddamn, I thought, maybe you've lived too long.

*B*ack when they first asked me to be on the Garnet Parish draft board in 1965, I got all puffed up. Figured giving me such a responsibility must of meant they thought something of me.

So I said, Yessir, I'd be proud to.

Our pictures were in the *Thornton Daily Monitor* and I wore a suit like the rest of them. But I was the only one with cowboy boots.

Vivi said, Shep, babe, why don't you wear your wing tips?

But I said, Vivi, let's don't get carried away with this thing.

The rest of the board was your downtown crowd— Neal Chauvin, the lawyer; two businessmen; and that orthodontist who was sending his son to Princeton on my kids' teeth. They needed somebody to represent those of us who farm out here along Bayou Latanier outside the city limits, and I was the one.

The meetings were at the parish courthouse at six in the evening so the rest of them could walk over from their offices after work. I would go home from the fields first, even though once the weather turned good, Chaney and me didn't know the meaning of the words "quitting time." We were making the changeover from cotton to rice back then. Had to get my land leveled perfect and make sure the ridges on the contours held the water like they should. Growing something under standing water was a whole different ballgame from what we'd been used to. We were working with new irrigation pumps and combines—the whole nine yards. Had folks from the Extension Service out there at least once a week to advise me. You got to try and diversify, so the land you inherited doesn't get worn out and useless. Not to mention, you also got to plant you a crop that'll bring in enough cash to keep a roof over your head.

Before the meetings I would shower and shave and

put on a suit—foreign to me, but there's such a thing as civic duty. Never saw any battle myself. Had my seventeenth birthday on a train headed for Navy boot camp in Great Lakes, Illinois. I wouldn't wish the kind of homesickness I had on my worst enemy.

Everybody who was anybody was for the Vietnam thing at that point. Get in and get out so the dominoes don't come tumbling down. They weren't even calling it a war then, just a "conflict." Up to that point, I hadn't ever realized that little swamp over there meant so much to democracy, but then I tend to pay attention to things more local.

Vivi would ask me questions about it, and the only thing I could say was, Well, Russell Long and his people seem to think it's important, and they've been in the know since Year One.

Then in September of '65, Hurricane Betsy roared across the Gulf of Mexico and hit the Mississippi Delta like no North Vietnamese mortar ever could. She knocked three-quarters of my rice to the ground and all I could do was stand on the carport with the humidity dripping off me and watch. We harvested the puny portion we could, burned off the rice straw, disked it, then put in wheat. Hurricanes remind you that it's the Old Podnah who's in charge, not you.

By the end of that year, we'd put ten times as many more men in uniform than when I first went on the board. I started reading more news, because I wasn't gonna have the other board members think I was some know-nothing tractor driver when I opened my mouth at the meetings. I read my *Thornton Monitor,* my *New*

Orleans Times-Picayune, Newsweek, and *U.S. News and World Report.*

One evening I just had to get up and walk down the hall to Vivi's room. I said, Babe, you still awake? Take a look at this, will you? You're a Catholic, explain this to me.

And I handed her a picture in *Newsweek* of this Catholic relief worker burning himself up in front of the United Nations building to protest us being over in Vietnam. The picture showed this young boy going right up in flames. You could still barely make out his eyeglasses and the shape of his sweater-vest and ears.

Vivi said, That's disgusting, Shep. Take it away from me.

I went on back to my room and tried to get some sleep but I couldn't. I sat up half the night with my asthma inhaler and Herman Wouk.

*C*hristmas that year was good enough, for just having come through a hurricane. Vivi charged everything.

I figured, Well, we can't have *two* years of hurricanes, can we?

We had a big Christmas breakfast with all kinds of kinpeople over, the little ones going nuts over their toys the way they do. While we ate our turkey and corn-bread dressing, the diplomatic muckety-mucks flew all over the globe pulling out the stops. They had a thirty-hour cease-fire, and man, did they burn some jet fuel hopping from one embassy to another.

I thought, Maybe they can stop this thing after all. I hope so. I'm a farmer, not a military recruiter.

Then '66 rolled in. After the so-called truce, we went all-out to bring the North to its knees. Good, I thought. Bomb the hell out of it and get it over with. I couldn't barbecue a sirloin without thinking about the G.D. war.

I had boys by the dozens coming in front of me, some of them hardly been shaving for a year. I never used to think nineteen-year-olds were so damn young. Well, we got ourselves into this thing; we got to get ourselves out. But I hated the idea of putting anyone through the hell I went through in the Navy. And I didn't even know any combat. Boot camp was bad enough. I had never left Garnet Parish without Mama or Daddy before, and I was sick the whole damn time. Had problems with my bowels and ended up in the infirmary, you can't count the number of times. An obstructed colon, they called it. I called it: Go ahead and shoot me now and get it over with.

*C*ivic duty or not, I could of done without those draft board meetings. I had enough on my hands just trying to run my own farm. I was going all out with the rice. If those Southwest Louisiana farmers could do it, I thought, then so could I. Cotton was a thing of the past by then. It got to where I'd laugh out loud when I'd even hear the phrase "Cotton South." When it comes to cotton, I'll wear it, but I sure as hell won't grow it anymore. It wasn't nothing but a sure way to go bankrupt.

Not that I didn't miss it. Not that I don't still miss it. There is some kind of beauty to growing cotton. First, you got to make sure it survives germinating when the ground is cool. Then summer comes and that plant grows so lightning-fast—it's like watching a kid shoot up from two to twenty in three hot months. You got to really love farming to grow cotton. Because you got to baby it, watch it every day, give it what it needs at every different stage. Keep the weeds out, watch for the boll weevils and bollworms. You can get emotional with that crop, I tell you. Sometimes I wonder if I wasn't better raising cotton than I was with my own children.

And the harvest. The kids used to come out to the fields after school. Vivi would bring a picnic supper and we'd eat under the pecan trees, with the oranges and pinks of the sky. Chaney and Lincoln and the other field hands sitting there with us next to the tin water cooler. Sometimes Willetta would bring out something special for Chaney, those tall, skinny girls of their tagging along. I liked showing off what we'd been working, and in those days my family was actually interested. Not like later, when they got ashamed of how I paid for their clothes and food and cars and colleges. Back in those days, the kids would climb up on the high-bed cotton truck and dive down into that freshly picked cotton like they thought they were in the circus or something. I'd watch them come up sneezing, picking fuzz off their eyelashes, then diving down for more.

Those were good times. Hell, we didn't even *drink* on those evenings. Just ice tea. And I'd keep working late into the night, because you didn't want to leave cotton in the field a day longer than you had to. No telling when the rain'd start.

I knew what I was doing then. My father taught me how to grow cotton.

But he didn't teach me how to sit still at no conference table with a bunch of air-conditioned men. At those draft board meetings, you knew you weren't part of their crowd, even though nothing was ever said. They had a club so private it didn't even have a name. Quick sure handshakes. Soft clean hands. Manicured fingernails. When we shook hands, I was always conscious of my calluses and the dirt that wouldn't come out, no matter how hard I scrubbed. I was the only farmer on the draft board and I busted my butt trying to get my fingernails clean as theirs.

There was something in me that would of liked to say: Listen, you SOBs, my Daddy could of sent me to Tulane too, but we had land to farm. While your people sat up at the country club during the Depression whining into their mint juleps, my father was trucking potatoes across the whole goddamn South to hold on to our land.

But I held my tongue. It was all deeper and sadder and more confusing then I had the words for. Sometimes I wondered if this wasn't how the niggers felt.

*O*h, I watched that war from my E-Z Boy. We're fighting a jungle war, a ground war, and one in the air. We're kicking ass now, LBJ said. Only no one was telling those VC bastards. They didn't seem to get the message. Maybe it was because they didn't speak English. Hah. They picked our jets off like kites in a storm.

I knew the numbers. We had our draft quotas to

meet every month. Quotas everywhere you turned. Started the year with 181,000 and ended up the year with 400,000.

And it wasn't just Vietnam. Meaner mouths than Dr. King were starting to holler. Whatever his dream was, it seemed like it was turning into a nightmare to me. It was war on all fronts. I just wish my own home hadn't been one of them. But don't get me started on that. There weren't any deferments from the battles in my house.

Christmas came again before I'd even paid off last year's charge slips. One night I was at Rotier's Bar having a drink and a bowl of gumbo with the boys. We were always bringing Rotier shrimp or duck, and the man could flat out turn it into something. If I'd eaten a bowl of that gumbo every time I ordered a drink from that man, my life might of turned out different. Anyway, the place was all decorated for Christmas, little fake trees up on the bar, the Playmate of the month next to it with her pink tits and wearing a red Santa's hat. And McNamara came on the TV, saying: Progress has exceeded our own expectations. We can now cut our draft in half during '67.

The only problem was, old Westmoreland kept asking for more boys—and what Westmoreland wanted, he sure as hell seemed to get.

*N*ineteen sixty-seven. Hottest G.D. summer I can remember. Bigger ground battles, more air assaults, same size body bags, only a helluva lot more of them.

That's when the calls started coming regular. Nine o'clock at night, that's when you'd hear the phone ring.

I remember the first one. It took me a while to even figure what it was about. It was Mrs. Alma Vanderlick, Charlie Vanderlick's wife.

I said, Hello, this is Shep Walker.

And she said, Mister Walker, I sure hate to be calling you this late at night. I know how early farmers got to get up. Charlie's asleep already.

I said, Don't you worry, Miz Alma. What can I do for you?

Mister Walker, she said, please don't tell Charlie I called. He wouldn't never get over it.

Miz Alma, I told her, you people been farming along this bayou as long as mine have. Now, what can I do for you?

Oh Mister Shep, you got to stop them from taking my son Albert to Vietnam. He's the only one left to farm this place when his daddy's gone. My oldest boy got him a real fine job with Texaco down in Morgan City. He's making good money. He ain't never gonna come back here and farm.

She was crying, and I sat up in bed and tried to unclench my chest.

I'll see what I can do for you, Miz Alma, I told her. Let me see what I can do.

She said, Thank you, Mr. Shep. I'm gonna run yall over a jar of my fig preserves next time I'm up your way.

That call shook me up something awful. Good thing I didn't know it was only the first. Once they started flying those body bags back to Louisiana, there wasn't any medals or patriotic sweet-talking that could hush up the farm mothers who live up and down this bayou.

At least not at night, when their husbands were in bed and the supper stuff was put away, and they got to remembering how they'd danced with those baby boys on their hips at Sunday afternoon pig roasts. Or rubbed Vicks VapoRub onto their chests when the bronchitis came around. These ladies didn't burn no flags. The looked up my number from the grain co-op phone list. I was the only country man on the draft board. They called me.

I had a bad taste in my mouth the day Albert Vanderlick stood up in front of us. Boy was asking to be deferred on sole-surviving-son status. He was wearing pressed khakis and a short-sleeve plaid shirt with a necktie. You could smell the homemade starch when he sweated. Healthy-looking boy. Those Dutchmen down the bayou feed their children good, raise them right. I remembered the boy from when he used to tag along with his daddy to the cotton gin. He sat there in front of us with his hands on his knees, fingers spread out. I could see where he'd scrubbed his hands, could tell by the redness around the cuticles. Shoot, don't I know that look. Don't I scrub my fingernails every evening of the world out in the utility room so Vivi won't have to see the dirt up under my nails? Using the fingernail brush, working it up under the nails, scrubbing my palms with Lava trying to get the earth out from in between the creases in my skin.

I could see Miz Alma, the way she must of called to him through the bathroom door, telling him: Albert, clean up good, you got to make a impression on those gentlemen.

We were scheduled to see thirty-one boys that same

evening. We had maybe five minutes to discuss Albert Vanderlick.

Neal Chauvin said, This boy doesn't qualify for sole surviving son. He has a brother.

I said, Well I know that, Neal, but what you got to understand is that his brother has got himself a good job with one of the oil companies down in Morgan City—the fellow's going places. Albert is the one his daddy raised to work that land. A man's gotta have somebody to hand his land over to, or what the hell's it all for?

The orthodontist said, Shep, it sounds like you know these people. Maybe we ought to be a little lenient in a case like this.

Chauvin said, This is all beside the point. There is no legal ground on which to defer him. The boy would make a fine soldier.

I said, Hold on, don't we have any give-and-take in this thing?

And Chauvin said, If we bend the rules for a boy like Vanderlick, we set a dangerous precedent in this parish.

So Albert got put to a vote, and the boy was in uniform before his daddy's cotton had grown another four inches.

We weren't escalating, though. It was just action over and above what had been taking place, is how they put it.

It got to where I had to pour me a quick drink before every meeting, then wash out my mouth with Listerine. Then—I don't know what it was, but I started waking up with the worst nightmares I'd had since Daddy died. I'd walk around the house, step out on the carport, try not to think about lighting a cigarette, pour myself a drink, try to read. Then the asthma would start up and I'd spend half the night sitting up in the E-Z Boy trying to keep my chest from closing up. You can breathe a little better if you're leaning back in that chair instead of flat out on the bed.

From where I sat, it seemed like we were talking two different wars. The one we were losing on the TV, and the one the Guv'ment said we were winning. But listen, I'm not a soldier. After that bowel thing, Daddy got me out of the Navy somehow. I didn't even ask what kind of strings he pulled. I was just so glad to be back home. We had a big cookup in the yard and he never said word one to me about it. The man handed me a lot of shit in my life, but he never said a word to me about leaving the Navy. My people never have been peaceniks or what-have-you. If somebody invaded Garnet Parish, you better believe we'd whip some butt. We just don't like the idea of traveling halfway around the world to fight when we got crops in the ground.

Come to think of it, Daddy never put on a uniform himself. He always said, The fat gonna stay fat. They don't need me to help them do it.

Then don't you know it, Lincoln Lloyd got called up. Chaney's younger brother. Chaney's been my right-hand-man since who laid the rail. Damn, Chaney's daddy worked for mine when we wasn't nothing but titty-babies. Lincoln was living down on Lower Levee Road with a sister of his who didn't amount to much.

Chaney and Willetta were the ones who got the boy to stay in school as long as he did. When you first met the boy, you thought he was slow because of his stutter he had. I thought it myself till I heard him talking to Chaney in the barn one day. Boy didn't know I was around and there he was, talking clear as any child of mine, not one stutter spitting off that tongue.

Later I asked Chaney about it and he said, I don't know, Mister Big Shep, I think the boy just be scart of white people.

Chaney and Willetta went up to the school one time to talk to an evaluator about Lincoln because of all the notes the teachers kept sending home. And this white evaluator and Chaney and Willetta and Lincoln himself sat up in that office, and the lady said, We have got to try and figure out whether to classify this boy as an idiot or a moron.

Chaney tried to laugh when he told me this but I knew he was mad. I know Chaney. I've spent every one of my working days beside the man and they don't come any better. He's a man who keeps his own counsel, a man you can count on.

Far as I'm concerned, Lincoln wasn't a idiot or a moron neither. He just had trouble getting his words out. He worked for me in the fields since he was ten, and I can't say I knew the boy good, but he rode Shetland ponies with my four kids and I'd recognize that donkey laugh of his anywhere. Yeah, he dropped out of school, but he wasn't as dumb as they thought. Lots of times people make the mistake of underestimating you on account of the way you talk. I've seen this in my own life. That stutter might of made him sound stupid, but it's by a man's eyes that you know his intelligence. And Lincoln Lloyd had some smart eyes. He was as good a worker as you could of asked for. Talked slow and worked fast. Little and wiry, but muscular like Chaney.

I'd never known Chaney to ask a favor before. But one Sunday afternoon he came up to the house and asked for me. I put on my slippers and went out on the carport, and Vivi said, Chaney, let me get you a Coke.

The two of us stood there and stared out at the rice. Chaney drank that whole Coke in silence. Then he said, Boss, I been with you since my daddy worked with Mister Baylor Senior and I ain't never axed you for nothin.

That's right, I told him, you've pulled your load.

Well, I gotta ax you for somethin now, he said.

Chaney wrapped his arms around his chest, the way he does when he's thinking. Rubbed his hand across his face and kept staring out at the fields.

Mister Shep, don't let them take Linc to the army, he said. He done got that stutter and he ain't never been nowhere. Boy ain't never even been as far as Mamou. He ain't gonna make it through no war. I know it up in my joints. See can you do somethin for my baby brother, could you please sir, Mister Shep?

He didn't beg. Just handed me the Coke bottle and said, Thank you for the cold drink. I gotta get on back, or Willetta'll be wonderin where I run off to.

*Th*is is what I got to live with. I didn't do a goddamn thing to keep Lincoln out of the draft. McNamara said the army was the best thing going for your disadvantaged Negro youth. The man stood up there with those glasses on and explained how they were going to give boys like Lincoln special classes to bring them up to par. Teach them skills so they could land jobs they'd never get without the army. Lincoln passed the entrance test, which I guess proved he wasn't no moron. And ain't nobody ever said a thing about the boy's stutter getting in the way of him shooting a gun.

I said to Chaney one day when he was working on the combine, Chaney, the army just might be that boy's ticket out of here. Give him opportunities you ain't never had.

Chaney didn't answer me, just kept on working. I stood there a full minute waiting for him to say something back, but he acted like I wasn't even there.

*O*ne day around in that time, I remember I went downtown to Weinstein's Men's Store and bought me a brand-new goddamn suit. The thing was brown with little flecks of green in it. Had the thing tailored and then wore it to the next draft board meeting. I thought: Your uptown crowd are not the only people in the world who can put a decent set of clothes on their backs.

I was walking out the kitchen door and Vivi said, Oooh, Mister Walker, I'd fight a war over you.

I was the first board member to show up at that particular meeting. Me and the draft clerk had to wait fifteen minutes for the others to get there. Well, we all get busy, I thought. But when the bastards waltzed in, they were all wearing madras slacks and topsiders and running on about their golf game. Every goddamn one of them had been out at the country club. You could smell it on them, that sun smell that comes from being outside without breaking a sweat.

The orthodontist looked at me and said, Hey, Shep, sorry we're late. Couldn't take the office one more afternoon. You know how it is.

Neal Chauvin looked at me and smiled. Said, New suit, Walker?

Then Chauvin sat down in his sissy-ass alligator shirt, and we proceeded to see a whole slew of college boys whose student deferments had lapsed.

One of them, the Jarrell boy, was in pre-law. And he actually sat there in front of us and said: If you gentlemen force me to leave school, my father might as well pour $12,000 down the drain. My education is costing him a lot of money. I'm going to be a damn fine district attorney one day.

Later, discussing his case, Chauvin said: You can't send a boy like that to die in the trenches. He's the kind of man Louisiana needs. Then he laughed and said, Besides, I'd never win a case in his father's courtroom again if that young fellow doesn't end up on the Louisiana bar.

And the others laughed along with him, like it was so funny, like it was all so goddamn funny.

*N*ineteen sixty-eight. Swatting the years away like flies. They kept saying we were winning. Westmoreland and old Ellsworth Bunker—what the hell kind of name is that anyway?—they kept on swearing things were fine. My rice was looking pretty good, but the price of everything you needed was sky-rocketing, and you had to read up every day on all the new pesticides and herbicides. Farming was changing fast, but I was there with it.

I ended up in the hospital for a couple days with the asthma, had to get on the oxygen. Lung guy told me, It's the dust.

I said, Great. I'll just farm without breathing any dust. That oughta be real easy. I'll just sit around and grow rice in a air-conditioned room. Listen, Doc, I got kids to raise. What you want me to do?

He said, Well, have you ever considered a change in professions?

I said, No, buddy, have you?

Chaney and Willetta got them a framed picture of Lincoln in uniform. The boy looked shipshape. They were so proud of him that Chaney gave me a wallet-size picture for myself. That Chaney has always loved his snapshots. Sits out under the mimosa tree on Sunday afternoons and pastes them in his scrapbook.

Sometimes I wonder if any of us are cut out for the lives we lead.

In the middle of the goddamn Tet New Year truce, we had to fight a VC assault against the Saigon embassy. They rained down enemy mortar on all those little towns and dropped napalm on the Mekong delta. We lost over a thousand boys.

Jesus! We are the United States of America, I thought. What the hell are we doing? We're talking a piss-ass little swamp! Can't we get in there and finish this thing off? I found myself getting in arguments with my buddies at Rotier's. Got to where I'd hear the sound of my own voice and think it was somebody else's.

I'd yell, *If we're fighting a war, then let's get it the hell over with!*

What in the world is happening here? I'd think while I watched things from my E-Z Boy. We tore up South Vietnam, the damn peanut-size country we were supposed to be saving. Dropped so many defoliants, that soil will never be the same. Now, I know defoliants. I been around them every day of my life.

I watched it all on the goddamn color TV—little Vietnamese girls running out of burning huts, carrying babies in their arms, squealing high-pitched like rabbits in a trap. They ran across the screen until I thought they were gonna run straight out of the set into my bedroom. I swear to God one evening I thought I saw the Vanderlick boy on the news, thought I recognized his hands.

Man, we beat the whole world and we couldn't even take that little swamp! We trained half those boys down the road at Fort Polk because Louisiana has the same heat and humidity like Vietnam. I know what a swamp is.

LBJ said, Now there will, of course, be nervous Nellies who will buckle under the strain.

I am an American farmer, I thought, I'm not a communist. What do you want from me?

I didn't want to be drinking as much as I was. Then even the bourbon quit working and I was up at 2:07 every goddamn night. I don't know why, but I bolted awake at exactly 2:07 A.M. If I hadn't already had a little problem with the whiskey, I would of gotten me some sleeping pills.

Then we fought back. This time we were really going to do it! Lost 2,000 boys pushing back the Tet Offensive. And it took three-and-a-half goddamn weeks to find out here at Pecan Grove that Lincoln Lloyd was one of them. Willetta's the one that told Sidda. And Sidda told Vivi, and Vivi told me.

Four solid days and Chaney didn't come to work, didn't say a word. Willetta took off too, and our house went to pot. All we ate was grilled cheeses. I left for the duck camp and went on a three-day drunk for the first time since Daddy died.

My son, Little Shep, finally drove out there one afternoon and said, Daddy you got to come on home. You're gone, Chaney's not working. I don't know what to tell the rest of the workers to do. We got crops in the field.

I looked at my son, dressed in his jeans and a starched white shirt. Trying so hard to be a man. Freckles, even on his eyelids. I wanted to pull him to me and say, Don't let them take you, Shep. The fat gonna stay fat. They don't need your help.

He dripped us some coffee and I showered and followed him on back home. Vivi thawed out some crayfish *étouffée* and I ate it with some french bread and two glasses of milk. That *étouffée* smelled like the best of everything in this state. The crayfish was from my own bayou. I sat there at the table and ate it, all hot and spicy, and smeared some more butter on the french bread. You can travel to Paris, France, and not do any better eating than we do here in Louisiana.

We were all sitting down together at the table for the first time in I don't know how long.

Sidda had on that goddamn eyeliner she wore back then. And I told her, Get up and wipe that shit off your eyes if you want to eat at my table.

She said, This is not just your table. Don't take it out on us because you're upset about Lincoln.

I went to slap her upside the head, but she ducked and ran down the hall. War, it was hanging up in the air, crawling on the ground, swimming in the sea. It was rolling across my supper table.

I screamed: IT'S NOT MY GODDAMN FAULT! YALL HEAR ME? I DIDN'T START THIS. I DIDN'T WANT TO SEE LINCOLN LLOYD GET HIS JAW BLOWN OFF! I'VE KNOWN THAT BOY SINCE HE WAS A BABY.

I had to fight from crying. Couldn't catch my breath. The kids were staring at me, open-mouthed. I could feel the tight fingers squeezing my chest in.

Then Sidda was back in the room, holding something out to me. It was my inhaler. She put it in my hand and I reached out and pulled her to me. My boys looked confused. Lulu stared down at her food.

Vivi folded up her napkin and said, I will shoot my sons' big toes off before I let them go off and fight in a war.

That's the thing about my wife—she is crazy, but sometimes the woman can nail things right on the head.

*S*he was the one who eventually drove me down to the Negro funeral parlor. It was drizzling slightly, and there were little lamps on either side of the entrance to the building that made it look like something from long ago. It's funny—Chaney, Willetta, all of them came to Daddy's funeral, but I don't believe I'd ever set foot in their funeral home before. Going to that section of town at night was like being in a foreign country to me.

I asked her, Please Vivi, would you go in there and tell Chaney I'm out here, that I'd like to talk to him?

Then I waited in the Thunderbird with the window rolled down watching all the Negroes walk in and out. Dressed to the nines, some of them carrying umbrellas. Holding onto each other, handkerchiefs in their hands, hats on.

Everyone used to wear hats, I remember thinking. When did they stop? Are the Negroes the only ones who wear hats anymore?

Vivi stepped out of the funeral parlor and came back to the car. She sat in the driver's seat and stared straight ahead. She wasn't acting like her normal self, but who the hell was? She told me, Chaney says if you want to talk to him, you'll have to go inside.

I took out my pocketknife and started to clean my fingernails. Finally I said, Vivi, what should I do?

Her hands were on the steering wheel, gripping it and letting it go, gripping it and letting it go. Then my wife said, I am dog-tired of all this, Shep. It's got to stop somewhere.

This was the first time I'd ever seen Chaney in a suit. It was tight on him and the pants pulled across the front. He was sitting down holding Willetta's hands, and a little group of women was hovering around them. Their hands together looked so brown and wrinkled. Those hands looked for a minute like the earth itself.

And for the first time, I thought: Rice. *Those people over there grow rice.*

I was frozen. Couldn't take a step. I just stood there, staring at Willetta and Chaney. The man saw me, saw I couldn't move. He whispered something to Willetta and they both looked over at me.

If you've ever done a kind act in your life, Chaney, please get up now and walk over to me and help unglue me from this spot. I am paralyzed. I'm in the middle of battle and I can't move.

Somebody was humming and it was sweet and warm in there. You could smell how dressed up they all were. I felt a dizziness come over me and I thought, Lord, I'm going to faint in this funeral parlor full of grieving colored people.

And then there was Vivi slipping in the door. She had on her chapel veil like the Catholics used to wear back then. She took my arm and we walked across the room to Willetta and Chaney. I was standing right in front of him.

Vivi said, I came to tell you how very sorry I am, Chaney. I'm so sorry, Willetta. I want yall to know you are in my prayers.

Chaney looked at her and said, Thank you, Miz Viviane.

He did not include me in the thanks. I couldn't believe Vivi didn't say: *We* are sorry. She should of said *We* are sorry. For God's sake, I thought, she's my *wife*.

Why was she saying, I'll be waiting in the car?

I looked down at my hands. I was left totally alone in the middle of those people. Tiny flecks of dirt up under my nails. Can't a man ever get his hands clean enough? Chaney's fingers were twined up with Willetta's. His palms had a pinkness to them I never noticed before. I had tears dripping down my face. I don't know where all the tears come from. My sinuses are going to be swole up for hours, I thought.

Chaney, podnah, I finally said. Can you forgive me, buddy?

He lifted his eyes, locked them on me, and left them there. I don't think Chaney had looked at me for that long since I'd known him. And all I could do is stand there and bear it. If he'd stood up and punched me in the stomach, I could not of lifted an arm to defend myself.

He didn't punch me. He reached up and handed me his handkerchief. It smelled like Clorox. I can still see that old white cannon handkerchief passing from his hand to mine. His bloodshot almond eyes, his full face, that big chest of his bulging out of what I realized was one of my old suits. I couldn't use that handkerchief until he spoke.

Until he said, Yeah, bossman, *I* forgive you.

He said it like there was a bunch of others who wouldn't forgive me. I kept on looking at him. Finally he said, Go on now, blow your nose.

I resigned from the draft board a couple of months after that. Figured if I was going to do my civic duty, I'd do it on the Garnet River Levee Board, something that might benefit us farmers. We got flooding and drainage problems throughout all this part of the country. Hell, the Mississippi, Red, and Atchafalaya are powerful big rivers. You got to pay some attention to the land and water in your own state.

Old Lyndon Baines decided not to run again. Said he was going back to Texas. Said his daddy once told him that down home the people know when you're sick and care when you die. I never really thought the man meant to keep us in that war for so long. I feel for him. He ain't never had Chaney forgive him. There's a lot of us on Judgment Day that will be ripped outta our E-Z Boys and thrown into a hell we never dreamed of.

These days, years after my time on the draft board, I'll sit up at night and watch the Gulf War on CNN. And I'll be damned if I can get to sleep, even hours after I turn off the TV. So I'll lay awake and talk to the Old Podnah. I wouldn't exactly call it praying. I just lay there and talk to Him. And sometimes when I listen close enough, I can hear—past the wheezing in my chest—the sound of a heartbeat that isn't coming from my own body at all, but from the fields outside, from the dirt, from the old Louisiana earth.

PLAYBOYS' SCRAPBOOK
Chaney, 1991

I be takin it easy in my twilight years. I sit out here under the mimosa tree with my ice tea and work on my scrapbook. Oh, I got pictures of it all. Miz Siddy call me the family historian. That what she say. I got pictures of her when she was the Mardi Gras Queen, her hair all long, wearin a green sequin gown. Pictures she done sent Letta from when she was gone to Europe and Paris. That child done been more places than any of us here at Pecan Grove, her Mama included. Done been ever'where and done ever'thing.

I got me clippins of what-all Mister Big Shep done on the Levee Board. He a big man in drainage. Got my own picture with my grandson, Macon, holdin that seventy-pound squash we growed in my garden. Man come out from *The Monitor,* took our picture, put it right up there in the newspaper. Got me the clip where Mister Big Shep done got one of his DWIs up on Davis Street. Got me the big write-up they done on Mister Baylor Senior when he passed.

But I don't need no clip to put me to mind of that.

*M*ister Big Shep called me from the Louisiana Savings and Loan the day after they put the old man in the ground. When the phone rang, I be just settin down to my noon meal. Coolin off in the kitchen with a ice rag on my neck in front of the fan. I member lookin over to the windowsill at a sweet potato Letta got growin in a jelly jar. Toothpicks stuck in the side to hold it up, roots spreadin down into the water. Letta love it when them sweet potatoes shoot green leafs out the top. She get them to spread out all over the TV.

Mister Big Shep say, Chaney could you come down here to the bank and pick me up?

Man cuttin into my lunch time, ain't no rest for the weary. I say, Your truck broke down, bossman?

He say, Don't ask me no questions now, podnah. Just get your butt down here. Please.

Somethin must be bad wrong. That man don't never say "please" to me. I grab me a chunk of cornbread, get in my truck, go down there to fetch him. He be settin up in that air-condition bank with his legs crossed like he don't hardly never do. Look pale as a ghost. His own truck parked right out on the curb, but when I see that man try to stand up, I know why he done hollered for me. His hands both shakin and he havin so much trouble breathin, got his wheezer clenched tight in his fist. Tryin to act like things be hunky-dory, but when he stand up, he like to fall down. I reach out to steady him but he pull away. The man got tears in his eyes and he walkin all whompa-sided. Lord, I be thinkin, Mister Big Shep better not be drinkin this early in the day or we all in trouble!

We get on out to the truck and then Mister Big Shep

haul off and start to cryin like a baby. I don't say nothin, no way. Act like it be a regular thing for a grown white man to be slobberin all over hisself in the cab of my pickup truck. He choke up and stop hisself, put his hands on the dashboard like he holdin on for dear life.

He say: Chaney, My Daddy done died and left me a one-hundred-thousand-dollar debt to pay off. That's what the bastard done left me!

Then he take out that wheezer and pull some breath out of it, stuff it in his shirt pocket and light up a Camel. He keep those Camels in his shirt pocket, right along with the wheezer, back in those days. (I still smoked my L&Ms on the sly, so I can't put the man down.)

Now I ain't never heard nobody talk that much money before. Not real-like. Oh, sometime the phone ring and Letta say, I answer it! Might be a man wantin to give me a million dollars! Somethin like that.

But Mister Shep not jokin.

I ax him, Boss, where you want me to take you? You want me to run you on back to the house?

He say, Hell no, the last thing I want to see is Viviane and the kids.

Okay, I say, then where we goin?

I shoulda knowed better than to ax him. The man don't know what he want. He a lost sheep settin in the cab of my truck. So I head out Jefferson Street like I got good sense.

Fore long, Mister Big Shep say, Chaney, why don't you just drive us around? Just take us for a ride, okay podnah?

Well, I carry us on out to Madewood where his Daddy used to farm. Out on Bayou Latanier where all the Dutchmen farm. All thick with pecan trees. Mister Vanderlick be farmin over there, we help him with his harvest from time to time when he in a pinch. I drive down the turn-row till we get to the bayou. Then I stop the truck, open the door, and get out. Mister Big Shep just stay settin there like he froze to the seat.

I ain't got no air condition in my truck like he do in his. I open his door, say, Come on out, Boss, it be cooler out here.

We go set under that big old pecan tree by the bayou where Mister Baylor Senior used to pull up his black car and eat his biscuits, drink ice tea Miz Hallie done packed him. It was shady and we sat there and Mister Shep just go on and cry and cry. He be pitiful. He take his handkerchief out the pocket of his khakis and wipe his nose. He say: Chaney, what am I gonna do? I can't farm this family one-hundred-thousand dollars outta the hole. I can't do it. I need me a goddamn drink.

That what he all the time be sayin: I need me a drink. The man be suckin on the juice since he was a teenager. I can't talk, cause I used to be sippin my cold Jax beer back then myself. But Mister Big Shep, he talk about a drink the way some men talk about wantin a woman.

I tell him what Letta be tellin me all our life, say: Mister Big Shep, you gotta turn it over, is what you gotta do. You gotta give it to the Lord.

He pull out another Camel, take a puff, then snuff it out on the ground with his boot. He got on his dressy boots. That cigarette paper so white there in the good sandy soil. That dirt by the bayou be what we call our "ice-cream dirt." Good ground. Easy to work.

He say, We used to play down here, huh, Chaney?

Yessir, I tell him, we play down here all the time when your Daddy be workin this place.

He say, Chaney, podnah, I'm thirty-three years old. I got four kids and a crazy wife. I should of went to Tulane. I should of been a goddamn sonovabitch lawyer.

Oooh Lord, I hate it when they start to talkin like this. You don't hear no black men rattlin off all they missed opportunities. They didn't have no opportunities *to* miss! I just want to slap Mister Shep upside the head and say, Pull yourself up, boy! Quit bein such a titty baby!

He be black, I mighta done it. But you don't talk like that to a white man, no how, no way.

Boss, I tell him, You gotta quit feelin sorry. You got you three plantations to farm. Your Daddy done built you a brick house. You white, you a man, and you got chilren what need you. You got you some good soil.

If I could, I'd give you this land, Chaney, he say. You're the farmer.

Shoo, I say, I don't want it.

He let out a laugh, say: Shit, it's pathetic! I couldn't give this land away if I tried to! No one would touch it. No. They're not gonna let me walk away from my Daddy's debt.

You oughta thank the Good Lord you got two legs to stand on, I tell him.

He go on whinin. Son of a goddamn bitch, he say.

Only thing I could do with my inheritance is run off into the night.

I been workin with Mister Big Shep my whole life, and all I can say is, he sure be takin his time growin from a boy to a man. He done had ever'thing a man could want. His Daddy done bought him a convertible Buick when he wasn't but eighteen. Many a time I sat in that outhouse and wiped myself with newspaper wonderin where justice was at. Many a time I axed the Good Lord why Mister Shep was the boss and I was the nigger.

But lookin at him snifflin by that tree, all my envy just fall away, and I get to feelin light-like. Feel like someone reach and take a heavy coat off my back.

I feel that hot air, swat a fly offa my face and think: Ain't a thing he got I need. Ain't a thing he got that I want. He ain't nothin but a sad, scart white man, can't even breathe worth a damn. Me, I got a strong body what my Letta love, and I done learnt to roll with the punches from my Daddy. That's one thing I know, is how to roll with the punches. Mister Big Shep, he ain't learnt nothin from his Daddy but smokin and drinkin and how to sign a check. I go to church on Sunday, sleep good at night, and when there's a rain comin in, I stand out on my porch and smell the earth I been workin. Even if I don't own it, it's still mine.

Get up, Mister Shep, I tell him. Quit your cryin. Your people done had this land too long for you to lay down and die now.

He look up at me like a little boy, instead of a man only two–three years younger than me. Then he stand up, straighten his khakis, run his hand through his hair.

He say, Let's get on back to Pecan Grove. We're wasting time down here.

*M*aybe I oughta not tole the man to stop cryin. Maybe I shoulda just let him set on that bank under that tree, cryin till he couldn't cry no more. Sometime I think about that. Think about maybe Mister Big Shep heart done got all hard cause of tears he ain't cried. Tears bricked up in there and turned hard. Dammed-up rain that couldn't water what needed it.

I wish somebody could tell Mister Big Shep how good he got it. I been knowin the man since we was little playboys together. Since my daddy and uncles was workin for Mister Baylor Senior. I been knowin the man since he was three–four years old. And I ain't never known him to be satisfied.

Oh sure, he might have him a minute or two at twilight, after he done had his highballs and come drivin down the lane, say, Come on Chaney! Ride on back with me to look at the fields.

It'll be gettin dark, way after my worktime unless we be harvestin. But I get in the truck with him, and he got that glass of whiskey in his hand. And we ride on back there and look at the beans or rice or cotton or whatever we got in the ground. And you can see him startin to settle down for a minute. But that don't happen much. And when it do, it don't last long. Mainly what happen is the man worry hisself sick till he can't breathe most every day of his life.

These days seem like he pullin that wheezer outta his shirt pocket and suckin on it every time I look over. When he breathe sometime he sound like a Mack truck in his chest stuck in the mud. That's how bad it is. Sometime when I get up to pee in the middle of the night and step out on the porch to look at the stars, there he be—settin up, the light on in his room down the lane. I can see him in the easy chair next to the window, fightin to get a breath.

He ain't even got Miz Viviane in there with him. He don't sleep with her since she done move out that room years ago and took over the chilren's little school-room. I had to go up to the brick house and take the blackboards down off the wall in that room. When them kids come home and seen they blackboards and desks out on the carport, they look around so lost. I just stared at the ground to keep away from they eyes.

After that, Mister Big Shep and Miz Viviane act like bidness people in that brick house. When Miz Viviane tell me to do somethin, she say, Get it done before *The Master* come home. She made it up to call him The Master. I ain't never called him that and don't plan to.

Pecan Grove a beautiful place. Quiet and green and full of sweet dirt. Oh sure, they was a whole lot more trees years ago. Whole grove of old pecan trees fore Mister Big Shep done ripped them out to plant the rice and soybeans. Me and Letta used to pick those pecans and sell them down the road at Mansour's Grocery. After Mister Baylor Senior died, Mister Big Shep come back here all young and sad and bustin to pay back bills, ready to tear up anything got in his way. He dig in the earth and pull them trees out by the roots—took near-bout every bit of shade off this plantation. He say he could get a whole lot more for rice and beans than for any old pecans.

I don't judge the man for that. I don't judge the man for any of it. Judgin up to the Good Lord hisself and nobody else. Bossman punished hisself enough, the way all that dust blow through his house and into his lungs after he pull up them trees by the roots.

I don't worry much. You can't. I done worked hard to help Mister Big Shep pay off his debt. Shoo, there was times when I just wanted to knock him to the ground. (And I coulda done it easy, cause I always been a stronger man than him, ever since we was little.) Times when he cuss at me in the fields or when he say somethin smart when he handin over the payroll on Fridays. Or when he sent my baby brother overseas to get his jaw blowed off, tellin me it was Lincoln's "big opportunity." There's a lot I coulda said to that white man.

I set under my mimosa tree and think on things and mostly I don't worry about Mister Shep or none of the Walkers. Some people, they is gonna be unhappy no matter what. You could give them ever'thing you have. Take the blood out you own body and give it to them and they'd still be miserable. That just be the way it is.

Oh, Pecan Grove full up with beauty. I got my vegetable garden full of tomatoes and string beans. Letta got flowers ever'where you want to look. Zinnias, hibiscus, hydrangeas. She got something growin outta most every empty coffee can we done used in our life. She even got flowers growin outta a pair of Mister Big Shep's old boots he done throwed out. I bet there ain't no more peaceful place on the Good Lord's earth than here at Pecan Grove. Ain't no violence, no noise, no shootin, no drugs, like up on *Miami Vice.* I watch the

TV, I know what's goin on. No drugs here. Just my blood pressure pills and what Letta take for her iron. Things might be different up at the Walker house, but I be talkin bout *my* Pecan Grove.

We done had us a good life here. A hard-workin life. And when we could, we done had us some parties! Catfish cook-ups like you never saw. Settin out in the yard till way after dark, laughin and laughin. We done good with the hand the Good Lord dealt us. We done loved each other, uh-huh. We done raised two girls, and five grandchilren, and we got a great-granbaby gonna need tendin pretty soon. That is just the way life happen. We done lived down the road from sadness all our lives. But you gotta know what sadness be yours and what be somebody else's, is what I say.

Sometime Letta she be up at the brick house, tryin to fix ever'thing. Lookin out for those chilren. I can understand that. That been her main job here at Pecan Grove. She ain't never lost no sleep worryin bout whiter-than-white towels for Miz Viviane or servin for the parties. Only thing my Letta done lost sleep over is those chilren. She know them chilren good. You hand-wash a family's underthings and you learn more about them than you ever want to.

Letta done stood over there many a time and bite her lip, watchin Miz Viviane tear into them. Miz Lulu not wearin a brassiere one time for a date, and right in front of Miz Lulu's boyfriend, Miz Viviane done rip that shirt off her daughter. Just rip it open down the front and show her little titties. Letta say the shame on Lulu's face make her want to hit Miz Viviane herself but she didn't. She just walk down the hall and vacuum

Mister Shep's room. He like it vacuum twice a day to keep out the dust.

Letta done seen it all, and sometimes it like to break her heart. She lay next to me in bed and say, Chaney, I wouldn't trade my life for that central air condition, no way, no how.

Same as me, I tell her, and rub my hands on the back of her neck.

Sometime she cook special sweet things for them chilren, tryin to make up for the things she can't do. Sometime I holler: Letta! Pearl and Ruby hungry for sweet things too! But Letta do what she got to.

Only one time we done crossed over and butted in. When Miz Viviane like to beat them chilren dead outside the house. We step in then and Mister Shep give me his truck after that and a small raise. Never made no fuss at all.

*W*hen the sun set on this land, it look like heaven. I ax Miz Siddy when she call us from up North, Do they got sunsets like this? And she say ain't no sunsets like Pecan Grove anywhere else in the world. Siddy know what it like. The sky be all Easter colors and you can see the light shootin against that flat green land. You hearin the birds, crickets, cows, dogs, the one or two horses they got left. Across the bayou now is Bayou Estates, buncha big houses tryin to look like the Old South or what-have-you. Sometime you can hear they little chilren out on the driveways playin, which I like cause we ain't got as many kids round this place as we used to. The sound of chilren ain't never bothered me. It always sound like singin to me.

I know we goin to Mister Big Shep and Miz Viviane's funerals one of these days. I know the inside of
that Cromer Funeral Home where all they people been
laid out real good. I wonder, will they come to help
bury me and Letta when we pass? Only time they done
set foot in our funeral home is when Lincoln got kilt.
When Lincoln got kilt cause Mister Big Shep done put
him in a uniform.

We all four of us been workin together, day in and
day out—for, oh Lord, I don't know how long. We
done raised crops and chilren together, done kept that
brick house so clean you could eat off the floors. But
like Letta always say, Who wanna eat off a floor?

You think somebody gonna throw us a party or
somethin for gettin through all this? No sir. You don't
get no trophies for livin the life you born into. It just
be your job, and you lucky if you can do the work set
out in front of you and not fret if it seem puny. Maybe
the Good Lord ain't give us nothin *but* puny things.
Little bitta things sparkin through our days and nights.
In the fields and in the mornin air, little bitta things
that if you blink your eye, they be gone and ain't never
comin back.

So I set outside in the yard and paste things up in
my scrapbook. Pictures and news clippins, old ticket
stubs—oh, just all kind of things. I gotta get them all
in my book fore I lose thought of them. Time fly so
fast, you gotta get it down in the book. I put all kind
of stuff up in there. Siddy, one time she throw out a
bunch of old school pictures, I just lift them out the
trash and paste them little Catholic white chilren in my
book. Some of them I don't even member they names,

but they friends of Miz Siddy's and call my mind back to that time.

And pictures of Letta and Pearl and Ruby. All my jewels. From the day we was married, to the babies on Letta's hips, to when Pearl got her the job over at the Wal-Mart. Pictures of Letta laughin. Oooh that woman, how she laugh and look at me like she do. How she walk in the house to take off her church clothes, lookin so good in her hat, and me followin behind. And her sayin, Chaney, who love you? And us crawlin up into bed in the afternoon with the sound of the girls playin on the porch, and the fan whirrin, and Letta lovin me till ever'thing that ever hurt me fall away.

Siddy she call me The Philosopher. Such a sweet child. I wish her Daddy knew that fore he draw his last hard breath. One of these days I'm gonna tell him. Gonna tell him, Mister Shep listen to me: It be good to know you chilren done turn out sweet. It make ever'thing less bitter. It be one of the savin things.

*M*e and Mister Big Shep was playboys that ran together when we was little, and now we old. That the way it is, old white man with your wheezin chest. I be settin down the lane watchin you. And whatever you took from me, I don't want it back. I didn't need it nohow. I'm gettin lighter every day and don't wish you nothin but easy breathin.

In my book I got it all. All what me and Letta done accomplished here. My book hold all my success, it hold my sorrow, it hold my harvests, it hold my heart.

LOOKING FOR MY MULES
Viviane, 1991

*I*t was getting near sunset. Shep had already come in from the fields and was back in his bathroom taking a shower. I was in the kitchen and could hear the evening farm report on the radio when I was sitting at the counter doing my nails. Over the years, all that droning on about drainage and moisture content—it bothers me less and less. Now it's like a kind of background chant, like Latin used to be at Mass before the Church went all Kumbayah and guitar Masses on me.

Charlie Vanderlick had just come by bringing us some of his snap beans. That Charlie's thumb gets greener every year. Little Shep had just left out for home after having a drink with me. That wife of his, Kane, won't let him drink in his own house. She runs that place like a lady general. The girl is so damn tall and tailored—it's no wonder she's no fun. Watched too much *Donna Reed* growing up, if you ask me.

I've already brushed my teeth and gargled with Listerine so Shep won't know I've had any whiskey. He can smell bourbon a mile off. The man hasn't touched a drop for six months now, because according to that know-it-all doctor he's seeing, it aggravates his asthma.

I pretend to go along with the drinking ban, just to try and keep things peaceful. Shep's had his beans in since mid-April and now he's putting in the rice. And he's planting trees. All I hear about is his tree-planting program. He's turning into an ecology nut, if you ask me. If I didn't still have a drink or two, I'd be bored into an early grave.

Nobody wants to have fun anymore. If they're not tee-totaling, they're cutting out sugar or fat or cholesterol. Drives me batty. I've been smoking and drinking and dyeing my hair since I was twelve years old. And I could do an Oil of Olay commercial if I wanted to—that's how good I still look.

I can tell we're going to have a marvelous sunset this evening the way the pinks are already starting to strut across the sky. God, I love my sunsets more than I do hamburgers! I try not to miss a single one if I can help it. I'm looking straight out the picture window when I see this old black man right out there on our gravel road. One I've never laid eyes on before.

He must be about eighty, but who knows? If I could bottle how well blacks hide their age, I'd be as rich as the Rothschilds. He's got him this old cypress limb for a walking stick and he's walking along pretty quick, like he's got to be somewhere. Real neat and respectable old fellow, you know—no bum or what-have-you. Got on a clean white shirt and a pair of overalls like all the coloreds used to wear. And there's all this gray hair on his black head that makes him look almost—well, you hate to say it: downright distinguished. He's not looking from side to side, he's looking straight ahead—like he's got an appointment to keep, like he's got a purpose.

Now I know that I haven't ever seen him before. He looks like an old field hand, but I'm absolutely positive I have never laid eyes on him. Not even when Shep first brought me out to Pecan Grove before we were married. Not even when I ruined umpty-ump pairs of high heels tromping through the mud, oohing and ahhing over the man's land. I can remember the faces of all the Negroes who have come and gone over the years, and I have not ever seen this one before.

I get the binoculars out of the recipe drawer and focus them on him. I always keep those binoculars handy. You never know when something will come up that you need to take a closer look at. The thing that gets me is how damn *determined* he looks. Determination is the one of the virtues I've always envied, believe it or not. I think, Well I'm just gonna leave him alone. Even though he is trespassing. Even though we have got the Private Property/No Trespassing sign out there clear as day.

He walks past the house without so much as a look my way. When he gets to the cattle gap, he just walks right over it like nothing is going to get in his way. I walk out to the driveway and keep looking at him through the binoculars.

Nothing much happens. He just goes on walking. I go on back inside and steal a little sip of vodka, take a steak out of the refrigerator. Shep likes to eat his supper on time these days.

I sit back down with the *Monitor*. No good news. I

can hardly stand to read the paper anymore. I read my "horrible-scope," like Shep calls it, and the funnies, and that's about it. We got enough to handle right here at Pecan Grove without worrying about the Iraqis and Kuwaitis and what-have-you. They bought up half of the Carolina coast as it is. Some of my favorite spots are now owned by sheiks, which doesn't really bother me one way or the other, as long as they still serve good soft-shell crab.

I had halfway gotten the old man out of my head when Shep walks into the kitchen, all clean from his shower, heading out to the utility room to clean his fingernails. I will always love the way that man cleans his fingernails after every single day in the fields. And does it in the utility room, not in the bathroom. Those are the kinds of things that keep you married to a man, even when everything else is not what you dreamed on your wedding day when your waist was still small and your feet were tiny.

I follow him out to the utility room and tell him: Babe, an old black fellow walked by a little while ago. Nobody we know.

Shep keeps on scrubbing his fingernails. I am sick and tired of people roaming onto this farm like they own the place, he says. Can't they read the sign? Goddamn it, I don't know what it's coming to, a man can't even own private property anymore.

Well babe, I don't know, I tell him. He doesn't look like he'd *bother* anyone.

Oh yeah, probably just an escaped convict, Shep says.

Shep does not like strangers on his property. In fact, I've wondered sometimes if he really likes *anybody* on his property. Seems like every single time I go and knock myself out to throw a dinner party, he'll get up soon as we finish dessert and walk back to his room. A few minutes'll pass, then he'll come back out with nothing on but his boxer shorts and say, Goodnight everybody. Don't let me keep you. Yall remember where your car keys are?

And that's the last we'll see of him. The Ya-Yas are used to this kind of behavior, but it mortifies me when he does it to somebody new. None of it has been easy on me. I'm a born socializer, I adore entertaining. I was born to throw dinner parties. They are one of the truly fine things in life. Even the Catholic Church hasn't been able to find a single bad thing to say against dinner parties.

Shep dries his hands and heads out to his truck. Well, I'm gonna see what the hell is going on back there, he says.

Well, I'm coming with you, I tell him. And we get into the truck and head out to the back fields.

I don't think Shep will ever know how lovely it still is for me to ride in that truck with him. There is just something so—oh, I don't know—sexy about the inside of pickup truck that a man has been working in all day. The smell of the sun and dust and Shep's body. I guess I will just always be a sucker for a man in a pickup truck. I guess that's why I have put up with so much shit over the years. I hear the sound of the man's voice on the telephone after a day of being apart and it still gives me goosebumps. I still have it bad for him, even though I've lived down the hall for so many years. There is no accounting for chemistry.

The day I decided to marry Shep, I was standing inside the River Street Cafe. It was after the War, after I lost my first love, my true love. I looked up and saw him pull up in a red pickup, watched him swing down out of the cab before hardly coming to a stop. He was wearing blue jeans, cowboy boots, and a starched white shirt with the sleeves rolled up. When I saw how the hair on his arms was bleached blond from the sun, it took my breath away. That very evening I told Caro and Necie and Teensy they could stop saying Novenas for me to get married. I had found my man and that was it.

Maybe if I'd been born later, I wouldn't have even gotten married. I'd have enjoyed what I wanted, then moved on. Enjoyed that convertible Buick Shep used to drive, and the way he'd lay his head on my lap when we'd park out at Little Spring Creek. And just let it go at that. Not sign up for life, for four kids and farm reports, day in and day out. But I was born before you could do what you wanted. That's what my children will never understand.

We head on back, not driving too fast. Shep points out the new drainage system he's been putting in for the rice. I swear the man knows more about drainage than the Army Corps of Engineers. It's a damn shame he didn't finish college. He could've made something of himself.

We slow down when we get back by the canal. Then we spot the old black man. You can just feel *intention* all over the man. He's got the look of a person who knows he's got a job to finish but can't find where he left off. He stands there looking at the ground, then out at the fields. Then he shades his eyes and squints off into the distance, like he's waiting for somebody to show up.

Shep calls to him from the truck. What you want, podnah?

Shep's got that gruff voice he gets when he doesn't know what's going on. I hope he won't be too rough on this old fellow.

The old guy says, Yassir. I be lookin for my mules. Name of Sary and Mike.

Shep says, Ain't no mules here, old man. This is my farm. All we got is my machinery.

The old man doesn't even hear Shep. He's in another world. He puts his hands back above his eyes and keeps staring out.

Sary! he calls out. Where you at, girl? Get you bad self over here. Sary! Sary! We got work to do.

Podnah, Shep says, We're gonna have to give you a ride out of here. This is my land.

And Shep gets out of the truck. He takes the man by the arm and helps him into the back of the pickup. Then we drive past the house and up toward Pecan Road leading into town. When we get to the paved road, Shep goes round to the back and helps the old man out, then he gets back in the cab. I can see the old fellow standing there on the blacktop, his head kind of cocked to the side like he's trying to get his bearings. Shep doesn't say anything and we drive back to the house.

Soon as we get there, he goes on back to his bedroom like he's hiding. Me, I stay in the kitchen. That sunset is taking its time, spreading out all over the flat fields, and I don't want to miss it.

If I miss a sunset, my next day is never a good one. It's one of my superstitions. If I miss a sunset, I have to consult the Ouija board. I've done that religiously ever since the kids left. It's part of my schedule. That's the reason I had so much trouble when all four of them were still at home: I couldn't stick to my schedule. They can laugh—but between Mass, sunsets, Ouija board, cocktails, and maybe a snippet of a prescription pill, I do fine. I've put together my own package. Anybody says something to me about it, I tell them: Don't knock it if you haven't tried it.

I've hardly started sprinkling the T-bone with Lea & Perrins when Freddy comes flying up on his little bike. Freddy's one of the kids I got to know after my four left. Lives up on Pecan Road, cutest little thing, big ears that stick out from his head. His daddy works for the phone company. I used to let his big sister crayfish in our bayou and she would bring him with her. I have known him since he was in diapers. I'm the one that helped him get over his fear of dogs. He just adores me, thinks I'm the greatest.

Anyway, he comes spinning up and calls out, Miz Vivi! Miz Vivi!

I light myself a ciggie and walk on out to the carport. How you, Mister Freddy? I ask.

Fine, Miz Vivi, he says.

Don't you ever start this filthy habit, you hear me? I tell him, pointing to my cigarette.

He's all worked up, though. He says, Miz Vivi, there's a black man just wandering around up on the road! You want me to bring him back to Mister Shep?

I think for a minute, then I tell him, Yeah dahlin, why don't you do that?

And he pedals off like his hair's on fire. I walk back to Shep's bedroom. He is laying back in his chair, watching Dan Rather on TV.

Baby, I tell him, That old man is still hanging around.

Damn, Shep says. A man works all day in the fields, he wants to be left alone. Can't I get any peace and quiet anywhere?

Don't get cross with me, I tell him. I just thought you'd want to know.

I fix myself a splash of vodka on the rocks and call up Caro. Her damn machine answers. All I get is that damn machine, ever since she started that travel-agent job. It makes me sick. I call Necie, but they're sitting down to dinner. I try Chick and Teensy, then I remember they're in Florida. I hate it when there's nobody to talk to on the phone with, I just detest it! I'd call over to Little Shep's, but that tight-ass wife of his told me that "any time after five is a very busy time in our home." I sit out on the swing and smoke three cigarettes in a row, because I will be damned if I start picking on food and gain weight just because this town is so goddamn boring.

Shep comes out and I stub out my cigarette. We both go out and stand on the carport next to the basketball hoop that we put up when the kids were little. It's funny to look at that thing now. Nobody plays basketball around here anymore, but if someone was to rip that thing down, the whole front of this house would look naked. Strange how things stick with a house. Like the insides of all my lampshades where Little Shep wrote his name when he first discovered Magic Markers. God, that child adored Magic Markers! Loved the way they smelled, love the way they squeaked when he wrote his name with them. I just hated having to whip him, he loved them so much. But still, the inside of every lampshade in my house was ruined by him scrawling: Little Shep, Little Shep, Little Shep.

I stand there next to my husband, not saying anything. When you're married nearly forty years, you don't always need to talk every second. I would go stark-raving nuts if I had to *discuss* everything, the way Sidda wants us all to do.

I'm just about to go in and powder my nose when Freddy and the old black man finally show up. Freddy's walking his bike, looking like he thinks he's a real important messenger.

Shep walks down there, and I can tell by the set of his shoulders he wishes this fellow had never shown up in the first place. Shep says: I told you to move on from here, old man. What you doing still hanging around?

I be lookin for my mules, the old fellow says, Sary and Mike.

Podnah, I done *told* you, there are no mules anywhere around here. This is my place, Pecan Grove, and there aren't any mules.

I step down closer to the two of them. What do you want those mules for? I ask.

That black man looks at me like I don't have good sense. He says, I gotta start my plantin is why.

And that's when Shep's gruffness just melts away, and I start to understand what's going on. Shep stands there silent. For a minute I think he's going to turn around and walk back inside and hide again. He's done that eighty-four thousand times before, God knows. Walked away and left me to deal with everything. But this time he just keeps standing there.

I say, Well why don't we go and have a seat?

I have always found that if you are ever in doubt about how to behave, just act like a hostess, and it'll get you over the rough spots.

The black man nods politely at me and I lead him and Shep over to the swing, where the two of them sit down. Shep has gone mute, but what else is new?

Why don't I go and get us something to drink? I say.

Thank you, ma'am, the old man say. Shep just nods.

I go into the kitchen and pour us each a 7-Up over ice in my plastic glasses. I put a splash of vodka in with mine, and reach up in the medicine cabinet and bite off half a Valium, which is almost nothing. Valium and vodka make a good cocktail, but you absolutely *have* to get your amounts exactly right. I have no desire to get carried off to The Betty Ford Center, I don't care how many movie stars I could meet there.

Back outside, I hand them each their cold drinks and they both say, Thank you.

Finally Shep finds his tongue and asks, Where you work, podnah?

The old man replies, Over to Dr. Jackson's place in Bunkie, Louisiana.

Uh-huh, Shep nods and stares down at the ground.

I wish he'd look at me, share something with me, but he just stares at the ground. We both know that Brainard Jackson's been dead for eight years. His children sold the farm for the new Garnet Parish Golf and Country Club. The only black men working over there now are the young ones who keep that golf course groomed and park the cars.

The old fellow just murmurs again, like he's chanting, like he's praying: Gotta find my mules. Gotta start my ploughin. A man can't dawdle this time of year.

I sit there in the lawn chair, holding my cigarette away from them so the smoke won't bother Shep. (He will only let me smoke outside now because it irritates his asthma.) The pinks and yellows and blues of the sky all over those green fields look gorgeous, and light spills on Shep and the old man. I can feel my cocktail start to leak through my bloodstream a little and my neck starts to relax. This is my favorite time of day.

All Shep does is look at his hands. Finally he talks and it's like it hurts him to make the sounds. Where you stay at now? Shep says.

Over to my daughter's, the man replies.

Where's that? Shep asks.

The old man looks at him, but all he answers is, Gotta find my mules.

I feel like a Peeping Tom, witnessing the look in Shep's eyes. He leans back in the swing and takes a sip of his 7-Up, and tears start to well up in his eyes. I swear that man just cries over everything these days.

Here he is, sitting on the swing, a sixty-four-year-old man with tears streaming down his cheeks. All the things he has done to me, all that he has taken from me and hurt me with, and he has never cried about them. But he can sit here and cry over an ancient colored man he doesn't even know. There is no justice in the world for me.

What about me? He's a stranger! I want to scream. But I don't. I don't say a word. I have worn myself out trying to help people. And I have never gotten a damn bit of recognition for all my effort.

You don't have to tell me why he's crying. He's seeing the shopping mall and the subdivision that took over the cotton fields he used to work. Seeing the 7-Eleven that took down his favorite pecan tree where they used to stop the flatbed trucks and set up the water cooler. He's seeing all the fields and fields of farmland that he'd known all his life, and the kids diving into truckloads of cotton. Seeing himself follow *his* Daddy around, learning how to tell exactly what was happening with a cotton plant. He's seeing Little Shep and Baylor when he taught them to farm. And then seeing both of them walk out of here with no interest at all in getting dirt under their fingernails.

Old man, he asks, how far did you have to walk to find my farm?

Well, nobody needs to answer that question. He knows the man had to walk at least five, six miles before he found anything except the Taco Bell and Wal-Mart, Carpet World and Minute-Lube. The old man doesn't breathe a sound. And Shep slumps over in the swing and sobs until his chest is heaving up and down, until he has to take out his inhaler and draw on it. In spite of all he has done to me, I still want to hold him. But I sit there and leave him alone. I have gone to him too many times and had him turn me away.

The old Negro sits perfectly at ease with his walking stick across his lap. Like he knows just what his business is and he can sit and wait just as long as he needs to, thank you kindly. The sun is getting lower and lower.

I look at the rows of pine trees that ring the yard, thirty feet tall now, and I can remember the day they were planted. I look out at the mailbox and think of the five-million times I ran out there in the middle of a hot summer afternoon, believing that something would arrive that would change my life. I stare at my own hands, the way the veins pop up now, no matter how much lotion I rub on them. My nails still look good, but these are the hands of an old person, and you can't go around wearing gloves in 1991 unless you *really* want them to think you're batty.

Vivi, will you go inside and get me the cordless phone? Shep asks me.

I'm relieved to get away from all this silence. It's just getting to be too much, sitting there with a strange Negro and a sobbing husband. I walk into the kitchen where you can smell the Lea & Perrins I'd started to put on the T-Bone. I stick that cut of meat back in the refrigerator, because we don't need ptomaine poisoning here at Pecan Grove, on top of everything else.

The kitchen and the breakfast room are spotless. Between having Letta in three times a week and no kids here anymore, this place is like a mausoleum. It's almost cool with the sun nearly down. I could turn off the fans if I wanted to, but I love our ceiling fans in the evening. I have to admit Shep was right when he had them put in, even though we've got central air conditioning.

I go back to Shep's bathroom, pick up the cordless phone, and walk down the hall with it in my hand. This is such a big house now with all of the kids gone. I swear—we've got more phones and TVs in this place then we do people. Sometimes I round a corner and think I hear one of the kids calling out, Mama, look at me! Look at me! And I'll turn my head, but nobody's there.

It was all so fast and furious—having them, raising them, watching them go. I thought when Baylor left: *Alright now, this is when my life can begin!* But it never did begin and I can't tell you why.

Walking through that house with the cordless phone makes me feel like an astronaut who got disconnected from his spaceship. With just the two of us living here, I have all the quiet I want. I have too much quiet. I mean there are just so many Sidney Sheldons you can read. I go to the movies with Necie twice a week, I get my hair done. I used to do my volunteer work at the Veterans Hospital—until they got so bossy about making us wear those tacky little uniforms that I had to tell them where to get off. I look at other women my age sometimes and I think: Maybe I should look all content like that. Maybe I should be pulling out pictures of grandchildren and oohing and ahhing. Maybe I should be happier. But those women are fat as hell and I still weigh only four pounds more than I did the day I graduated from Thornton High. I look ten years younger than any of them.

I don't know, it all just came and went before I had a chance to realize. One day I was head cheerleader at Thornton High, then I lost the twin, and the next thing I know, Sidda is grown-up and talking to me like she's some kind of refugee with a Ph.D. in psychology.

You can't blame me for any of it. I had no idea in God's world that DDT was poison. We didn't know what was and wasn't poison back then. You didn't even think about such things. It is not my goddamn fault if it caused Sidda's breathing problems. I didn't know about smoking, either. A mother can't know everything in the G.D. universe. I did my best.

You don't have to tell me what Sidda was thinking when she asked for that picture of me and Caro taken at the kitchen table in 1952. I'm eight-and-a-half months pregnant in that photo and so is Caro. Both of us sitting at that round oak table. Had our feet propped up on the table, smoking Luckies, sipping a little bourbon and branch, reading Dr. Benjamin Spock. Necie took the picture. I remember where she was standing, right next to the drainboard where I had some chicken thawing out. I know why my oldest child wanted that picture. I am not ignorant. To bring it to her group, where they all sit around and whine while she tells lies about the way I raised her.

But I just handed over the damn photo like she asked. I didn't want my saying No to be one more thing she can add to her litany of abuses. She's got the world thinking I'm Joan Crawford as it is. Even though I never once touched them with a coat-hanger.

Hell, I was just trying to stay alive. Four kids in four years and eight months, and a husband who did nothing but farm and duck hunt. Even when he was home, he wasn't really here. Cook, clean, wash crappy diapers, wipe runny noses, listen to him run on about goddamn drainage ditches. That's not what I was raised for, that's not why I was created! I am not a goddamn maid. I have a bachelor's degree from Ole Miss in Speech, not in Home-fucking-Ec. I used to be so much fun. I lived to laugh, to make other people laugh. Then I started praying, I started confessing once a week, I studied the lives of the G.D. saints. I tried to be holy, but nothing stopped the shakes like a bourbon and branch.

Sidda can't explain this to her friends, I don't care how many books she reads on the subject. She hates me now. She divorced me without even handing me any papers.

When I get outside, I hand Shep the cordless phone and he calls the sheriff's department. Evening, he says. This is Shep Walker out at Pecan Grove. I got me a old black man out here and he is, well he's. . . . Then he chokes up with tears and can't talk.

For heaven's sake! I think. And he has always said *I* was the dramatic one. I reach over and take the phone from him. Hello dahling, I say. Vivi Abbott Walker here. Look, we've got an old man out here at our farm and he says he's looking for his mules.

The man on the other end says, What?

I say, Mules.

Shep yells out, Mules, damn it! Doesn't anyone even remember mules?

I tell him, Shhh, babe, I'll handle this.

My husband is acting like a big fat baby, I swear to God. You simply must have decent telephone manners in this world or you will get absolutely nowhere.

He is looking for his mules, I explain to the man on the phone. Mules, like they used to plough with. We're calling because the old fellow can't remember where he lives. And I think one of yall should come out here and get him and help him find his daughter's house. Yessir, that's right. Pecan Grove.

Only undeveloped land at the end of Jefferson Street Extension, Shep says.

Did you hear that? I ask the man. No, it's *past* Bayou Estates subdivision.

Shep takes the phone away from me and says, Listen, podnah, send out one of your black officers, would you? This is a fine old gentleman here, this is a fine old man, I don't want you to shake him up.

Shep clicks off the cordless phone and stares out at the last of the sunset. The old man starts humming a song Letta and them used to sing. It amazes me to watch how comfortable the old man is, sitting there like we had just called up and ordered the sheriff's department to bring his mules out to him, right on the double.

We all three of us sit there not saying a word. Part of me wants to sob, and part of me wants to scream bloody-murder. Part of me wants to take Shep by the throat and yell, You care more about this old black man than you do about me!

But I don't say a word. I will not be dragged away from Pecan Grove in my old age because they claim

I'm nuts (like certain people have implied when they thought I wasn't sharp enough to know exactly what they were saying). They don't know what sharp is. I have been sharp as a tack my whole life, so nobody better even *try* to fool me. No, I have suffered too much on this plantation to get carted away because of one unguarded moment.

We sit that way for—oh, I don't know—about fifteen minutes. Until I'd seen at least two lightning bugs over by the clothesline. When the sheriff's car pulls into the driveway, Shep gets up and walks over to the officer and I follow behind him. The officer is indeed a black one—young and handsome, I am ashamed to admit. But I have always loved a man in uniform.

Shep says to the officer, Look you know how us old farmers get when spring rolls around. Got to get those seeds in the ground. The old man's looking for his mules. Help him find where he lives. Help him find his home.

And then Shep opens the front passenger door and helps the old man in most respectfully. The car backs out, and the old man rolls down the window and calls out to Shep: I sho nuff hope the Good Lord give us enough rain this year!

Shep walks over to the car and leans down to him, puts his hand on the man's shoulder and says, I do too, podnah, I do too.

Then the sheriff's car pulls out of the driveway with the headlights on and takes off down the gravel road toward town. Shep watches until it's out of sight, then he stares out into the field where the beans have disappeared in the dark. He stands that way for a good long time with his hands in his pockets. When he turns to me, his eyes are so soft and serious.

He says, It goes by so fast, Vivi, it just goes by so goddamn fast.

I know, babe, I tell him and try to hook my arm through his.

But he turns and walks up the drive saying, I'm hungry. It's way past suppertime.

Oh God, I think, it's such a good life, but it *hurts!*

*A*fter supper I fall asleep, but for some reason I wake up after only a couple of hours. I get up and go into the kitchen and fix myself a Coke over crushed ice. *I will tell him that I still love him,* I think.

I will tell him that when we are old and looking for our mules, we don't have to be alone, we can help each other.

I rinse out my Coke glass and put it in the dishwasher. Then I walk down the hall to Shep's room. I start to knock on the closed door, but I think, No, I will just go and sit on the edge of his bed, touch his shoulder, and say his name softly so I don't startle him.

I reach down to open the door, try to turn the knob to the right.

The door is locked.

There are only the two of us in this house and he has locked his door before going to sleep.

I will never let him hurt me again as long as I live, I say to myself. As I walk back down the hall, I say it over and over to myself. One of these days I will learn.

I grab my cigarettes and walk out into the back yard.

That candy-cane striped swing set we bought the kids years ago still sits out there, looking ridiculous. I look up at the stars and say a prayer straight up to Heaven: Please, do not give me any more than I can handle. I am a strong woman, but don't push me. *Don't push me, Lord, you hear me!*

I finish that cigarette, then I go in and get back into bed. I need to lay back and give up. I need to surrender for at least one night, for at least eight-and-a-half hours. I look like crap if I don't get enough sleep. My eyes get all puffy and I'm cranky as hell. I need my beauty rest. I always have.

THE FIRST IMPERFECT DIVINE COMPASSION BAPTISM VIDEO

Siddalee, 1991

I'm a godmother now.

Baylor called me while I was directing a new play at a small house on Theater Row.

We've named her after you, he said, and we're going to call her Lee. She's beautiful, looks exactly like you. We'll wait till after your show opens to have her baptized.

End of October alright? I asked.

Sure, he said. October is the only decent month in this state.

I direct plays. It's nice work if you can get it. I make about the same amount of money as a teenage golf caddy, but I like what I do. When I'm not in Manhattan, I'm at regional theaters in places like Milwaukee or Seattle. I go where the work is, season to season. Like a migrant worker. I love studying a script on the page, then presiding over the accidents that occur when the actors let their bodies lead them. The whole process, from first read-through to opening night, feels like a series of tiny miracles to me—one person's thoughts getting transformed into flesh and movement and conversation and thousands of gestures.

I don't go back to Louisiana very often. It makes me too sad. I get an emotional hangover for months afterward. There's too much danger of getting sucked back into the swamp I've learned to crawl out of—or at least swim through.

I'm not what you'd call a serene person, but I'm not a walking nerve-end either. Let's just say that with a lot of work, I've managed not to become a full-fledged Junior Ya-Ya. I have one main rule for myself these days: *Don't hit the baby.* It means: Don't hurt the baby that is *me.* Don't beat up on the little one who I'm learning to hold and comfort, the one I'm trying to love no matter how raggedy she looks. It's sort of a code, a shorthand of the heart.

I murmur *Don't hit the baby* when I wake up, when I ride the subway, when I board a plane, when I step into a theater. I whisper *Don't hit the baby* before I go to sleep. And on the nights when I make it through without a futon-soaking nightmare, I know I've breathed it like a prayer during my sleep. You can read all the books and spend a small fortune on therapy, but that one sentence just about covers it all.

It takes me weeks to prepare myself for the trip home for Lee's baptism. One day I'm fantasizing how warm and loving and familiar it will all be and how much everyone will have changed. Then that same night I'm having one of the old familiar nightmares where I must swim for hours through a black ocean looking for the boat Mama and Daddy are about to capsize in. I swim until my whole body aches. I wake with my neck hurting. I wake up needing to rest from the night's sleep.

It's a blessing to have to show up at the theater each day. To block the show, to feel for pacing, to go over last-minute lighting cues and costume changes, to bird-dog the ten-thousand things that lead up to opening night—when you stand in the back of the theater and hold your breath.

The day after the show opens, I sleep fourteen hours, see my therapist for one last emotional rehearsal, then have dinner with my best friend, Connor.

He gives me six of those little Guatemalan worry dolls in a little pouch, and says, Don't forget: While you're in Louisiana, blue-green coral is still growing on the ocean floor.

Connor is a scenic designer/carpenter/sometime writer with a fascination for Salinger. He leaves messages on my machine like "Sidd! Listen up! J.D. was spotted in Queens at a retirement party for an old policeman friend of his. This is fact. Believe it." For the past year we've worked together and played together, and even spent the night at each other's apartments after late nights at the theater or watching videos about Delta folk artists. We haven't made love yet, though. Not because the chemistry isn't hot, but because Connor feels too important for me to risk blowing everything by sleeping together. On good days, I tell myself: Hold on. If it's meant to be, it'll happen. You have all the time in the world. Our friendship, or whatever you want to call it, is one of my main comforts. With Connor I get to rest.

You get to Thornton by flying through Dallas–Fort Worth, usually with a long layover. From there, you take a Royale Air Lines commuter plane, which does not even have a bathroom. There isn't a big demand for flights to my hometown. I can't imagine why.

During my layover at DFW, I locate the non-sectarian chapel. It's a small room with about eight wooden benches that face this huge oil painting. Someone received divine inspiration and probably a hefty commission from the Port Authority to paint a Boeing 747 flying through a terrible storm. Flying right alongside the plane is this huge figure of Jesus. His hands hold the plane up, like if it weren't for Him, that plane would crash in a second and kill everybody involved. His hands curl under the belly of that plane, like the Boeing engineers had designed the body of the plane with just such a thing in mind. I stand in front of the painting for so long that it finally stops looking like the sentimental trash that gets sold on the side of the highway and begins to make a deep kind of sense to me.

I am really losing it, I think, and go to sit on one of the benches. I swallow half a Xanax, then take a *People* magazine out of my carry-on, but I cannot get too worked up about Madonna's latest exploits. I keep thinking about Thornton in October. I haven't been back to Louisiana in three years, and my heart starts pounding and my breathing gets ragged every time I picture the streets of that town. I put down *People* and take the worry dolls out of my purse, checking to make sure my asthma inhaler is still there. I pour the tiny figures out of their little blue striped handmade pouch into my hand. Six of them—one each for Mama, Daddy, Little Shep, Lulu, Baylor, and me. I walk up to the painting and line them up along the frame like little offerings.

Here, J.C., I think, You take care of them. I'm tired.

It's nighttime when my plane lands in Thornton. I get off the plane and walk across the cracked tarmac to the terminal. I can see the same tired hair-netted waitresses still serving hamburgers in the airport café. Or maybe these women are their daughters. Every Sunday night when I was seventeen, I used to drive out to the airport to watch planes and dream about where they would someday deliver me.

I can still smell that chemical-sweet, faint aroma of cotton poison hanging in the autumn air, exactly the way it smelled twenty years ago. There is the forgiving coolness in the air that Louisiana gets in late October, a coolness that seems kinder than anywhere else in the world—if only because the heat and humidity which preceded it were so cruel.

Baylor comes forward and hugs me. Welcome home to Wackoville, he says. See? I told you it'd be nice when you got here. It's football weather!

He checks me into the Theodore Hotel, the restored 1920s hotel downtown on the river. It's a gracious old building with potted palms and ceiling fans in the lobby. There are desks where you can actually sit and write letters, like people used to do when they were away on a trip and thinking of the folks they had left behind. Mama and Daddy had their wedding reception in the huge hotel ballroom with the mirrors and the crystal chandeliers. There are very few pictures of that event, however, because the photographer got as smashed as the rest of the guests.

After Baylor carries my bags and unlocks the door to my room, he turns on one of the brass lamps above the bed. See, Sidda? he says. There's a ceiling fan even in the room! He turns it on and its whirring freshens the stale hotel air. Bay walks over to the French doors and pulls open the curtains, and we step out on a small balcony that overlooks the Garnet River. I can smell the water and the loamy earth.

Baylor says, It's not so bad, huh? I mean, it's not the Plaza, but it's not bad for Thornton.

Then he opens up the antique armoire that holds a huge color TV. He turns the TV set on for background noise and walks into the bathroom to break the toilet-seat banner—our ritual as kids whenever Mama and Daddy took us to hotels.

It makes me laugh. Aw, why didn't you let me do it?! I say.

He walks over and leans down to open the small refrigerator. Look, he points out proudly: Anything you want. You're uptown, baby. Toasted almonds, Godiva chocolate, they even got a split of champagne in here. You want anything else, just call room service and charge it.

Then he turns to me and asks, Is it okay? I mean, the room and all?

Oh sweetie, I assure him, it's lovely. It must be costing you a fortune.

This is not New York, he says. Don't even think about it. These are to the rental car, he explains, and hands me a set of keys. It's down in the parking lot. A red Tempo. It has a good air conditioner. I checked. And FM. No tape deck, sorry.

Thank you, Bay, I tell him.

He sits on the bed awkwardly and examines my luggage. I can tell he doesn't want to leave. He stares at the 1930s suitcases I bought at a thrift store in upstate New York. They're plastered with decals from all over the country, so I can feel like an old-time vaudeville artist when I job-out to direct plays.

Have you been to all of these places? Bay asks.

Uh-huh, I tell him in my best Chaney voice. Been ever'where. Done ever'thing.

He looks up at me and smiles.

I love you, Baylor, I say.

Thanks for coming back for the baptism, he says.

Well, I've never held my godchild in my arms. It's a big deal.

Blood of my blood, flesh of my flesh, Baylor says. Then he kisses me and says: Good night! Sleep tight! Don't let the bedbugs bite! Like Mama said to us eighty-four thousand times when we were growing up.

The next day, I almost faint when I pull the Tempo into the circular drive of Baylor's new house. He'd sent me photos, but still, I had no idea! It's a mini-mansion straight out of *Southern Living!* Columns running the length of the porch. Ten white rocking chairs lined up, with pots of flowers next to them. A manicured lawn that must take scads of workers to keep up. There is something almost embarrassing about how new Old South it all is.

The twins, Jeff and Caitlin, run out to greet me.

They haven't seen me in three years, but they yell out, Hey! Aunt Sidda! Hey! I talk to them on the phone every Sunday morning from wherever I am, so it's not like we're strangers. But still, I almost burst into tears to see how much they've grown since I last visited. How can they change like that without me being here?!

Their accents are thick as Louisiana coffee. I love it. I drop my cultivated Yankee accent right then and there and relax into my mother tongue.

Angel-twins! I call out. Come here! Oh, I've missed-missed-missed yall!

They hug me and say, We missed-missed-missed you too, Aunt Sidda!

They're dressed to within an inch of their lives. Melissa loves dressing them up. It's her art form. She comes out and gives me a small kiss on the cheek.

Oh Siddalee, she says, we're so glad you could come. Now come see Lee! She's been waiting for you.

Melissa gives me a quick peek of the house on our way to the nursery. Huge formal dining room, a pool with a deck that I can see through the floor-to-ceiling windows. Live oaks lining the yard. At least Bay built on an old lot, I think. Jesus, French doors everywhere. A master bath the size of my studio apartment in Manhattan. A study with 1840s mahogany and glass bookcases and antique butler's tables. A handsome antique globe of the world. Mile-high carpet everywhere you step. Baylor's kind of house.

The nursery is straight out of a dream catalog. But who can look at the decor? It's Lee who pulls me in. Lee with the huge black eyes that stare straight up at me, as if to say: Okay, introduce yourself, Godmother.

Lee of the dolphin forehead. Lee of the jet-black hair
and thick eyelashes. Lee, the only force on earth that
could make me move back to Thornton just to be in
the same room with her every time she wakes from a
nap.

We waited until you got here to dress her, Melissa
says.

Baylor's in the doorway knotting his tie. He comes
over and hugs me, Hey God-mama! he says. Is your
goddaughter a doll or what?

A white linen and ecru lace baptismal gown is laid
out on the changing table, along with a pair of white
satin booties and a little white cap that ties under the
chin.

I can hardly believe all this stuff! I exclaim. You guys
don't kid around.

Melissa says shyly, The gown was my great-grand-
mother's. I bought the booties and cap in New Orleans.
You don't think they look too new, do you? she asks
me worriedly.

I look at my sister-in-law, who I used to consider
beneath my brother, who I once described as a "classic
Southern bimbo who reads only dime-store romances."
I was wrong about her. She is kind. One time, in a
pique of jealousy, I called her "mindless" in front of
Bay. He didn't get angry with me. He just said: Sidda,
what can I tell you? When I wake up with nightmares,
she holds me and she doesn't ask any questions. She
loves me. Don't talk bad about her.

I shut up after that.

I look at Melissa and say, The hat and booties are

beautiful, sweetie. Everything is beautiful. Thank you for waiting to let me dress her.

I lift Lee and begin to put the gown on her. I'm so awkward, I keep saying under my breath, Forgive me, Lee, I'm new at this. She helps me (I swear) put her little arms into the sleeves of the gown and she doesn't squirm when I slip the tiny socks and satin booties on her feet. I hold one of her feet before I slip the socks on. Her toes are so pink and perfect. Her tiny foot sits in my hand like a new potato just out of the ground. I pick her up in my arms and for a moment the wisdom of fairy tales sparkles through: We all need blessings in our cribs, we all need protection from the witches.

I hear a phone bleating down the hall. A moment later, Bay sticks his head in the nursery. It's our alleged mother, he says, and hands me a portable phone. I put Lee down and step out into the hall. I need to focus all my concentration when I attempt a conversation with my mother.

Dahling! Mama says breathlessly. Why didn't you call us as soon as you got in last night?

It was too late, Mother, I tell her.

Oh well, anyway—I simply must ask you a crucial question.

I can picture her in the bathroom, rushing to get moisturized and made up, cigarette perched in the bathroom ashtray with "Vivi Dahling, Happy Forty!" engraved on it. The Ya-Yas love giving anything that's silver and engraved.

Is it too late in the year to wear aqua?! my mother asks. I've got to know!

She says this like she has 9-1-1 on the line and is asking for instructions on how to give CPR.

I've got eighty-four-thousand things to wear, she gasps, but I just feel *called* by the aqua!

Mother, I reply, you've got to be kidding! Aqua was made for this time of year. You will be the belle of the Baptism.

Oh, thank God, she says. I am so relieved to have you home! I didn't know who I was going to ask for advice! All the Ya-Yas are down in Baton Rouge for the LSU-Auburn game. What are you wearing?

Oh, I tell her, I just thought I'd go with my basic rhinestone tiara and my green sequin Mardi Gras Queen gown. You know, the complete fairy-godmother look.

You crazy fool, she said. Sounds perfect.

You can say a lot about my mother. Jungians, Freudians, Reichians—you name it, they'd all have a field day with her. But she is funny. She is quick and she is funny.

*A*t Our Lady of Divine Compassion Church they've moved the Baptismal font up to the side of the altar. Mama's wearing the aqua with a matching hat, her hands still shaking like always. She hugs me and whispers: I think you've lost weight!

Daddy is shifting his weight from one foot to another the way he has always done inside a Catholic church.

Hey babe, he says, you looking good. New York not treating you too bad, I guess.

I hardly recognize Little Shep. He's gained about

forty pounds and his face is all puffy, like a middle-aged man, which I suppose he's moving in the direction of being. (Strange, I never think of myself as anything near middle-aged, but when Mama and Daddy were in their late thirties, that's certainly what they were called.)

Little Shep gives me a starched hug and says, Hey, Miss Broadway, how you doin?

Kane looks tall and tailored as usual. I've always liked her because I've never once seen her wear high heels, which is a monumental statement of individuality for a woman in the Gret Stet of Loosiana.

She shakes my hand and says, Welcome home, Sidd. Dorey and Kurt, do yall remember Aunt Sidda?

No, Kurt says.

I try not to die.

Dorey says, I remember you. You're the movie star in the picture on Uncle Bay's desk.

Uncle Bay has a picture of me on his desk? I ask.

It's one of the glamorous ones from the big play you directed, Kane explains.

I've directed a "big play?" I think.

Oh right, I say. The head shot where I looked gorgeous for one hour after spending a hundred dollars for a professional makeup job? Looks sort of like I'm auditioning for *Dallas?*

Kane laughs and says, Glad you could make it, Sidd. Then she turns to say something to Melissa.

Then Lulu shows up in a mauve silk suit with a slit up the side of the skirt, and heels so high she stands six inches taller than me, which she is definitely not. Her hair is about three inches long—far shorter than her fingernails. We hug and her perfume is so strong it makes my eyes water.

So you made it down, huh? she asks.

How could I miss it? I say. I'm the G.M.

Right, she says. I figured you would be. I'm Dorey's godmother, you know. She adores me.

Yes, Lulu, I remember.

I'd kill for a cigarette, she says, wouldn't you? Being in a Catholic church still gives me the fucking willies. Reminds me of all those lesbo penguins.

Still sweet-lipped after all these years, I remark.

I try, Lulu says, and rolls her eyes. Think anyone'll mind if I light up in here?

Hell no, I tell her. The Catholic Church now actively encourages smoking in church, just to try and bring stray lambs back into the fold!

Lulu laughs and gives me a kiss through the air and says, Love your hair color.

Thanks, I tell her. I like yours too. What there is of it.

My new approach is just to cut off all the damn gray.

How are you? I ask her.

Like the Ya-Yas, she says: Simply mahvelous, dahling. Couldn't be better.

Oh God, you can smell her perfume throughout the entire church. Her makeup is perfectly done, her blush applied like a Lancôme ad. Isn't she going to just die standing in those heels for the whole ceremony? I want to run and get her a chair.

Calm down, I think. You do not have to take care of Lulu.

I hear Mama squeal, and I turn to see Willetta and Chaney slip in through the side door of Divine Compassion. Willetta is wearing one of her glorious hats and Chaney has on a suit of Daddy's I remember from Bay's law school graduation.

Mama crosses over to them at the same time I do. I didn't know yall were coming! she says.

Yas'm, Willetta says, Mister Bay say we better be here.

Then Willetta gives me one of her hugs. This is the woman who invented hugs. When Letta and I hug, my arms reach right about at her sternum—that's how tall she is. She hugs me with every cell of her body.

Oooh, Miz Siddy, I done missed you so much! It ain't the same just talkin on the phone. Babygirl, you looks *good.* You looks real good.

Willetta still smells the same: like Lipton tea and Ajax. As far as I'm concerned, if you could bottle that smell, all the companies that make Xanax, Prozac, and Valium would be out of business. You could just open the bottle and smell Willetta and never feel panicked or depressed again.

Chaney takes my hand in his and says, We sure glad to see you, Miz Siddy. Been too long. You be lookin healthy.

He has gray curling through his hair and he is more stooped over than the last time I'd seen him. Even though I call them twice a month, I never realized they were actually getting old. Time is a strange thing when you live so far away from your home soil.

Mid-afternoon light shines through a large stained glass above the baptismal font. Even though that glass has been there forever, seeing it in that particular October afternoon light, it looks all new to me. Like I've never seen it before. In blues and purples, it's a window of Our Lady holding Baby Jesus. The infant has a round baby belly and the slightest of dimples. The Virgin looks as holy as ever, but I have never noticed the sadness in her eyes before. They are eyes that have seen all the suffering in the world and have managed to still stay open.

Maybe that is a new stained glass, I think, *I don't remember those eyes. Maybe some artist has changed those eyes.*

Monsignor Messina appears just like priests do, silently, out of nowhere. Short and chubby as ever, he smiles at us and actually reaches up and knuckles Baylor's head the way he used to do when we were little. Monsignor Messina was a green young priest when he was first sent to our parish. Back then he was in the shadow of Monsignor O'Ryan (or "Pig-face," as we lovingly called him). Pig-face was the man of God who snowed Mama for awhile with the idea of becoming a saint right here on earth. But Monsignor Messina was the kind of priest who always reminded me of spaghetti dinners and bright purple and gold satin robes and Blessed Virgins all smothered in jewelry and flowers.

Then I am holding Lee in my arms, with her body facing out so all can witness her baby beauty. Her baptismal gown falls in perfect folds against my hip. This is a princess baptism. My mother is recording it all on the video recorder. I feel Lee's tiny, fragile hand curve over my finger. I wonder who held me like this when I was baptized. I can't remember my godmother. Surely it must have been one of the Ya-Yas. Lee's godfather stands next to me, a shy CPA, one of Melissa's brothers. He looks to me for his cues.

Monsignor Messina pours the holy water over Lee's baby head. She lets out an indignant little cry as the water drips over her sweet, defenseless brow.

May you be born again in the spirit, Monsignor Messina says.

He anoints her with oil. He touches her eyes: May your eyes be open to the beauty of God's world all around you. He touches her ears: May your ears hear the sound of God's voice and the comfort of His words.

Her, I silently correct him. *Her* words.

Then he asks Melissa's brother and me: Will you care for Siddalee Durant Walker's soul in a world filled with storm and temptation?

Yes I will, I answer out loud. I think, *I will love you, little baby, I will do my best to protect you from harm. I will not be able to stop you from suffering, but I will do my best to protect you from deliberate cruelty.*

The smell of the Knights of Columbus BBQ dinner is drifting over from the parish hall. It mixes in with the age-old smell of incense and prayer books in the church. The Saturday afternoon light pours in through the stained-glass window. Little Shep snaps a million pictures, his flash popping in our faces. Mama stalks the baptismal font with her video recorder like she's a professional documentary maker. She always loved Super-8s, but she really flipped once she discovered home video recorders.

Now Baylor stands with his hands clasped in front of him and he cries. Daddy cries too and does not try to wipe away the tears. Lulu puts on her sunglasses. Then Lee starts crying. At first it is only little whimpers and I softly pat her back. But then she cranks it up to rock-concert level. She is gasping and her little body convulses with the sobs. So much stimulation, I think. She can't relax.

I turn her face away from the flash and the video camera and hold her against me. I can feel the tender pressure of her head against my breast. Mama makes a frantic gesture for me to turn Lee back around to face the camera, but I ignore her. Finally my godchild begins to calm down. She is tired, I think, this is a big day for her. Her gown is all wadded up and people can no longer witness her little sacred face. She is offstage now and soon she grows very quiet and starts to nod off. Mama steps forward and tries to straighten the baptismal gown, but Daddy reaches out and pulls her back. She winces as though he has slapped her, and then she glares at me as she angrily flicks off the video recorder. I can see her mouth say something to me, which I choose to think is just a little prayer.

I make myself breathe slowly. I begin to feel the beating of my heart. I feel Lee's young heartbeat. *I feel your life, baby girl. Can you feel mine?* Then I begin to feel the beating of each one of their hearts: Baylor's, Little Shep's, Lulu's, Daddy's, Mama's, Letta's, Chaney's. All of our hearts beating in concert. I remember the picture at Buggy's house when we were little: the Sacred Heart of Jesus with the crown of thorns, the blood dripping out. The heart cracked open again and again and again. The heart utterly open. A tree could grow out of a cracked heart, tears giving moisture to the dry places so the roots can live. Mama and the Ya-Yas: *Spring Creek has always been in a dry parish and it's our job to moisten it up!*

And I realize for the first time in my life: All their longing was pure! My parents stand in front of me, two people growing old. Mama in her aqua outfit. Daddy in black dress shoes. Where are his cowboy boots? All their longing was pure. All the longing was for the Spirit. It got trapped in the bottle, but some of the pure longing got through. That is why we are standing here in the sacrament of this moment.

I feel a hairline fracture of pain in my heart. Can I continue to breathe or will I have to reach for my inhaler? I can see the outline of Daddy's in his shirt pocket. Keep breathing, keep breathing with baby Lee. And I feel it: the sweet pure longing of each of us, still intact. Our Lady of Divine Compassion, no wonder you look so sad. My family stands in a circle around me. All the innocence, the old woundings. It grows so quiet. I feel my godchild's breathing, but it is also the breathing of parched babies in drought-stricken lands. I feel each member of my family's breath dropping in and out, until it seems like we are all part of one giant bellows. And all the suffering spirals down into one shaft of sunlight, which shines through one stained glass window in Thornton, Louisiana. *This is what I come home to.* I do not have to crawl across the desert on my knees. I do not have to swim through turbulent oceans to stop the drownings. All I have to do is watch and pray, and love what I love. I can hold the baby and not hurt her. I can hold them all and not hurt them. Not save them, not hurt them, just hold them.

And then Baylor catches my eye. And we are standing perfectly balanced on a tractor inner-tube at Little Spring Creek. Perfectly balanced and the sky is a big blue dome above us and there is room for everything—for every thought, for every feeling, for every speck. And I catch his eye back and he winks, and Mama is bringing him home from the hospital and I am four years old talking on the phone to Aunt Jezie and I hang up the receiver and walk toward him. And I see him in her arms and the sun is hitting the rag rug next to the hassock. Baylor is so tiny. Mama says, Count his fingers, Sidda. I proudly count: One two three four five. Mama says, You are so smart, Siddalee, you are brilliant.

I'm not brilliant, Mama. I can't lead you out of the darkness. But I will not close my heart.

*M*ama and Daddy are the last to leave the post-baptism party. Daddy hugs me goodbye and when the hug ends, we're both teary-eyed. Love you, babe, he says. Lemme know if you need anything, hear?

It strikes me for the first time how much my father cries now that he is older.

As my mother hugs me, she says out loud, You're a gutsy woman, Siddalee. Then as she hugs me tighter, she hisses, You ruined my entire baptism video!

What? I ask, stepping back, only mildly shocked.

You deliberately turned that darling baby girl away from me so I could not shoot her.

Mother, I respond, I turned her away because she was crying. I was trying to comfort her.

No you were not! Mama says, You were deliberately

defying me, just like you have done since the day you were born.

Daddy and Baylor stand there and watch. Baylor lights a cigarette. Daddy takes out his asthma inhaler and sucks in a few puffs.

I say: Tough shit, Mother.

Baylor starts to laugh.

Daddy says, Viviane, get in the car. It's time to go.

This is just like you, Siddalee Walker, Mama says, to come down here for two days, ruin my baptism video, and then fly off to New York and leave me here. I have four magnificent baptism videos of every single one of my grandchildren, and now you have ruined the entire series!

Go home, Mother, Baylor tells her. You don't work for Public Television.

I love you, Mama, I say, meaning it.

Don't be sarcastic, she replies. She looks at me for a long time, the way drunks do when they're studying you.

Then she says, That's the *perfect* outfit for a baptism, Sidda. I want to learn to dress more New York like you do.

I love you, Mama, I say again.

I love you too, Siddalee Abbott Walker, and don't you forget it, or I'll kill you.

And she gets in the mauve Cadillac convertible she talked Daddy into buying, and they drive off.

*L*ater that evening when the twins are in bed and Melissa is watching TV, Baylor and I stand out on the carport. There is a nip in the air and I wear one of Baylor's windbreakers over my dress.

I say, God there is no place in the world like Louisiana for Halloween.

Baylor looks surprised to hear me say that. Why don't you stay longer and spend Halloween with us? he asks.

I'm sorry, Bay, I can't I've got to get back. Maybe some other year.

Maybe some other lifetime, I think.

I want to stay and trick or treat. I wish I could stay in my hometown for more than two-and-a-half days without becoming five years old again, without hurting like I was hurt then.

We look out at the night. It is clear, with a good half-moon.

Almost a harvest moon, Baylor says, and lights another cigarette. He smokes cigarette after cigarette. The tips glow red in the dark.

Baylor says, God, Sidd, that new baby girl is so pure. Lee is just so damn innocent. Were we ever that innocent, you think?

Yeah, Bay, I tell him. I think we were.

He laughs that little half-laugh he's had since he was a kid.

If we had been in a movie, a shooting star would have swept through the Louisiana sky. But it didn't. All that happened is that my baby brother and I stood together on his carport in the October night for a long time. Until Melissa stuck her head out and called, Yall okay out there?

Yeah, we call back in unison, we're okay. And I kiss him goodbye.

I roll down all the windows in my rental car and turn on the radio. Aaron Neville is singing "Tell It Like It Is," just as pretty as he did when I was in high school. One thing I will say for my hometown: They play decent music on the radio. They play the kind of music that New York City has to have special "Delta Nights" in order to play. Funky old music, African-Louisiana music from deep in the heart—and they don't label it anything, they just play it.

I drive through my sleeping hometown. Through City Park, past Buggy's old house, past the old Community Center where I tapped my heart out. I drive past the Abracadabra Liquor Store, closed now. I can hardly make out the sign that used to terrify me so. Now it's all so puny and where there was once bright, cruel light, there are only a few broken bulbs left. When I look closely I can make out the letters "I-F-T." The "G" must have dropped off at some point, but I still remember what it used to read.

Then a memory comes to me so crisp and clear, it takes my breath away and gives it back again: the Christmas that Daddy bought all of us cowgirl and cowboy outfits. He actually talked Mama into letting us wear them to Mass! We trooped in late to Our Lady of Divine Compassion, looking like a family singing group that got lost on the way to the Grand Ole Opry. I remember walking up to the Communion rail wearing my orange cowgirl skirt, shirt, hat, and boots. I opened my mouth and received the body and blood of Jesus, and for one fine moment I knew what it meant to be pure, to be true, to be clean and unashamed. I actually thought the reason that everyone was staring at my family was because our get-ups were so magnificent. I actually felt like everything would be just fine. Not perfect, but just fine.

On good days now, I can feel that way for hours. Feel like there is a big pair of hands holding me up. Feel like underneath the terror there is some kind of wonder waiting for me. And sometimes I believe what I knew for a split second on that Christmas morning: that the mother who holds me isn't Mama. She's somebody bigger, somebody much older, somebody so tender that just looking into her eyes is like a sweet, much needed nap. She speaks to me daily, this mother, with little private signs. And all I have to do is keep walking, with my ears tuned and my eyes wide open.

ABOUT THE AUTHOR

Rebecca Wells, a Louisiana native, is an author, actor and playwright. She has received numerous awards and fellowships, including the Eastern States Book Award for *Little Altars Everywhere*. Wells's follow up novel, *Divine Secrets of the Ya-Ya Sisterhood*, inspired a grass-roots literary following that sparked the creation of Ya-Ya clubs around the country while the book rose to number one on the *New York Times* bestseller list.